MAFIOSA PRINCESS LOYALTY

LIZA MALLOY

CHAPTER 1

Adrian

*M*arco Conti raised his brows as I spoke, but gave no other indication he even heard me. "Excuse me?"

"I said I want in," I repeated, sucking in a few shallow breaths.

The tall, well-dressed man leaned back in his chair. "In what?"

I tilted my head to the side. He had to know what I meant. Was this a test? Was he trying to see if I would say it out loud? *Could* I even say that aloud?

"The family business?" I finally said, hating that I made it seem like a question. Marco would never take me seriously if I didn't come across as certain.

"I'm not hiring."

I blew out a sigh. "Look, if this is about Giada, I'm done with her. I mean, no disrespect, but she's a better fit for Luca."

Marco chortled. "Yes. Yes, she is. It's good that you realized that sooner rather than later."

I paused, wanting to stay on track but also desperate to know the truth. "You never would've let me have a chance with her, would you?"

"Hard to say. Giada is a difficult woman to control. If she refused the life we prepared her for..." he shrugged in lieu of finishing his sentence.

"Luca is not a good man."

Marco tapped his fingers on the smooth mahogany desk. "Luca and I have a lot in common. Am *I* a good man, in the gospel according to Adrian?"

I didn't answer, but Mr. Conti continued anyway.

"Luca's good for her. He'll keep her safe, and she'll find her way eventually."

I pondered what Marco might mean by that.

"Why did you do what Giada asked of you if you're no longer interested in her?" he asked.

I wasn't sure how much information he had— about the marriage, the baby, or anything, really. And I was unclear on the technical lines between Marco's business and Luca's. Divulging something I shouldn't had bigger consequences when it came to men like the Contis and Marinos, and I wasn't about to take any risks. Having just stepped up as an alibi for my arch-nemesis, I'd earned a lot of goodwill in their world. I didn't want to ruin all that now.

"I heard he was a bad man, the guy Luca was accused of killing," I said.

"You just told me Luca wasn't a good man."

I shook my head. "This man was worse, much worse, according to Giada."

"You didn't look into it independently?"

"I did. And she was right. He had no morals, no...limits. He hurt children and women. The world is better off without him."

"So now you're the judge and the jury?"

I shrugged. "Now I realize the world isn't so black and white. I always thought there were two sides, good and evil, and that's not the case. And if it is, well, I'm not so sure playing for the good team helped anyone. That side is losing."

"What does that mean?" Marco leaned forward and reached for his glass. He tilted it to the side, letting the ice cubes clink against the edge of the glass as the amber liquid swirled.

"It means I'm done playing by the rules."

He chuckled softly. "There's only one way out of the game, and you are not dead yet. And until that day, you will have no choice but to play by the rules. Which set of rules, I suppose, depends. But there are always rules."

Nervous energy filled me, but I forged ahead. "I've got skills you could use, and I've already proven myself."

"Have you?"

"Yes," I replied, my resolve firm.

Marco leaned back in his chair, glanced at his phone, then flipped the device facedown before lazily gazing up at me. "I think it's the Marino family that owes you a favor, not me."

"I'm not looking for any favors. And my loyalty isn't to the Marinos."

"What do you know about loyalty?"

I considered the question carefully. Truthfully, I knew nothing. I'd always viewed myself as a loyal person. I didn't cheat on girlfriends, I didn't betray friends. But that wasn't what Marco meant by the term. Mafia loyalty carried a lot more weight.

"I understand what it means to you," I finally said.

Marco eyed me warily, then reached under his desk and pulled out a gun. His movements were so abrupt that I jumped, which probably didn't help my case.

"Let's say I told you to take this gun and shoot Antonio down at the docks. What would you say?"

I held my breath, uncertain if this test required a mere response or if he'd expect action on my part. Whatever I'd envisioned when I came to Marco, I wasn't prepared to shoot someone.

"Well?" he prompted, becoming impatient.

"I'd say no."

His eyebrow shot up.

"You're not the type of man to order people to shoot someone, and if you were, you sure wouldn't want it done with your personal gun."

The corners of Marco's mouth tipped up, but the smile didn't fully reach his eyes. I knew I'd passed a test. Marco slid the gun back under the desk.

"I appreciate your honesty Adrian, and again, I thank you for stepping forward on behalf of Giada. But I don't need any more workers at the dock right now, and my security team positions are all filled."

"I'm a hard worker. I'm not asking for a handout or a pity hire. I'm a qualified candidate."

"Do you even know how to shoot a gun?"

I hesitated. "No."

"Are you skilled in hand-to-hand combat? A black belt in some martial arts? Or maybe you're an award-winning knife thrower or archer like that comic book character?"

He was teasing me, but I wasn't ready to give up quite yet. "No."

Marco nodded. "But let me guess—you're a real quick learner?"

I shrugged. "I am, but I'm not going to take up any of those…things."

"Why would I hire you if you're not even willing to learn the necessary skills?"

"You just finished saying you don't need any more security. But you could always use another smart, hardworking, loyal, upstanding citizen on your side."

Marco drained his drink, flinching as the ice clanked into his teeth. "You have one more year of law school?"

I nodded.

"I could maybe use some help in my legal department."

"You have a legal department?"

Now he smiled comfortably. "No, but I know some people."

I wasn't sure how to respond to that, but Marco shifted in his seat then stood.

"If you'll excuse me, I have some matters to attend to."

I rose to my feet, unsure of where I stood.

"I'll be in touch," Marco said, extending his hand. I accepted and firmly shook his hand. "But in the meantime, get the permits. Buy a gun. And learn how to use it."

Mr. Conti brushed past me and was out of his own house before I even knew what hit me.

By the time I reached my apartment, I still wasn't sure what to make of the meeting. He hadn't outright agreed, but he also hadn't shot me, so I supposed I'd just have to wait and see what he meant when he promised to be in touch.

Luckily, I didn't have to wait long. My phone rang right as I sprinkled seasonings onto a pork chop for my dinner. I didn't recognize the number but answered anyway.

"Is this Adrian?" The caller's voice was familiar, but I couldn't place it.

"Yeah, who is this?"

"Angelo. Look, my dad wants a copy of your resume. You can send it to this number, and I'll get it to him."

All of that was so unexpected that it took me a moment to answer. "Um, okay. What resume?"

Angelo swore under his breath. "Aren't you a lawyer or something? You should have a fucking resume. Or don't ask for favors if you aren't serious about getting a job."

"I didn't ask for..." I began, but Angelo had already hung up. *Super*.

Giada

A repetitive thumping jolted me from a deep slumber. I awoke as though wading through a dense fog, slowly treading my way back to reality.

Beside me, Luca groaned. "Arrivando!" he yelled. "I'm coming."

He slid his arm out from under me and rolled out of the bed. I smiled, noting that he'd slept in the nude. He stumbled towards a chair across the room and stepped into a pair of thin gray sweatpants. I definitely appreciated the sight of Luca in sweats, especially with nothing beneath them. Muscles stretched along his waist like cords, and suddenly, I missed him in bed beside me.

I snuck a glance at the clock. "It's not even seven," I said.

"Sorry." He started towards the door.

"Do you want a shirt?"

Luca paused then turned back to me, revealing that he already held a tee shirt in his hand. "Do you?" he asked, lunging closer and lifting the covers just enough to reveal my breasts. He dragged his tongue along my nipple, causing me to shiver.

"Not if you promise to do that more," I said, eager to tempt him into staying in bed longer.

"Don't move. I'll be back," he said.

I pulled the sheets higher as Luca slipped out the door. Exhaustion riddled me, which wasn't surprising since I'd barely slept the entire time we'd been apart. I wasn't entirely comfortable lounging around naked in Luca's parents' house, but I also didn't want to get dressed if he was returning right away.

I decided to give Luca ten minutes, then get dressed.

Except, apparently, I fell asleep while waiting, because when I next checked the clock, it was nearly ten A.M.

Luca had scribbled on a post-it note beside me.

"Come get some breakfast when you wake, sleeping beauty," read the note. Smiling, I inched out of bed, stretched, then made my way to the bathroom. Certain at least a handful of men remained in the house, I dressed in leggings and a tank top before peering into the hallway.

I followed the sound of voices to the kitchen, frowning when I only saw Alessio and Thomas. They both gazed at me like I'd imagine one would evaluate a wild animal to determine if it were rabid. After a moment, Alessio spoke.

"Luca's in the office with some of his dad's guys. Want some coffee?"

I nodded. Alessio motioned for me to sit at the counter by Thomas, so I did. Alessio brewed a fresh cup of coffee, then slid it across the counter to me along with a small tray containing cream and sugar.

"Did you sleep okay?" Alessio asked, eliciting a chuckle from Thomas.

Both Alessio and I scowled at him.

"What?" he asked. "Luca's back now. You probably don't have to keep treating her like an orphaned kitten."

"I slept well, thank you," I replied, ignoring Thomas.

Thankfully, before any of us could attempt more awkward small talk, a door down the hall clicked open, and a flurry of voices filled the foyer. I listened as the front door opened, then shut, then a solitary set of footsteps started towards us. My pulse raced as he rounded the corner.

"Luca!" I exclaimed, popping from my seat as though I hadn't just spent the night roped around his body.

His smile broadened as he closed the distance between us, wrapping his arms around me and pulling me close. "Amore," Luca breathed against my hair, his nose tickling my neck. He maintained the embrace longer than usual, only releasing me when my stomach growled painfully loud. Then, he pressed his lips to my forehead before issuing a single command, "Eat."

I gazed up again and noticed an entire spread of delicacies arranged on the table behind me. Scones, bagels, muffins, and other pastries filled one large tray, while fruits occupied another. I filled a plate, then sat at the table, where Luca joined me with his own cup of coffee. I didn't bother asking what the meeting was about, since Luca couldn't tell me much with Thomas and Alessio still in the room. So instead, I asked about the rest of the day.

"The guys are coming back at noon. I'll probably be stuck in meetings here until at least mid-afternoon, and then I need to check on things at the club." He paused and lowered his voice. "You could call Enzo and see if he could drive you to the drugstore so you could pick up some items. Discretely, of course."

My brows furrowed as I tried to imagine why I would leave Luca just to go to a store, and then it hit me. I choked on the muffin in my mouth, then gulped my coffee to wash it down.

Had I seriously forgotten? What kind of a terrible mother woke up and forgot she was pregnant?

Well, *probably* pregnant. As Luca so subtly pointed out, I still hadn't managed to procure a test, let alone take it.

I dropped my gaze to the coffee cup, wondering if I should even be drinking the caffeinated liquid. I debated hiding the fact that I'd somehow forgotten about the actual human possibly growing in my uterus, but instead peered up at Luca. Warmth filled his soft brown eyes, and I couldn't help but smile.

"I was so happy to have you back that I sort of forgot when I woke up this morning," I admitted.

He cast a glance towards Thomas and Alessio, but they didn't seem to be paying us any attention.

"That's a good thing, right? It must mean you're feeling better," he said.

I shrugged. "I don't know if I'm supposed to drink this," I whispered, gesturing to my coffee.

"I have no idea," he admitted, standing and making his way to the counter. He poured a glass of orange juice, then brought it back to me. He talked with his friends while I finished eating. Then he nodded for me to join him in the bedroom.

I figured we would talk, but the moment the door shut behind me, Luca pounced. His mouth captured my own, and his tongue teased the slit between my lips until they parted, granting him full access. He nudged my back against the wall, working his hands up my torso.

I grinned against Luca's lips, so damn grateful to be with him. Two days before, he'd been in jail, and I wasn't sure I'd ever be able to speak with him again, let alone touch him. I'd felt terrified, hopeless, and cheated. But now… now everything was good. Perfect, really.

Luca pulled back abruptly, his thick lashes almost fully hiding his deep brown eyes. "What's wrong?"

I shook my head. "Nothing. I was just thinking how happy I am to have you back. We owe Adrian…" I was about to say "everything," when Luca's expression cut me off.

"I was rounding second base, and you were thinking about your ex?"

I wrinkled my nose, but appreciated that Luca had relaxed enough to make jokes. I tugged at the hem of his shirt, and he tore it off in a flash. My fingers stroked the chain around his neck, then dipped into the ring hanging against his chest. "No one commented on this when you were…detained?" I shuddered, still unable to speak aloud where he'd actually been.

Luca kissed the finger fondling his ring. "No, not even a stray joke about how much jewelry I wear."

My smile relaxed, and I smoothed my palms up and down his bare chest, relishing the silky warmth of his skin.

"We only have a little while," Luca said. "Do you want to talk, or…?"

I answered his question by stripping off my own shirt. He didn't hesitate unclasping my bra and then he hauled my face closer, kissing me roughly as his fingers pinched my nipple. I groaned into his mouth as a delicious heat spread through my limbs before settling in my core.

We stumbled to the still-unmade bed, shucking the rest of our clothes before laying back. Luca kissed his way down my body, settling between my thighs. I shivered at the first, feathery-light stroke of his tongue, but as he increased the pressure, my hand drifted to his head. I opened my eyes, stricken by the realization that nothing would ever be more erotic than the sight of this beautiful man feasting on me like he was the luckiest person alive.

Luca gazed up at me, his mischievous grin telling me he knew exactly what he was doing to me. I gave his hair a gentle tug, urging him back up my body. He obeyed, covering my body with his perfectly masculine form.

"You're not sore?" he asked, his mouth so close that I felt his words on my lips.

"No," I lied. "I want you."

"Baby girl," he groaned, "You have me. But I'm happy to finish—"

"No," I cut off his words by reaching between us and gripping his hard length. I pressed it against my entrance, then returned my hand to his lower back. "I want this," I said, wiggling my hips towards him.

Luca drove into me fully, and the slight twinge of soreness was soon overpowered by my intense relief. I gripped his waist, holding him to me as he brought our lips back together. He slid an arm under my hips, We built up a rhythm with our bodies as I began to meet him thrust for thrust.

Pleasure curled deep and tight within my belly, threatening to unleash itself at any minute. I tried to hold on longer, desperate for just one more minute to appreciate the perfect moment. I wanted to memorize the feel of Luca's body—against me, beneath me, above me, and inside me, all at once. As long as we were joined in every way possible, I couldn't remember the icky cold feeling of being apart or the bottomless dread that had seeped into every breath I took when he was gone.

Luca shifted to a new angle, and an explosion of colors burst in front of my eyes. I heard myself cry out as pleasure exploded from my core in wave after exquisite wave. I was so lost in my own ecstasy that I didn't even realize Luca had slipped over the edge with me until I felt his warmth inside of me.

He dropped his lips to my shoulder and mumbled something in Italian. I wasn't sure what the words meant, but I was confident I shared the sentiment.

"You're good at that," he said a minute later, once we'd both caught our breath.

"We are good at that," I corrected, combing my fingers through his hair. I kissed his ring, then he climbed off of me, heading into the bathroom and returning a moment later with a warm washcloth. He climbed back into bed beside me, pulling the covers over us.

"It's good to be back home," he said, sighing into my hair.

"This is not our home," I reminded him.

He lifted his head to catch my gaze. "You are my home, Giada. Wherever you are, that's where I need to be."

A few minutes later, we were jolted out of bed for the second time that day by someone knocking on the door. Luca dressed quickly, this time in black suit trousers and a button-down shirt. I dawdled, debating what to do with the rest of my afternoon. I supposed I should get dressed and run by the drug store, but I wasn't sure how to purchase such a personal item with Enzo following me around. Maybe if I told him it was feminine products, he'd back off. Or maybe I should just wait.

I tied a robe around myself and went to brush my hair while making up my mind. Right as I emerged from the bathroom, I heard the bedroom door open.

"Oh!" a startled female voice greeted me.

I swiveled around and came face to face with Luca's mom.

I was so surprised to see someone who was supposedly still in Italy that I couldn't even formulate a polite hello.

"I would've knocked, but I didn't realize anyone was in here."

I nodded and tried to smile.

"You're quite comfortable in my home, I see," she said, her eyes slowly drifting down my robe then back again. "That's good, I suppose." She turned but not before I caught her eye roll. "It's after noon…"

"Luca didn't mention you'd be returning this soon," I said, finally finding my voice.

She raised an eyebrow and mumbled something under her breath.

"Well, I was just about to get ready to head out…" I said, hoping she'd catch the hint and leave.

"Clearly," she said, her voice dripping with sarcasm. Luckily, she fled the room, shutting the door behind her.

~

Luca

I hung up the phone just in time to see Alessio round the corner into the office. "Uh oh," he said.

I didn't have time to ask what prompted his comment before my mom barged into the room. I raised an eyebrow, silently asking Alessio why she was here when my papà's flight wasn't arriving until evening. He simply shrugged.

"Luca," my mom said, her voice sweet. "How are you?"

"Good, Mamma," I said, leaning forward so she could offer me the traditional greeting of a kiss on each cheek. "Did you catch an earlier flight?"

"Obviously. Your father went straight to one of the businesses, but he will be back later. I see you've completely taken over my house."

I glanced around, noting no mess whatsoever and no sign I was even there aside from Alessio, well, and my things—and wife—in my old bedroom. "Maximo said that Papà wanted me to stay here until he returned."

"Well, did he say the Conti girl needed to come too? I ran into the little trollop in the guestroom. She's half naked, you know."

I cringed. Alessio's eyes widened, and he excused himself from the room.

"If I'm staying here, Giada is staying here. You can assume she's always going to be wherever I am. But now that you're back, we can both leave, especially since you clearly can't play nice."

My mother made a face. "Oh, lighten up. If she'd put some clothes on, we could go over some of the wedding plans."

I sighed, wondering if I'd ever stop feeling torn between the two women in my life. "Mamma, she's had a rough couple of days. I don't think she's in the mood for wedding plans."

My mother rolled her eyes. "It's not like she has anything else to do with her time."

I started to answer, but my phone rang, saving me. I gazed at the caller ID, suppressed a chuckle when I saw it was Alessio, then turned back to my mother. "Sorry, Mamma, but I have to take this."

"Pronto," I answered, walking quickly towards the bedroom. Once I was safely inside with the door shut, I thanked Alessio for the save and hung up.

Giada was already packing up her things. "She hates me," she said. "I'm going back to our apartment now."

"Me too," I said. "I'm sorry. I didn't know she was coming back early."

"It's fine." Giada crammed something else into a bag, dropping a sock. She bent down to pick it up, rose quickly, then stumbled. Her hand drifted to her head.

I flew to her side. "Sit down, Giada."

For once, she obeyed. I dropped to my knees in front of her.

"I'm fine," she insisted. "Just tired and dizzy."

"And pregnant," I added, frowning.

"We don't know that," she said, shaking her head.

"Yeah, why haven't we taken the test?" I'd known of the possibility of her being pregnant for close to twenty-four hours now. I understood why she didn't test before I was home, but she could've done it last night when we'd gotten home or first thing this morning. In a city that never sleeps, surely someone could've delivered a pregnancy test in a matter of hours.

"I don't know. I was just so tired last night. I'm still overwhelmed with everything that's happened this week. I'm not sure I can handle anything else thrown our way."

I understood what she was saying, but at the same time, I got the impression she was putting a pregnancy in the same category as a felony arrest. I decided not to share my thought aloud, though. "Lay down for a few minutes. I need to pack my stuff, and I'll get yours together too. I'll push back my meeting an hour so we can stop at a drug store on the way home and buy a test."

Giada winced, but stretched back on the bed to watch me pack.

CHAPTER 2

Giada

We bought a pregnancy test on the way home from the Marinos' house. I was mentally prepared to learn our fate, but then Alessio called and needed Luca at the club right away. Luca insisted we had five minutes to take the test before he left, but I refused.

Yes, I wanted us to be together when we learned the results, but I also wanted him by my side in the hours after. I couldn't imagine my stress if I learned we were indeed about to become parents, and then moments later my husband left me for the rest of the day.

Luca was reluctant but agreed. As soon as he left, I changed into sweats and went back to our bedroom to lie down. I didn't think I'd fall asleep, but I did, only to be awakened by sharp cramping deep in my abdomen.

I sat up and rubbed my eyes. It was only ten p.m., so I wasn't surprised that Luca hadn't returned yet. I was more concerned that I was still so tired. I winced at another twinge of pain, then made my way to the bathroom.

One minute later, I exhaled with relief. I couldn't be pregnant. I had my period. *Finally.*

Just in case though, I took the test. I started to get nervous during the three- minute waiting period, but once my phone timer dinged, I confirmed the negative result and tossed the stick in the trash.

"Not pregnant," I texted Luca. My phone rang seconds later.

"You took the test without me?" he asked the moment I answered.

"Yes," I admitted, "but only because I got my period."

"But you said it was late."

"It was. That happens sometimes. It can be stress-induced."

He was quiet for a minute. "You were dizzy and nauseous. Alessio said you fainted."

"You were arrested by an entire fleet of police, Luca. I was stressed."

This time, he paused even longer. "So you're positive? I mean, the test is negative?"

"Yes."

"Okay then," Luca sighed, "and you're happy about that?"

I hesitated. I'd gauged from Luca's reaction at his office the day before that he was excited, but the timing wasn't right. "Yes. You know I want children with you someday, Luca, but our wedding is soon. And we're just starting out together. We need time before we start having babies."

Luca exhaled hard. "You're right. I have to go. I love you."

"Love you too," I said.

I somehow managed to fall back asleep before he came home, but when I awoke the next morning, I was finally refreshed. I went into the bathroom and noticed the instruction pamphlet for the pregnancy test on the counter. I distinctly remembered having thrown that away the night before.

There was a tap on the door, and I turned to see Luca, with coffee.

I thanked him for the coffee and held up the instructions. "Didn't believe me?"

He shrugged, leaning in for a kiss. "I just wanted to be sure."

"I'm sorry to have gotten your hopes up for nothing."

"I wasn't hoping for anything. I just…I don't know. This is better though. I'm not ready to share you with anyone else yet."

I gazed at him, trying to read his expression, but mostly he just looked tired. "Did you sleep any last night?"

"Yeah. I'm good."

Since I'd called in sick to work the past several days, I figured I should make an appearance there. Luca offered to drive me on his way to some meeting in that part of town.

Surprisingly, having something to do—something normal—distracted me from my thoughts in a welcomed way. I'd been looking through some design files for about an hour when Suzie, one of the receptionists, came into the conference room.

"Hey! You're back! How are you feeling?"

For a moment, I thought she'd somehow heard about my pregnancy scare, and I panicked. Then, I remembered I'd told everyone I was sick when I had to miss work because of Luca being arrested for murder. And that reminded me that I was actually married to the man that everyone thought was just my fiancé. *Jeez.* The amount of lies ruling my life at the moment was staggering.

"I'm good. How's everything here going?"

She shrugged. "Eh. Same old, same old. Cami said your fiancé dropped you off but that nobody got to meet him. Is he picking you up later?"

I laughed. "I don't know." For some reason, the office staff was fascinated that I had an Italian fiancé whose business allowed us frequent cross-continental travel. The fact that none of them but Cami had actually seen him seemed to make him even more intriguing.

"Okay, but he'll definitely be there next Friday, right?"

"Next Friday," I repeated, trying to figure out where he was supposed to be then.

"At the decorator's party? Remember? They're renting out a whole restaurant for it. You've got to bring your fiancé. And maybe a friend or two. Especially if any are potential clients."

I nodded, and she scampered off down the hall.

I really liked Suzie and Cami. Actually, everyone at Sash & Lowens Interior Design was pleasant. Audra and Diana, the partners who ran the place, had both been skeptical of my work at first, but they'd warmed to me once they saw the amazing treasures I found in Italy. There were a handful of other designers at the firm, and all of them occasionally asked me for input on projects and treated me respectfully. But Cami and Suzie, the receptionists, were the only other employees close to my age, and the only ones I'd actually consider friends.

Before I forgot about the upcoming event, I pulled out my phone. I added it to my calendar, then texted Luca.

"Don't forget," I typed, "You, me, and a very tiny dress have a date next Friday at some dinner party my design firm is hosting."

"Not on my calendar," came his near-instant reply.

"Is it now?" I asked, tossing in some smiley and heart emojis in lieu of begging.

"Yes, I better not miss it, or someone else will steal you and your tiny dress."

I smiled and slipped my phone away, then stood to see if Suzie wanted to grab a coffee at her break.

~

Adrian

The next afternoon, my eyes were glued to my phone as I approached my apartment, so I didn't notice the black Escalade roll up beside me until the tinted windows rolled down.

"Get in," a voice called.

I turned to see Angelo in the back seat. I could make out a driver and another passenger in the front. Quickly, I tried to brainstorm an excuse, but then I remembered… We were on the same side now. I had no reason to be afraid. Or did I?

"Where are we going?" I asked, stepping closer.

"Nowhere. Walk around," Angelo gestured to the other side of the car.

I glanced around, dismayed to see there were no neighbors or other witnesses watching me disappear into the sedan. Still uncertain of the purpose of the visit, I clutched my cell phone in my hand as I climbed in.

"Hi," I said to Angelo. I peered into the front seat. The two men looked familiar, but I wasn't sure if I'd actually met them before or just seen them around the Conti estate.

"I'm Adrian," I said to them.

"Jesus fucking Christ, this isn't an AA meeting," Angelo said. "No one gives a shit about your fucking name."

I couldn't hide my scowl. "Wow. Bad day?"

He rolled his eyes and handed me a small card that read "4pm Tuesday." I flipped the card over, surprised to see the name and contact information for a local attorney on the other side.

"What's this?"

"My father set up a meeting for you. I assume you can make that work?"

I nodded. My classes ended early most days. I'd scheduled it that way so I could do all of my studying in the afternoons, but I supposed it worked well for interviews too.

"Good." Angelo paused. "Okay, you can get out now."

I didn't see why he couldn't have just handed me the card without forcing me into the car, but I turned towards the door anyway. Then I hesitated, daring to ask a follow-up question. "What sort of attire should I wear for this meeting?"

Angelo made a face. "You are such a girl," he mumbled. "Wear a suit."

I nodded and reached for the handle again before remembering another potential issue. Unsure of how freely we could talk with the two guys in the front within earshot, I lowered my voice.

"Your dad told me to get a gun, but I um… well I applied for the permit, but I don't yet—"

Angelo sighed loudly and leaned into the front seat before I even finished my sentence. "Eddie, you have a spare Glock?"

The man nodded, reached to the floor, then tugged a gun out of a holster by his sock. He casually handed it over the back of the seat. Angelo grabbed it and offered it to me.

"There," he said, dropping it on my lap when I didn't reach for it. "Is that all?"

I didn't know where to begin. "What I was saying was that I don't have the permit yet."

Angelo chuckled, the other two guys joining in quickly. "That's alright, Adrian. This isn't the type of gun you need a permit for. The numbers are scratched off anyway."

"So…" I wasn't sure what he was even saying.

"So don't get caught with it."

I opened my mouth to protest further, but no words came.

"You're welcome," Angelo said. "Now get out. I have a meeting to get to."

I glanced anxiously at the gun on my lap, then quickly stuck it in the inside pocket of my jacket, pointing down. I was half convinced I'd shoot myself climbing out of the car, but by some miracle, I didn't. And even though I clutched my pocket awkwardly as I walked the last fifty yards to my apartment, no one stopped me.

Luca

The following day was filled with tedious, insignificant tasks, and it showed no signs of ending. My papà summoned me to a late dinner, so I swung by the house to change clothes and greet my wife before heading out again. Giada had spent her morning at the gym, then dedicated the rest of the day to wedding plans with her best friend Gabriella.

I couldn't help but smile when I saw Giada. She looked relaxed and happy, especially compared to the first two days after I'd been released from jail.

"If you're heading out again, I think I'll see if Gabby wants to go out for dinner. That's okay with you, right?" she asked me.

"Of course. Listen though, can I talk with you for a minute?"

Giada raised an eyebrow, then followed me into the bedroom. As soon as I shut the door, she wrapped her arms around my waist and tugged me to her, kissing me deeply.

The kiss caught me off guard, but I wasn't about to complain. Except I did actually need to talk to her. I nudged her away.

"I could do that all night, but Alessio will be here any minute now, and we need to go meet up with my papà."

She made a face.

"I really want to tell him about the wedding."

"Your dad?" Her eyes widened exponentially.

"Jesus, no! Alessio. And he won't tell a soul." I paused, trying to decide how to explain my fear without making her anxious, too. "It's irrational and I know it, but I really worry that if something were to happen to me, and no one knew. They couldn't take care of you. Nothing is going to happen, but the thought that I haven't done everything I can to protect you is distracting to me. I need to know that you're safe no matter what. I have enough stress in my days that I can't avoid, and it would just be really reassuring if—"

She pressed her fingers to my lips until I stopped trying to talk. "Okay," she whispered.

"Okay?"

"Yes. Tell Alessio. Just make sure he knows not to tell anyone else."

"Of course." I paused, certain she'd agreed too easily. "You sure?"

Giada nodded. "Yes. I didn't know it was stressing you out."

Once we were alone in the car, I blurted my news to Alessio.

"I have to tell you something," I began. "It's about Giada."

Alessio didn't even glance over, so I added, "it's important."

He sighed and turned his full attention to me at the stoplight. "Let me guess. You cheated on her?"

I couldn't even hide my annoyance that my best friend thought so little of me. "No, I didn't cheat on her. I married her."

Alessio stared blankly.

"We eloped in Italy."

"I don't understand."

I'd long suspected he didn't understand anything about the institute or marriage or anyone's motivation to enter into such an arrangement, but I didn't think that was the source of his present confusion. "It was her idea. She wanted something just for us, so we did it. But she still wants the big public ceremony too, and it's important that everyone else believe that is the real ceremony. So don't tell anyone."

"Is she pregnant?"

I winced. I didn't want kids yet. I knew that. I needed more time alone with Giada before I had to share her with anyone else, especially someone else she was sure to love more than me. But that awareness didn't stop the pang of disappointment over the results of the pregnancy test. "No," I said finally.

"You sure?"

"Yeah."

Alessio frowned and shook his head. "Why are you telling me this now?"

"Because someone needs to know who she is to me if anything bad happens."

"Like if you get arrested for murder? Sure would've been good to know then."

"I'm sorry. She really didn't want anyone to know."

"She doesn't know you're telling me now?"

"She does. She trusts you."

"No she doesn't."

I laughed. "Well, she trusts me. And she told Adrian. I guess that was how she convinced him to talk to the cops."

Alessio was uncharacteristically quiet for a moment, then grinned. "Congratulations, amico. She's way too beautiful for you, and more trouble than you've bargained for, but I wish you nothing but happiness."

"Grazie."

He chuckled. "And now I can stop worrying about her leaving you at the altar."

I felt the same relief, but wasn't about to admit that aloud, even to my best friend. Instead, I switched the focus to work.

"My papà is going to want a name for the rat," I said.

"Then he'll have to work harder to figure it out," Alessio snapped back. "You know as well as I do that we may never find out who it was, and I'm not convinced it matters anyway."

"Just because the charges didn't stick doesn't mean we are off the hook. Until we find out who turned me in to the cops, we won't know why they did it."

"Na, I could tell you now why they did it. They want us out of the way."

"Okay, but was it revenge, or—?"

"It doesn't matter. We have enemies. That's not news. Going

forward, we'll be more careful. You won't be involved in anything from now on. That's how we keep you safe."

I remained skeptical, but when Alessio touted his theory to my papà an hour later at the restaurant, the elder Mr. Marino latched right on.

"That's exactly my point," he said to us. "You need more men."

I exchanged a glance with Alessio, certain neither of us had meant that. I didn't trust a lot of people, and as long as my stint in jail was fresh on my mind reminding me what could happen if I trusted the wrong people, I didn't feel too inclined to widen my circle of trust.

I started to explain as much, but my papà interrupted. "I'm not asking you to bring on a whole new team and rely on their loyalty overnight," he began. "But you need to start vetting them. Alessio, if you and Thomas, Roberto, and Giovanni each bring three of four new men on board, that quadruples your manpower. Don't introduce them to Luca, don't trust them with any critical information. Just start vetting them and gradually give them bigger jobs. Let them handle security at the docks. Let them collect debts. You guys save your energy for the bigger fish."

Alessio tipped his head towards me. "We're going to need more manpower if we want to break into the casino business," he said.

I suppressed a grimace at the fact that he was actually agreeing with my papà. What he was suggesting wasn't a novel idea, but it was risky. The reason I personally oversaw everything done at all of my businesses was because that was the only way I could guarantee shit got done correctly the first time. If I wasn't involved, sure, I couldn't be charged with a crime when things went wrong, but I also couldn't control that things went right.

"I don't think—" I began, but my papà raised a hand to shush me.

"Alessio is right. He kept me abreast of your plans with the casinos while you were otherwise occupied, and I think the plans sound promising."

I nearly choked on my salad. That statement had so much for me to unpack I wasn't sure where to start. My papà had never supported Alessio's ideas—or mine, for that matter. Why would he start now. "You make it seem like I was on vacation," I said. "I was in jail, remember?"

My papà's lips tightened to a thin line and he shot a harsh stare at the waiter refilling our water glasses. I mustered all my willpower not to roll my eyes at his unnecessary theatrics. For years, my papà had conducted a sizeable chunk of all of his business meetings from this restaurant. My mention of my time in jail surely was not the most sensitive information those waiters had overheard.

Alessio muffled a laugh, raising his wine glass to his lips.

The waiter left, and my papà leaned closer. "I did want to tell you, though, we were all pleasantly surprised with how you handled that situation, Luca."

I wasn't sure who exactly comprised the "we all," but I was too focused on the fact that my papà had actually paid me a legit compliment to ask for clarification.

"You too, Alessio. Really, your whole crew did just what they should have," he continued. "And Giada, well, let's just say no one expected her to manage those circumstances well, but she seems to have kept her composure. I understand she played a role in making sure Adrian came forward with his alibi."

"Giada was great," Alessio agreed.

I quirked a brow since Alessio had told me the opposite in confidence. He said she'd cried, refused food, and thrown a fit about Enzo staying. His exact words to describe her composure —or lack thereof—had been "hot mess express," but I appreciated Alessio not telling my papà the same.

"Speaking of that, I did think we'd owe that Adrian kid something, but I guess now that he's working for the Contis, we—"

"Hold up," I cut in. "What?"

My papà lowered his fork to the plate and turned to me, staring as if no one had ever interrupted him before. Maybe they hadn't. But I didn't care. I couldn't believe my ears.

"Did you just say that Adrian Patras is working for Marco Conti?" I asked.

A slight nod was the only confirmation my papà offered.

"Since when?"

My papà shrugged. "Couple of days at most. I assumed you knew. Marco called me to check that it was okay if he connected Adrian to some of his defense attorney friends. Sounds like the boy enjoyed helping out the right side for once."

I reached for my wine, choking down a large gulp while trying to process that revelation. I'd gotten the feeling Marco had been grooming Adrian back when he was still with Giada, but never in a million years would I have guessed Adrian would've sought him out after finally escaping the Conti web.

My papà continued with his debriefing, yammering on about the goals for our casino project the entire time we ate our meals.

During the drive home, I felt invincible. Never before had my papà bestowed such praise, or hinted at offering me so much freedom. From the sound of things, he planned to begin spending most of his time in Italy, and my reign would be largely unchecked in the States. I didn't love his ideas about bringing on more men, but if that was what we needed to do for him to sign off on the casino project Alessio and I were planning, so be it.

I went home and celebrated with Giada for a solid hour in the bedroom that night, then repeated the whole performance in the morning.

Life was good.

CHAPTER 3

Adrian

By Tuesday, I was a nervous wreck. I wasn't sure what Angelo had meant when he told me I had a "meeting," and I wasn't about to ask him. I was scheduled to meet with a lawyer, and Angelo had said to wear a suit, so it was probably a business meeting. But, it seemed clear that I was expected to bring the gun. Why else would Angelo have given it to me?

I had zero experience with meetings that required a gun. I also had zero experience with an actual gun.

I'd taken two firearm safety classes, so I could at least turn off the safety and shoot the gun, but I still hadn't gotten my official permits. Angelo acted like it was no big deal for me to carry around an illegal gun that I wasn't permitted to possess, let alone to carry concealed. But I had more than enough legal expertise to know it was actually a very big deal. Like a felony-level deal.

I'd ordered a variety of holsters, not sure what would work best. I liked the appeal of the ankle holster because if I did somehow manage to shoot myself, well, a shot to the foot seemed a lot more appealing than one to the abdomen or thigh. But if I actually needed to use my gun, crouching down to my ankle certainly wouldn't give me any tactical advantages. The hip holster was more convenient, but terrified me. And the holsters which secured the weapon to my chest felt neither comfortable nor convenient.

In the end, I went with the ankle holster for the meeting. It was the only gun placement where I didn't constantly fidget. Still, as I rode the elevator up to the twelfth floor, I was painfully aware of the weapon strapped to my person. The moment the elevator doors slid open, an inkling of relief hit me. The suite in front of me was clearly a law office, and on the surface at least, it was a legit one.

I strode inside, gave my name to the receptionist, then took a seat in the nondescript waiting room. I wiped my palms on my suit pants when the receptionist motioned for me to head back to the office. As I stood, I was acutely aware of the handgun. It felt like it weighed a million pounds. I walked awkwardly, certain it would come loose and fall to the ground, even though I'd tested the holster dozens of times and confirmed it was secure.

"Mr. Patras?" The man greeting me appeared to be in his late fifties. He wore a suit and resembled any other law firm partner.

I sighed with relief, then nodded and offered my hand.

The man's smile matched my own. "I'm Gino Russo. Please call me Gino."

"Nice to meet you. You can call me Adrian."

Mr. Russo motioned for me to sit, then closed his office door behind us.

"Thank you for meeting with me," I said, hoping that was the right thing to lead with. The man smiled, so I supposed it was a good guess.

"Mr. Conti spoke highly of you. How exactly are you acquainted with him?"

I hesitated. Normally, I'd tell people I dated Giada, but in light of the circumstances, I wasn't sure that complete honesty was the best policy.

"I'm a family friend."

He quirked an eyebrow. "I see. And you've done some work for him?"

I chose my words carefully. "I wouldn't say that, but I've helped him out from time to time. That's what friends do, right?"

Mr. Russo nodded slowly. His eyes lowered to a paper on his desk. "Well, your resume looks good. The firm doesn't typically hire at this point in the year, but with such a high recommendation, we're certainly willing to give you a try as an intern this semester, and I don't see why we wouldn't be able to take on a new associate this summer if we all seem to get along."

I opened and closed my mouth several times, uncertain of how to proceed. I had so many questions, but if there was one thing I'd learned from Angelo, it was that mobsters liked to keep their meetings brief. Of course, I didn't know if this guy actually was a mobster, and I was positive *I* didn't qualify as one. Still, it seemed poor form to interrogate the guy, even if I wasn't completely sure I wanted the job he seemed to be offering me.

When I'd gone to Marco, I hadn't anticipated legit work in my chosen career field. And yeah, I'd begun researching permanent attorney positions after graduation, but I wasn't yet sure where I wanted to end up. I certainly hadn't planned to accept an internship without knowing the hours and pay.

"I appreciate that," I finally said, forcing a polite smile to my face. "Shall we work out the details now, or—"

He waved dismissively. "You'll get an email from HR. They like to keep things official and documented. You know how that is."

I nodded politely, then stood as he stood. "Thanks for your time. It was nice meeting you."

∽

Luca

The morning after my meeting with my papà, I awoke in a spectacular mood. Giada shifted beside me as I pried open my eyes, so I figured she was awake. I ducked under the covers, grateful she hadn't bothered to dress after our second round of lovemaking the night before. I fumbled with the sheets, working my way closer, then pressed a soft kiss just below her belly button.

Giada's sigh sounded almost like a kitten purring. I kissed her again, shifting lower this time, and was rewarded with another adorable sound. I inched lower still, finally stroking my tongue directly on my target, and she squirmed against me. I repeated the motion, and her hands found my hair, tugging gently.

"Babe," she murmured, sounding half awake.

"Mmm?" I replied, the sound vibrating against her soft flesh.

"Don't you have a meeting this morning?"

Crap. She was right. But Alessio could wait. The task at hand, decidedly could not. "Priorities," I said, debating whether to add a finger to the mix. I opted not to, instead simply feasting on her until her breathy sighs turned into moans and the soft tug of my hair turned into a fierce clutch pinning me in place.

As I untangled myself from the sheets after, I was fully prepared to head to the shower and go about my day. After the activities I'd enjoyed with Giada the night before, I hardly expected her to reciprocate this morning. When she followed me into the bathroom, though, I wasn't about to complain. Still nude, she watched me shower, brushing her teeth instead of joining me. When I stepped out of the shower, she raked her eyes up and down my torso before handing me a towel.

I blotted myself in a cursory attempt to dry off, then she snatched the towel back and knelt on it. "Surely you have a few more minutes to spare, right?" she asked, peering up at me beneath thick, dark lashes.

I bit back a groan, certain what she was about to do wouldn't take long at all. Between the taste of her still on my tongue and the sight of her tanned, familiar curves, my arousal was at an all-time high. She dipped her head down, wrapping her lips around the tip of my cock. As she began to work her soft, warm mouth up and down the first couple of inches of my shaft, I gripped the counter behind me, certain I'd fall without the support.

I kept my eyes open, enjoying the sight of her licking and sucking me almost as much as the sensation. As my breath picked up and I inched closer to my climax, Giada gazed up at me, her beautiful eyes locking on mine. That pushed me over the edge.

I groaned her name through gritted teeth, and my entire body shook as pleasure zapped through me like electric shocks. I loosened my grip on the counter as my pulse evened out, eventually shifting my hands to her arms, helping her to her feet.

"Holy shit you're good at that," I panted.

She smiled shyly.

I reached for the towel, then gazed up to admire my beautiful wife.

"I should probably brush my teeth again after that," she mused.

"I wish you wouldn't," I replied, alarmingly aroused by the thought of my taste on her tongue all morning.

Giada actually blushed at my words, but I was already running behind and couldn't spare anymore time staring at her perfection. Alessio was due to pick me up in under a half hour, and I still hadn't dressed.

"I'll make you some coffee to go," she offered, wrapping a robe around herself.

I was practically whistling as Alessio began our stops for the day, but my friend wisely refrained from asking why. We had roughly five debts to collect that morning and then planned to finalize some plans about the casinos over lunch.

Giada

With all the craziness of the month, I was a little surprised Luca agreed to accompany me to my work party the next weekend. Well, technically, he said he'd "stop by," but I took that as a win. As an added insurance on his attendance, I selected a slinky purple dress Luca was sure to appreciate and dressed early enough for him to see it.

"Alessio and I just need to run one quick errand, and then I'll…" Luca began. He stopped dead in his tracks when he came out of the bathroom and saw me standing by the mirror, fiddling with my necklace. "Damn girl. You win," he said, grinning as he came to help me fasten the necklace.

Luca's breath tickled the back of my neck, and I leaned into him as he kissed the sensitive spot just behind my ear. His hands worked around my waist then pressed upward, squeezing my breasts.

I swatted his hands. "Oh no, buddy. If you want that, you've got to show up tonight. Whoever takes me home gets that grand prize."

He grimaced. "Well, Thomas is driving you there. You're not going to reward him for that, are you?"

I shrugged playfully. "We'll see. How late will you be?"

"Forty five minutes. An hour at most," he promised, licking his lips as his eyes roamed up my body one last time.

I kissed him goodbye, then climbed into Thomas's Range Rover. We somehow arrived right as Suzie did. She walked over to the SUV as it idled along the curb, waiting as I climbed out. Thomas wasn't leaving until Luca arrived, but he also didn't trust valets enough to leave his car unattended.

"There's an open bar," I told him, but he simply shook his head.

I turned to my friend.

"Is that your fiancé?" she asked eagerly, only slightly confused when he started to pull away from the unloading zone.

"No, that's his friend Thomas. You'll know when my fiancé arrives."

She laughed, and we made our way inside. We started at the bar, both of us selecting the featured mandarin orange martini.

"So, your fiancé's friend," Suzie began, "Is he single?"

I bit back a smile and nodded. "Not sure he's your type, though."

"Umm…my type is tall, dark, and handsome. Check, check, and check."

I giggled. We chatted for a few more minutes, then separated to mingle with current and potential clients.

Right as I met up with Suzie again, ready to relax for a few minutes before resuming my schmoozing, I felt the energy of the room change. My body buzzed with excitement as I turned to the door, immediately spotted Luca. Drinking him in, I waited for him to find me in the crowd. The moment our eyes locked, his expression softened. Luca didn't go so far as to smile, but he raised his eyebrows, letting me know he'd head my way soon.

"*That* is my fiancé," I said to Suzie, continuing to gawk at Luca instead of pointing him out.

"Ooh, he is hot," she said.

Giovanni whispered something to Luca, and I followed his gaze to the other side of the room where he was eying some man I didn't know.

"He looks intense," she joked. "Like maybe he kills people for a living?"

I loved Suzie for her sense of humor and her honesty, but sometimes, her comments hit a little close to home. I swiveled back to face Luca and noted his expression had changed. His eyes were darker now, and his lips pursed tightly. I watched him respond to Giovanni, then nodded my way. Whatever business had come up, he was going to make them wait.

"He hasn't killed *that* many people," I replied. "He's Italian. They all have that sexy, serious look."

The crowd parted as Luca approached, and within seconds, he was standing in front of me.

"Tesoro," he said, cocking his head to the side and raking his eyes down my body. Then he leaned forward and pressed his lips to my forehead. "Beautiful," he said. He brushed another kiss to my ear and whispered, "Those shoes are staying on when we get home tonight."

I felt my cheeks heat at the erotic promise, but Luca remained completely calm and collected. If his life of crime didn't pan out, he could probably make a decent living playing poker.

"Luca, this is Suzie," I said, remembering we weren't alone.

Luca extended his hand to her. "Ah, the entertaining coworker," he said. He then leaned in to offer a quick Italian greeting in the form of a kiss on either cheek. Suzie appeared uneasy from the unexpected gesture, but I smiled, aware it was a sign that he was accepting her into our lives.

"And you're the mystery fiancé," she said, quickly regaining her composure.

"Mystery?" he repeated, gazing at me with a questioning eyebrow raise.

"I've been talking about you for weeks, and every time I think she'll get to meet you, Giovanni or Thomas or Alessio shows up instead."

"Ah. My apologies. Business has been…busy."

"Busy is good," Suzie said.

"Not always." Luca eyed my empty glass. "Can I get you a drink?"

I pouted. "You're planning on leaving early, aren't you?"

"Just a bit. Thomas will take you home."

"Or Thomas can take care of business, and you take care of me," I countered.

Luca's eyes widened. "Excuse us," he said to Suzie. He tugged my hand gently till I followed him to the corner of the room. He leaned into me, placing his hand beside my head so I was pinned in place.

"I will definitely be home in time to handle that job myself," he promised.

Luca was so close that I could smell his cologne. I wanted to pull him against me and kiss him until he forgot where he needed to go or who he was supposed to beat up.

"I want more," I said instead. "I want you to delegate this crap that doesn't matter, then have a drink with me, talk to my new friend, and possibly fuck me in the coat closet later."

He leaned forward and kissed me roughly, ending it too soon. "I'll see what I can do," he promised.

I bit my lip, savoring the taste of him on my tongue as he walked off. As I watched him grab Thomas and Giovanni, I made my way back to Suzie.

"He'll be right back," I told her.

She fanned herself dramatically. "He's hot. And apparently, you're like, the alpha male whisperer or something."

CHAPTER 4

Giada

The next two months blew by like a popup shower in spring. I divided my days evenly between work and wedding plans, but Luca consumed my nights. I adored every moment of our secret newlywed life, and I couldn't help but wonder if our relationship would still burn this hot after our public nuptials.

Much to my mom's relief, we had made huge progress on the wedding plans. We'd sent out the invitations, chosen the reception location, and hired a caterer. The bridesmaids' dresses and groomsmen's tuxedos had been ordered. We'd selected a florist and baker, although we still had to work out our final orders with both. We'd even made progress on the reception we were holding in Italy the week after our New York wedding. I still hadn't found my dream veil, but I told myself I could always buy a simple one and pay someone to alter it to match my fantasies.

Gabriella was the best maid of honor, carefully tracking every task I needed to complete and keeping me company on any wedding-related missions that Luca didn't join. Actually, she'd tagged along on a couple of wedding errands with Luca and me. By some miracle, Gabby and Luca were now friendly. She was comfortable hanging out in our house, and when the three of us went out, she and Luca talked and laughed like old friends.

I was so relieved.

And I still couldn't believe my luck. Two months ago, I'd been terrified that I'd be raising a baby alone while the man everyone else thought was still my fiancé rotted in prison. Now, we were together and everything was perfect.

Luca was working crazy hours the next week, trying to break into the casino market in Atlantic City. So, I figured I might as well spend extra time at the office, too. Audra, one of the designers, let me tag along on all of her appointments and home visits that week, so I finally felt like a real intern for once. Seeing the homes I was shopping for in person made such a difference. Being inside, exploring all of the rooms and not just the areas we were tasked with designing, really gave me a better feel for the owner's true style.

"When is your next trip to Italy?" Audra asked as we left the final client meeting of the day.

"I actually don't know," I admitted. "Luca's work here has been nuts lately, and I've got all the wedding planning to do, so—"

"Ooh, how is the wedding planning coming along? Have you picked out a dress yet?"

I nodded, but the topic stressed me out nonetheless since I still needed to find the perfect shoes and veil. I'd always loved fashion, which meant I'd been picturing my wedding attire since I was a child—the gown, shoes, and veil. I was thrilled with my dress, but the shoes were important too, and the veil was critical. I didn't want to settle for anything less than perfect.

I spent the entire day Friday shopping with my mom, then I rode back to their house with her. We'd found the perfect shoes, but still no veil. My entire family was at the house for dinner, plus Angelo's obnoxious girlfriend Julia. Luca had promised he'd come, but since my parents' house was a good ninety minutes from where he seemed to spend most of his working hours, I wasn't surprised that we were already finishing dessert when Luca arrived.

When he buzzed to be let in through the gate, I hopped up to greet him. Things between my brother and Luca had been tense for a while now, and since that was largely my fault, I figured I should try to ease the awkwardness as much as possible.

Luca smiled as he jogged up the front porch steps to meet me. "You're a breath of fresh air," he said, lacing his fingers around mine.

"I was going for sunshine, not air," I teased, alluding to my bright yellow top.

His grin widened, then he leaned in and planted a soft kiss on the corner of my mouth. "Find a veil?"

"No," I replied, pouting only slightly less than I otherwise would since I was flattered that he remembered I'd been veil shopping.

"Sorry. Why don't you go with Gabriella tomorrow?"

I thrust my bottom lip over the top one. "Does that mean you're working all day?"

Luca gazed just past me instead of answering, and I turned to see my brother Matteo standing behind me.

My brother nodded politely to Luca before asking if he would join us for dessert.

Not a big dessert person, Luca was sure to say no. So, I answered for him in the affirmative, then tugged him inside. If he was going to leave me to work all the time, the least he could do was acknowledge my family when he wasn't working.

My parents both greeted him warmly, and I realized that the only person in my family who didn't clearly adore Luca was Angelo. My father seemed to prefer Luca over his own sons some days. I didn't make Luca linger, though, and soon we were in the car on the way back.

"How was your day?" I asked, gazing out the window. It was dark already, and riding in the car at night tended to make me sleepy. I figured my chances of staying awake increased greatly if I kept talking.

"Stressful," he answered curtly. After a moment, he continued. "My papà is pushing ahead with his plan to bring in some new guys. He says it'll lessen my work and hopefully keep me off the radar with the cops."

"That all sounds great," I interrupted. "You aren't allowed to get arrested again. Ever." I stared at him until he finally glanced to the side, acknowledging my words with a simple nod.

"Yeah, it could be. I mean, right now half the stuff I have my guys doing is way beneath them, but I just don't have anyone else that I trust to do it right. Alessio has all these good business ideas, and we'd really like to focus more on that, but we don't have the time or manpower now."

"What are his ideas?"

Luca hesitated. "I don't want to jinx it. I'll tell you if we make any of it happen."

"Luca…"

"Nothing dangerous, Giada. Just more with the casinos. Sort of another branch of our club business." He paused. "I don't really want anything to do with some of the business my papà operates, so this would be a way to avoid getting too involved in his side crap."

"Sounds perfect. What's the problem?"

"Well, the reason I trust Giovanni and Thomas and Roberto is because I know them. They've proven themselves and earned that trust ten times over. New guys are wild cards. And the way my papà wants to bring them in feels even riskier."

"So don't do it his way." That seemed obvious to me.

Luca chuckled. "As if I have a choice. He is the boss, you

know? Besides, he might be right. I just don't know. His plan is basically to have each of my guys bring in their own crew. They'll vet them, they'll supervise. The new guys won't even know my papà or I are involved. Then if something goes south, there won't be any way of anyone tracing anything back to us."

I yawned, feeling the full relaxing effect of the car's motion. "Sounds like a win-win to me."

Luca reached over and stroked my fingers. "Yeah, you're probably right." He lifted my hand to his lips and kissed it, then switched on the radio.

I waited a few minutes before following up with my next question. "Not to stress you out more, but how is everything with Carla?" Ever since we'd learned Carla lied about sleeping with Luca and that her son, Jacob, was actually Luca's half-brother —*eww*— Luca was a little less sensitive about the topic. But she still was far from his favorite person.

Luca had been giving Carla money to help support Jacob since we returned from Italy, and he'd started spending a little time with the toddler, too. With Salvatore in town, Luca had been hesitant to ever visit Carla or Jacob in public, and so far, I still hadn't even met Jacob.

"Eh, I guess fine. Carla found a daycare she likes. I'm going to pay for that, and let her handle the rest of Jacob's expenses."

"That seems fair," I said.

Luca scowled.

I supposed I'd misspoken. "Fair" wouldn't involve Luca paying anything, since Jacob was not his son. But Carla didn't want Salvatore knowing about the kid and as long as Luca was financially involved, he could be otherwise included in his half-brother's life, too.

"Any idea when I could meet him?" I asked.

Luca gazed at me for a moment, then refocused his eyes on the road. "I don't know, Tesoro. Maybe once my papà is back in Italy?"

I reached my hand over to his thigh. "Sounds good," I agreed.

Adrian

A full week passed without any word from the Conti family, but a courier had delivered the formal offer Gino had promised the day after my sister showed up at my door. She was only in town for a few days, visiting me and scoping out the job market.

Gino's employment offer detailed my hourly pay, expectations, and status as an hourly employee. The packet included some confidentiality agreements to read and sign and the full benefits package, even though I wasn't eligible for the vast majority of benefits.

Gino's practice was a medium-sized firm, by New York standards, and between the few dozen partners, there was someone who practiced virtually every area of law. Some of the firm's higher profile cases drew media attention, but really nothing that stood out. It all seemed alarmingly legit.

The offer letter detailed the possibility of this internship leading to a full-time associate position upon graduation and successful completion of the bar exam. I actually felt a glimmer of hope. Maybe I had failed to convince Marco Conti I was a suitable recruit for his criminal enterprise, but he had, apparently, believed in my potential as an actual lawyer.

I signed the papers then called my parents to tell them the good news. I was still on the phone with them when Angelo called. I accepted his call, surprised to hear he was calling to congratulate me. I declined his offer to head out for a celebratory drink, using my sister's visit as an excuse, but Angelo never took no for an answer. So, two hours later, my sister and I found ourselves at some Italian-owned bar a half hour away.

I wasn't eager for Annie to meet Angelo or the other guys, so I didn't mind when she immediately ditched me to flirt with some investment banker at the bar. Angelo didn't waste any time sidling up beside me.

"Wait, that's your sister? Damn Patras, you've got some good genes. I didn't know those Greek girls were so—"

"She isn't Greek, and I swear to God, Angelo, if you finish that sentence…" I stopped myself and glared. Luckily, Angelo broke out into a wide grin. It actually might have been the first true smile I'd seen from him ever.

He patted my shoulder. "It's fine, Patras. Your hot sister is off limits." He paused and cocked his head to the side. "Although, that doesn't seem completely fair since you had no trouble violating *my* sister."

I opened my mouth to defend myself, then shut it.

Angelo let out a low chuckle, almost like a growl, clearly proud I'd accepted defeat. "Speaking of your love life, do you have a date for the wedding?"

"Wedding?"

Angelo rolled his eyes, and my stomach churned as I realized what wedding he meant.

"I'm not going to your sister's wedding."

"Yeah, you are."

"No. That's weird. We used to date."

"You were invited."

"I'm sure only because Giada wanted to be polite."

I couldn't tell if Angelo agreed with that or not, but he shrugged. "Doesn't matter. You have to go."

"No."

His expression turned serious. "Look, I don't know if Giada wants you there or not, but Luca does, so you're going."

"Why would Luca want me…" I started to ask, then shook my head. Maybe Luca just wanted to torment me. Or maybe it was all for show. He knew Giada had told me about their secret wedding, but to the rest of the world, this was real. Luca would love for everyone to know that I watched her choose him over me. Again.

"I can get you a date," Angelo offered. "Hell, I can get you a whole table filled with hot girls willing to do your bidding."

I struggled to mask my disgust at the thought of the type of woman Angelo would find for me. "No thanks. I'll find my own date." I'd have to bring a friend, though, because no way would I bring anyone I was actually interested in dating to my ex-girl-friend's wedding to my mortal enemy.

~

Luca

I was just finishing up some paperwork at the club when there was a light knock at the door. I glanced up as Thomas poked his head in, a ridiculous grin on his face.

"You won't believe who just dropped by," he said, not pausing long enough for me to guess. "Chiara Gambino."

He was right. I didn't believe it. I had no words.

"You know, your old girl from—" Thomas continued.

"I know who she is," I interrupted. "Why is she here?"

He shrugged. "To say hi?"

I'd meant why was she in my country, not in my club, but whatever. I blew out a sigh and dragged my hand through my hair. "How does she seem?"

"Hot."

I rolled my eyes at his second misinterpretation of the conversation. "Does she look angry? Do you think she wants money? Or revenge?" I paused, then a terrifying idea hit me. "Jesus, she isn't pregnant is she?"

Now he laughed. "No, but have you even been with her that recently?"

I hadn't, but that didn't mean she wouldn't still make some claim. I had never cheated on Giada with Chiara. But, out of all the other women I'd dated, Chiara was the only one who ever actually reached girlfriend status. We'd first hooked up in Rome right after Giada and I broke up the first time, back when she was still in high school. The sex had led to friendship, then to an actual relationship. But I'd never actually loved her.

We'd parted ways a couple years back when I'd moved back to the U.S, right before I wormed my way between Adrian and Giada. When Giada left me shortly after to go back to Adrian, I'd started seeing Chiara again. But that was mostly because I needed someone to take my mind off Giada.

Looking back, that was all Chiara had ever been to me—a substitute for Giada. On first glance, they had a lot in common. They were both beautiful brunettes, with long hair, dark eyes, and gorgeous smiles. They both had the kind of body that made heads turn, and they both knew it. They were also both rich. But the similarities ended there. Chiara was every bit as obedient and subservient as Giada was independent and stubborn. Chiara was also sneaky and cunning and, unlike Giada, she rarely used her gifts to help others.

"So…shall I bring her back?" Thomas asked.

I glanced at my watch. I'd promised Giada I wouldn't be late, but it was not yet nine. I had a few minutes. "No, I'll come have a drink with her."

I followed Thomas down the long hallway that led into the main bar area of the club. He pointed to a woman at the end of the bar, but his gesture was unnecessary. I could've spotted Chiara from a mile away. It would be hard not to, given that she was wearing a fire-engine red, sequined dress. She turned right as I reached the opposite end of the bar, raising her eyebrows as she dipped her head. Chiara always had been an expert flirt.

I asked the bartender, Chad, to bring a gin and tonic and

another of whatever she was drinking to a private table. Then, I went to greet Chiara.

She smiled broadly as I approached, pulling me in for the traditional kiss on either cheek.

"Luca, you look even more handsome than I remember," she said, speaking Italian. "And this…is this whole place yours?"

I bobbed my head up and down twice, then tilted it to the side. "Join me for a drink? We can catch up." I offered her my arm, and she happily gripped my elbow and followed me up the stairs to a more private table. Chad arrived with our drinks a moment later. I thanked him, then turned back to Chiara as she surveyed the club below us. Her hair was much longer than I remembered, and I wondered if she wore extensions. The moment she glanced back at me and caught me staring, she beamed, clearly assuming I'd been checking her out.

"So, what brings you to New York?" I asked.

"Other than you?"

I raised my glass to my lips in lieu of answering.

"Just wanted to explore. I haven't been here for years. Last time I was in the city actually was right before you and I enjoyed our first little stint together."

"Is your family with you?"

"My sister is in town. She moved here a few months back, actually. She's a model."

Somehow, I felt like I should know that, but I hadn't.

"How long are you staying?"

She shrugged. "Until I get bored."

I downed another swig of my drink, then dared to make eye contact. "My wedding is at the start of next month."

"So I've heard," she replied. "Guess that means we only have a few weeks of fun. For a while, anyway. Right?" she winked and returned to her own drink. "I'd love to meet the little woman someday."

I chuckled and shook my head. "I forgot how bad you could be."

"You always did love that. I hear Giana can be quite the handful too."

"Giada," I corrected, despite my certainty that she'd intentionally said the wrong name. "And who have you been talking to about her?"

"Small world," she began.

I cringed and awaited the rest of her explanation. It was not a small world. In my experience, every perceived coincidence was actually part of a larger scheme.

"My sister is friends with this girl Julia. She does the makeup for the models before the shoot. And I guess Julia is dating your fiancée's brother."

"And how did you discover this tiny coincidence?"

Chiara waved her hand dismissively. "We were hanging out at the apartment having drinks, and—"

"Who?"

"I don't know. A group of us girls. Maybe seven or eight of us? I don't know. Like I said, I was drinking. And someone brought some coke because, well, you know models. So I don't recall every last detail. But anyway, Julia was there. At some point, Concetta asked me about you and if I planned to see you when I was in town, and Julia heard and so we started talking and figured out you were the same Luca she knows."

Chiara sipped her drink casually, peering out over the dance floor beneath us. She wasn't a good enough actress to make that all up, nor did I think she had any reason to. Maybe it was a coincidence that she met Julia.

"She does not like you by the way," Chiara added.

"Who? Your sister?"

"No, Concetta always loved you. Julia. She said you were cranky and that you and Angelo are always fighting."

I didn't disagree with that assessment.

"So how are the wedding plans coming along?"

I gazed into her big brown eyes for a moment, trying to decipher her end game. But all I saw staring back at me was the same Chiara as always, friendly and up for some fun. "You came all the way to New York to chat about my wedding plans?"

Chiara laughed. "Well, no, Luca. If I'm being completely honest, I'd rather you take me to your office and fuck me on the desk." She paused. "Or at least dance with me. But since you're getting married so soon, I'm guessing those activities are off the table."

I leaned back in my chair, inhaling slowly through my nose. It had been so long since someone had flirted with me in my native tongue. Actually, aside from my mother, no women ever spoke Italian to me. It was nice. Refreshing. I didn't have to work to figure out any of the slang.

"We have a cake tasting tomorrow," I told her. "We already spent one afternoon sampling cakes from different bakeries, but I guess now we have to decide which flavor we want from the bakery we chose."

Chiara winced. "That sounds complicated and time consuming."

It was, to be honest, but I wasn't dreading it. Watching Giada eat dessert was one of my favorite past times. "We want the wedding to be perfect. And Giada really likes food."

"She's fat?"

Chiara asked without malice, but I pulled out my phone to find a recent photo of Giada that was appropriate to share but still showed more than her face. Scrolling back, I found one of her in a bikini from our last trip to Palermo. "No. She's perfect," I replied, holding out my phone.

Chiara accepted it, zooming in on the photo as though searching for something. "Wow, she's gorgeous. And you clearly have a type, Sir." She paused to observe my response to that. "Would your fiancée be up for a threesome?"

"No," I replied dryly. "Neither of us would."

"I didn't say you were invited," she teased before reaching for her drink. "So when do I get to meet her?"

"Never?"

"Oh, come on. Aside from my sister, I have no girlfriends here. It's boring."

"I don't see you and Giada being friends."

She feigned offense. "What? Everyone likes me."

"No one likes you," I countered, and it was true. Chiara was a bitch to nearly everyone she met.

"Men do."

I conceded that point.

"How's business?" she asked.

"Good." I gestured to the crowded room beneath us.

"Not the business I was asking about."

I hesitated, certain I'd never let on anything about my off-the-record activities to her. Then, I realized she'd always been interested in all of my shipping.

"The shipping industry is growing. Lots of environmental backlash over trucks and airplanes, but boats and trains seem to be slipping under the radar."

She seemed pleased to hear that, then asked about my mother. The conversation flowed, and I'd actually relaxed and stopped searching for any suspicious undertones in her words. Then, my phone buzzed and ended the spell.

"Shit," I mumbled, glancing at the caller ID. I didn't swear because it was Giada, but because it was late. I didn't like to keep her waiting.

I clicked to answer, pushing away from the table. "Baby, I'm so sorry I'm late. I completely lost track of time. I'll head out in a minute."

She sighed into the phone, and I could actually picture her, curled up on our couch under her favorite fuzzy blanket, twirling her hair around her finger while we spoke. "No, it's fine. You might as well stay now. I should get to bed anyway. I want to go by the office for a couple hours tomorrow before the cake tasting."

"Are you sure? Because I'm done working now. I can be yours in under a half hour."

"Nope, have fun with the guys," she said. "In fact, stay out all night if you want. Live it up, Luca, because once we make this official…again…I'm not letting you out of our bed for at least a week."

I bit back a groan at the thought. "A week? But I've cleared my schedule for a whole month."

"Liar. Love you."

I dawdled in my vision of Giada all ready for bed for another minute before turning back to see Chiara eying me expectantly.

"So that was her?" she asked.

I nodded.

"Let me guess, she's angry that you're out late?"

"No, she told me to stay out and have fun.

Chiara frowned but stood from the table. "Seems like you have time for a dance then."

I considered it, then walked her to the dance floor.

CHAPTER 5

Giada

The cakes were amazing. I loved every variety I sampled, which meant I had to taste a second bite of each to make a decision. Luca nibbled a few flavors, but was zero help at narrowing down the options.

"Luca, it's your cake too. You have to have an opinion."

He shrugged. "I'm just not a cake man." He bit back a smile and lowered his voice, brushing his lips across my ear as he spoke. "I'd rather eat what I had after the last ceremony. You are the only dessert I enjoy."

His hand slid from my outer thigh towards my groin as he spoke, his fingers dangerously close to my core. Heat flooded my cheeks, and I scooted a few inches further away. When I dared to gaze up, the bakery manager was peering back and forth from Luca to me as if she was waiting for some explanation.

"We have some lovely pies if you prefer something non-traditional," she began.

"That won't be necessary," Luca said, flipping back to his professional tone. "Giada adores cake, so we will have cake. I think her favorite was the one with the lemon cream filling." Luca gazed at me for confirmation, and I nodded, assuming he guessed based solely on how loudly I'd moaned while tasting that.

He grinned and brushed a kiss on my knuckles. We finalized the details on the order, then walked hand-in-hand to the coffee shop down the street. Luca ordered for both of us while I slid into a corner booth. I'd expected Luca to sit across from me but wasn't surprised when he scooted in beside me. He hated having his back to the room. Luca leaned his head against the top of the leathery seat and reached for my hand.

"I need a nap after all that sugar," he groaned.

"That's what the coffee is for," I reminded him. "Although, maybe if you hadn't stayed out so late last night, you wouldn't be so tired."

His eyes popped open. "You told me to."

I squeezed his hand. "You don't have to do everything I tell you."

Luca lifted my hand, pressing my fingers against his chest where his original wedding band hung from a simple chain.

"This hidden ring here says otherwise."

I laughed just as our coffees arrived. "Did you have fun at least?"

He seemed to consider that, then nodded. "I did actually."

"Who all was there? Just the usual?"

A flash of worry crossed his face. "Uh no. An old friend from Italy dropped by, and we were catching up. It was completely unexpected, so—"

I leaned in and kissed him, then offered what I hoped was an encouraging smile. Luca had so few genuine friends that it was always nice when he spent time with one. Alessio and Thomas and them were obviously his friends, but it seemed beneficial for him to also have some relationships outside of the business.

"So, shall we discuss the other desserts?"

His eyes narrowed. "What other desserts?"

"Well, so in addition to the cake, we'll have a table with a bunch of other sweets. Obviously tiramisu, maybe some fruit tarts?" I paused but Luca still looked confused. "And those candied almonds…those are supposed to be given to the guests as a favor to take home, right?"

His frown morphed into a grin, then a laugh. "You want more desserts at our wedding?"

"Yes, of course. It's tradition."

"It is?"

I rolled my eyes. "The cake is the American tradition. A table of sweets is the Italian tradition. Haven't you been to Italian weddings?"

Luca reached for his coffee. "I'm happy to go along with whatever you'd like, as long as you don't make me taste anything else for a few days. I think I'm becoming diabetic."

I swatted him playfully. Luca's stomach was flat and muscled. His body showed no evidence of any excessive indulgence of any kind. And if he did start to have health problems, it would be from alcohol, not sugar.

"Well, the tiramisu is nonnegotiable."

"Of course," he quickly agreed, smiling.

The bell above the door chimed, and his expression shifted instantly.

Luca swore under his breath, so softly that I couldn't even discern whether he spoke English or Italian. I turned to the woman walking into the café, assuming she was the reason for his annoyance. My first guess was that she was a relative or friend of Carla's, since I didn't know any other women who'd make him swear.

She looked insanely tall, but that could just be the excessively high heels she wore. Her skirt barely covered her ass, and the long blazer she wore over the skirt dipped so low in the front that I completely understood why every man in the café was staring.

She walked immediately to our table, beaming widely.

"Luca," she purred, leaning down and kissing each of his cheeks.

I grimaced as the position thrust her cleavage way too close to my face.

The woman then turned to me, smiled, and said something in Italian. I caught my name, but nothing else. Then she gazed back at Luca and spoke more.

"Giada, this is Chiara," he said to me, squeezing my hand before addressing her. "Giada doesn't speak Italian."

Chiara frowned and then said something else, which I could only guess was some disparaging comment about my inability to speak Luca's native language.

"Luca and I are…old friends. I visit from Italy," she said slowly, her words heavily accented.

As she spoke, it hit me. Chiara wasn't an old friend. She was Luca's ex-girlfriend. She was his Adrian.

I forced a cordial smile onto my face. "So nice to meet you. I was glad you two had a chance to catch up last night," I said, staring pointedly at my husband.

Luca flashed me a brief sheepish grin before Chiara began chattering away again, this time reverting to Italian. He did his best to translate, but I lost focus quickly. Why had I encouraged Luca to stay out so late? Or why hadn't I at least asked whom he was with, or where he was? And why did he invite her to meet us for coffee?

"I should get back to work," I said, standing abruptly. "Nice to meet you Chiara. Hope to see you again," I lied.

I snatched my coffee cup off the table right as Luca grasped my other hand, squeezing until I glanced his way. His eyes spoke volumes, pleading with me to stay, apologizing for the awkwardness. But I didn't have the patience for any of it. I shook my head dismissively.

"I'll drive you back to the office," he said.

"It's faster to walk from here," I replied. With traffic, that was the truth. "You should stay and catch up more."

Luca nodded, and I thought that meant he was going to do just that. Thankfully, he didn't. He said something to Chiara in Italian, then jumped up after me, following me to the door.

"I'll walk with you," Luca said.

"It's broad daylight. I'm perfectly safe walking alone."

"I want to walk with you."

"My office is in the opposite direction from your car," I said, speeding up. I didn't want to pick a fight with him, but I could feel the jealousy brewing in my core. If Luca didn't back off and give me space to cool down, I was going to snap.

"Giada, slow down."

I didn't.

He grabbed my bicep, possibly harder than he intended. He tugged me to him, gripping both of my arms once I was facing him. "Look at me," he commanded.

I did, but only briefly. I didn't want to start crying, not when his stupid model ex-girlfriend was probably still watching us.

"I haven't seen her in years, until last night. I didn't know she was coming to town, and I certainly didn't tell her to meet us today." He paused. "Nothing happened."

I drew in a sharp breath and gazed up at him. "Then why didn't you tell me you were with her last night?"

"I told you I was with an old friend. That's the truth. You were the one who told me I should stay out."

"Luca," was all I said in response.

He sighed, squeezing his eyes shut and dipping his forehead to touch mine. "Amore, I'm sorry. I didn't tell you because I didn't want to annoy you or make you feel jealous. I should have. Now can I please walk to your office with you? I need the exercise after all that sugar."

I relented, and by the time he kissed me goodbye outside my office, I'd forgotten all about the leggy brunette at the coffee shop.

~

Luca

The next morning, I left the apartment early so I could squeeze in a workout before meeting Alessio at L'Occhio. The club was quiet when I arrived and smelled of a pleasant mixture of lemon cleaning solution and wood polish. Alessio was seated at my desk chair, talking on his cell phone while combing his hair.

He disconnected his call when he saw me but didn't cede my chair or pause his primping. I sunk into a chair facing my desk and waited until he shoved his comb and mirror into his pocket.

"What's on the agenda today?" I asked, glancing at the photo I'd taken of Giada that morning. She was half asleep still, sprawled out in bed with her hair fanning her face. She looked like an angel.

"We should go meet with the car dealer."

"The Audi guy?" The day before, Alessio had informed me that an Audi dealership had been vandalized. Word on the street was that a low-level gang mostly operating out of Jersey took credit. We looked into them and discovered they were actually part of one of the groups dabbling in the casino scene.

Alessio nodded. "I took the car for a test drive. It purrs like a kitten."

I laughed. He'd been stalking the dealership for weeks since they got in the new model, so it wasn't surprising he'd been so quick to find a way to "help" them. Still, Alessio wasn't an idiot, and he wouldn't suggest we get involved if it was a bad deal.

"Alright. Lunch first?"

"Sure." Alessio's eye twitched, so I knew there was something else. "Remember my cousin I told you about? He really wants to meet with you. The kid needs money, bad."

"So loan him some."

He shook his head. "He needs long-term funds. He wants in." he paused, then stood, walking towards the door. "He's here now, if you have a minute."

I winced. Alessio had impeccable judgment, and I trusted him with my life. But getting involved with family was one thing, and getting involved with your best friend's family was a whole different ballgame.

"Just meet him," Alessio said, opening the door.

"I just don't want to have to shoot the closest thing you have to a brother," I said.

Of course, his cousin had already started into the office and visibly paled at my comment. *Great.*

I gave Alessio a look, then shook the kid's hand and motioned for him to sit down.

"Alessio seems to think I'll like you," I said. "What's your name?"

"Lincoln."

I frowned, not having expected that.

"Like the car," he added, as if that was where I'd gotten confused.

"How's your Italian, Lincoln?" I asked.

He shook his head. "I don't really…" He perked up suddenly. "I'm not bad at Spanish, though. It's my minor."

That actually could come in handy, I decided. "Your minor? You're in college?"

Lincoln nodded. "Studying business. That's um, why I need

money. I can't work enough hours at a minimum-wage job to pay tuition and still study enough to graduate."

I sighed. "Working for me isn't the sort of thing you put on your resume. I'd recommend asking your cousin there for a loan. He can handle it."

"I've been working for you for almost a year now. I help the dancers with their music, stock the bar, clean up, random stuff."

I wondered if Alessio had told me he was hiring his cousin for that. He probably had, and I'd simply forgotten.

I asked him some basics, like his grades, long term career goals, and if he had a criminal record.

He gave all the right answers, then started talking about how his girlfriend wanted to be an elementary teacher, and she had a bunch of school loans he wanted to be able to help out with. I held my hand up to shut him up.

"Look, you seem like a good kid. You'll make someone an awesome employee someday. But the kind of work you'd do for me, it might get you killed. Or arrested. And if it doesn't, you still can't go home at the end of a hard day and vent to your girl about it. You can't say anything to anyone, ever." I shook my head. "This isn't the right move for you."

He looked me straight in the eye. "I'm not a kid, and I'm smarter than my cousin."

His confidence amused me. "Do you know how to shoot a gun?"

Lincoln nodded.

I blew out a sigh. This wasn't going to end well, but I just didn't have the heart to disappoint Alessio. "Get your cousin back in here," I said.

He did, hesitantly lingering in the entryway. Alessio nudged him all the way in and shut the door behind them.

"Go over some basic rules with him," I said.

Alessio smiled then turned to Lincoln. "Okay, it's pretty easy. If he tells you to do something, you do it. If I tell you to do something, do it. Never repeat a single word of anything you hear from either Luca or I either in this room or out to anyone, even if you think they already know or are in on it too. Never tell anyone anything you did for us, even the completely legal stuff. If they ask about your work, you say you work for a company that handles exports and imports. You're like a glorified personal assistant, and you sometimes help load or unload shipments."

Lincoln nodded eagerly, so Alessio continued.

"If the police ever question you, you say nothing. And I don't mean nothing that would implicate anyone, I mean nothing. You act as though your tongue has been ripped out. And know that if you break that rule, even in a harmless way, your tongue will be ripped out, along with some other parts your girlfriend might really miss."

Lincoln winced.

"Don't lie to Luca or any of your superiors, don't steal, and don't even think about starting any shit on the side. Oh, and don't touch the princess."

"That isn't actually a rule," I interrupted.

Alessio shrugged. "I'm just listing the things that'll get him shot," he said. "And if he touches the princess, you'll shoot him."

I had to agree with that.

"The princess?"

Alessio chuckled. "Luca's girl. Giada Conti."

"Is she related to—"

"Yeah. So, like I said, don't touch her."

Lincoln gazed back and forth from Alessio to me.

I turned to Alessio. "He told me he's smarter than you, by the way."

Alessio flipped his middle finger to his cousin.

"Alright, so Lincoln, why don't you tag along with Alessio and me today," I began. "First though, take his car and get it cleaned—full detail inside and out, then meet us at the Audi dealership on the east side in an hour. Can you handle that?"

He and Alessio both eyed me with confusion.

"If you're getting an Audi, you're sure as shit trading in that Dodge Charger you drive around."

Alessio grinned, then tossed his keys to his cousin. He followed him out of my office, presumably to get his personal items from the car.

An hour later, when we arrived at the dealership, Lincoln was already there, sitting in Alessio's car. I hadn't seen it that clean since the time he beat the shit out of some punk on the hood and then had to scrub for hours to erase the evidence.

"I hope they don't mistake him for one of the cars, with a name like that," I teased.

"He can't help his name," Alessio said with a scowl.

When Lincoln saw us, he waved eagerly then jogged over to greet us.

"Okay, one more rule," Alessio said. "Never wave."

He and I both laughed, then walked into the dealership.

"What's this guy's name again?" I asked.

"Ryan DelFino," Alessio said. Then he turned to his cousin. "Don't say a word the entire time we are here. Your job is to learn."

An eager sales guy greeted us at the door and launched into his spiel.

"Actually, we need to speak with Mr. DelFino," I interrupted.

"He's in a meeting right now, but I'd be more than happy to assist you..." the sales guy trailed off as Alessio spotted the owner's office and nodded his head in that direction.

"Thanks," I said, brushing past him.

The salesman sprinted ahead of Alessio and practically blocked his boss's door with his body.

"It's urgent," I said. "Maybe you could interrupt him."

The man hesitantly knocked on the door. "Hey, uh, Ryan, there are some men out here that need to see you and say it's urgent."

"I'm in a meeting," a voice from the other side of the door said. It sounded breathless and beyond annoyed.

Alessio raised an eyebrow. I nodded for him to proceed.

"Ours is more important, Mr. DelFino," Alessio shouted through the door. "And we'll only take a few minutes of your time."

We waited about one more minute before Alessio tried the knob but it was locked. Luckily, the door opened a moment later.

A red-faced woman, probably in her late twenties, rushed out, adjusting her skirt.

"That explains why she didn't respond to my flirting yesterday," Alessio mumbled.

Next, a heavier middle-aged man came to the door. He glared at his salesman, then turned to us. Alessio brushed past into the office. Lincoln and I followed. Alessio shut the door behind us.

"Luca Marino," I said, offering my hand to Mr. DelFino.

"Pleased to meet you," he said, his tone not matching the polite words. "I apologize if there was some confusion, but my sales team is more than happy to assist with…" his voice trailed off as Alessio held up a framed photo from his desk. It showed him, with what was clearly his wife, kids, and two golden retrievers.

"Your wife good friends with your receptionist?" Alessio asked.

The man glared. "What can I help you with?"

I motioned for him to sit. Alessio walked around to join me in the customer seats facing the desk, which left Lincoln standing by the door. Perfect.

"We're actually here to help you," I said. "I heard you suffered some vandalism the night before last."

"How did you—"

Alessio shook his head and shushed the man. Not one to enjoy interruptions, I appreciated that.

"Not important. What matters is that I know who is responsible for the vandalism and why they did it. Better yet, I can make them stop."

"The police are looking into it, so—"

"I bet your insurance is going to go through the roof after that claim goes through. Can you imagine what it'll be like after they hit you a second time? Or the third? And you know they won't stop until you pay them. Why would they? Hell, I wouldn't be surprised if they kept messing with you even after you pay your debt."

His face paled. "You work for them?"

I shook my head. "No. But I know of them, and the good news for you is that they know me, too, which means they're terrified of me."

"I don't follow."

"DelFino—that's an Italian name, right? Well, us Italians should stick together. That is what my associate and I like to do. So here is our offer. We will take care of your vandals. I can't undo what they've done, but I can make sure they don't harm you or your business again. How much do you owe them?"

His eyes flitted nervously from me to Alessio.

"I need a number."

"Maybe ten thousand."

Alessio made a face.

"Maybe?" I repeated.

"That was the original debt, but they keep saying there's interest now, and…"

"So what is it up to now?"

"Nineteen grand," he said sheepishly.

That wasn't so bad. "Alright, so here's what we're going to do. I'll personally take care of your debt, and I'll let you repay me interest-free and in a tax-deductible way. As an added perk, I'll make sure no one messes with you or your business in the future."

"I don't…well, why would you do this?"

"He needs a new car," I said, motioning to Alessio. He told the man the exact model he wanted, both of us watching the panic in the man's eyes grow.

"Don't worry, he has a trade in," I added, gesturing to the parking lot. "You're going to appraise it at seventeen thousand dollars."

"It's not worth…I don't even appraise the vehicles myself," he stammered.

"Sure, I understand. But you're the guy that can make sure it happens. And we both know it's not the first time you've overestimated the value of a trade in to entice the sale. You're also going to drop the price of the new car by fifteen thousand. We'll give you five thousand cash down payment today towards the difference, and then we'll talk in a couple months and see where we're at on the rest."

Mr. DelFino looked thoroughly panicked, which I interpreted as a good sign.

"Oh, as for the tax-deductible repayment part, you're going to hire our friend Lincoln here to do some marketing. He's in college studying business, and he could really use the money and the boost for his resume. Of course, he's too busy to actually do any work for you, but all of the paperwork will be legit. If you have the employment forms now, this would be a good time for him to fill them all out while we finish hammering out the details of everything else."

Mr. DelFino looked at Lincoln then back to me. "I don't know…"

"Page your girlfriend," I suggested. "I mean secretary. Tell her you have a new hire and need the paperwork. Trust me that you'll need all of that completed to make sure you can deduct your payments to him from your taxes."

Alessio shifted in his seat, ensuring Mr. DelFino got a clear view of his gun.

Mr. DelFino did as we'd asked. A moment later, there was a

knock at the door, and the secretary brushed in, gave him a questioning look, then sauntered out with a smile after delivering the papers.

"Nice ass," Alessio mumbled when we were alone again.

I stood and motioned for Lincoln to take my seat. I grabbed a pen from the cup on Mr. DelFino's desk and handed it to him.

"What do I write?" Lincoln asked.

"And there goes the rule about talking," Alessio mumbled. "Write your name, address, social security number. None of these are hard questions."

"You will get regular paychecks," I told Lincoln. "You will be taxed on your regular paychecks. And because we'll be keeping Mr. Delfino very happy, he will make sure to leave glowing reviews to any future employers who inquire, right?" I turned to Mr. DelFino, who simply nodded.

"Look, I get that this is a lot to take in. And I know right now you're probably questioning which is the lesser evil, the debt you have now or the one you think you're incurring with us. But I'll say this much—I'm a very good friend to have. Under our protection, your business will grow and thrive despite your pesky gambling habit and tendency to borrow business funds for personal use."

"I have children…" he said.

"And a wife and a girlfriend, it seems," I said. "Good for you. I'd really prefer that none of them—or anyone else—ever know anything about our little arrangement." I paused, unsure whether this guy needed more clarification. I decided he probably did. "And when I say I'd prefer, I mean you may end up at the bottom of a river if you talk to anyone."

His eyes widened appropriately.

"Otherwise, I'm a pretty easy guy to get along with. You can keep paying Lincoln here on a biweekly basis until you've given him a total of nineteen thousand, and let's aim for about sixteen hundred a month so you've paid him off within a year. We'll make sure he stops by periodically to make sure no one is giving you any trouble, but you can also call Lincoln 24/7 if any emergencies crop up."

Mr. DelFino frowned. "You want me to call him…"

I nodded. "Yeah. We work for you. Until we've fairly paid off that brand new Audi."

"Minus the trade in," Alessio chimed in.

"Until then, we are at your beck and call. You need protection from vandals, help with the competition, you name it."

He nodded slowly.

"Oh, and pro tip, tell the cops you just noticed three employee laptops are missing too. If you're filing with insurance anyway, might as well get reimbursed for a few extras."

I turned to Alessio. "I assume you can finalize your car purchase without me?"

"Hell yes. Joy ride later?"

I gave him a fist bump, chuckling, then started out. I paused and turned to Lincoln. "You want a ride back to the club or you waiting for your cousin?"

He hesitated, then came with me. Wisely he waited until he was in the car to talk.

"That was awesome," he said. "You just solved that guy's problems, and mine, and got Alessio a new car and it took…what… twenty minutes?"

It wasn't often that I received sincere praise, so I basked in it for a minute and didn't explain it had been a little more complicated than that.

"But what do I do if he calls me?"

"You answer. Don't say anything that could be used against you on the phone ever. Just ask him what's up and say you'll get back to him. Then tell your cousin."

He seemed okay with that answer and didn't talk for a few minutes. Then, he had more questions. "You guys aren't really going to track down the guys that vandalized his place, are you? I mean, like that was all just talk?"

I frowned. "I'm a man of my word, and I recommend you be one as well. A good step towards staying alive is never making a promise you can't keep." I paused, then answered the initial question. "I'll deal with the vandals. They won't mess with him again."

"Like, what are you going to do? How do you know they won't..."

I cut him off with a glare. "Remember when Alessio told you never to question me? It's for your own good. I understand it must be confusing seeing me interact with Alessio, but the rules are different for him because he is like a brother to me. You are not."

When we got back to the club, my phone buzzed. It was a picture of Alessio behind the wheel of his new car. I shook my head, smiling, then turned to his cousin. He was standing beside me still as though waiting further instruction. "You, uh, have a ride, right?"

"Yeah. That's my bike there," he said, pointing to a Ducati Monster.

I blew out a sigh. *Of course,* the kid drove a motorcycle. At least it was Italian. I nodded to Thomas, who was joining us from inside the club.

"If you ever let Giada on that, I'll kill you," I said to Lincoln before turning to Thomas.

"Wait, why would I ever take your girl..." Lincoln began. He stopped himself, appropriately interpreting the look in my eyes.

"You know she'll ask," Thomas said, a slight upward tick at the corner of his mouth. "And good luck saying no to the princess."

"I need about three or four more guys to go with Alessio and I when he gets back. We need to talk to Scotty Lance. I'm guessing he's at his casino."

"Alright. Giovanni is around somewhere. And I can call Roberto."

"I can go," Lincoln piped up.

"Who's that?" Thomas asked.

"Lincoln. Alessio's cousin."

He waved like a new kid in school. Fuck.

I turned to him and stepped closer. "Let's get something straight, Linc. You are not part of my crew, or whatever you think this is. You are not one of us. You are a lowly errand boy, and that is it. If you want to tag along today, I'll let you. But this isn't going to be a regular thing. I don't want you hanging around the club or volunteering for odd jobs when you're not working. You are staying as far away from any real work as possible."

"Dude. Why do you hate me?"

"I don't hate you. I actually really want to keep you alive. But if you ever call me 'dude' again…"

"Right."

Adrian

Mr. Russo called me that morning and asked if I was available for a meeting later that afternoon. As it was, I had plenty of availability, having arranged my schedule for the final year of law school so as to grant me time to work part time. I'd also finally gotten my gun permit a few days before, and after a bit of research, I'd purchased a gun and a safe in which to store it. But, I was so confident in the legitimacy of my new paid internship that I didn't bring it with me.

When I arrived at the office, Mr. Russo met me in the lobby. He introduced me to another partner, then walked me back to his office and motioned for me to sit.

"Coffee?" he offered.

I shook my head.

"I realized we hadn't discussed your availability, but really, at the moment, I don't have anything too time-specific. So as long as we make sure to touch base maybe once a week, that should be good. Just set something up with my secretary. In the meantime, I have some research that needs updating."

He slid a manila folder across the desk to me. "It's a compilation of some legal tips and regulations for small business owners and the like."

I nodded as I opened the folder and began flipping through.

"You can review it later," he said.

I snapped the folder shut.

"It covers a whole slew of information that our clients might find useful. What's important is that it stays up to date. Read through it, update everything, make sure you add any local ordinances and note any variations between New York, Connecticut, and the other surrounding states. Then once you finish that, if you could pare it down to a bare-bones version we could give some of our clients, that would be great."

I nodded. What he was asking seemed fairly self-explanatory. I didn't have the greatest understanding of complex business rules, but surely I could handle this. "When would you like this by?"

Mr. Russo shrugged. "Sooner is better than later, but no real rush. Let's say maybe a month?"

"Okay."

"One other thing. I drew up some leases for a couple of new properties Marco Conti wants to rent out. Could you run these by his house? Just have him review, and if there's no changes, he can sign."

I paused, confused as to why Gino would pay for me to go rather than just fax or email the information to Marco.

"Just track your time for both projects, and we'll make sure you're paid. Oh, and fill out the online application to become a notary. We'll reimburse the costs."

I accepted the folder with the papers for Marco, shook Gino's hand, then left.

When I reached my car, I looked through both folders. I started with the papers for Marco, because that folder was smaller.

Apparently, he was renting out two properties. One of them I recognized as a restaurant Giada had taken me to ages ago when we were dating. I hadn't realized he even owned the place then.

Switching to the second folder, I was pleased to see that the research had been performed once before, albeit several years prior. And it wasn't complex business laws like I'd worried. This was more basic stuff, like rules pertaining to weapons, extortion, money laundering, racketeering, and loansharking.

As I flipped through the folder, the realization hit me like a rogue wave. Apparently, I was a mafia lawyer after all.

❧

Luca

The drive to Scotty's casino was much faster than expected due to light traffic, but still painful. I hadn't anticipated such a long day when I'd left home that morning, and I was ready to be back in bed with my girl.

We didn't waste time exploring the casino floor before making our way to the private hallway off to the side. Alessio knocked on the locked door, then gazed up to the ceiling-level camera pointed down at us. He flashed a wide smile then tapped his watch. A moment later, the door unlocked.

A couple of guys let us into the empty hallway, shutting the solid metal door behind us. I assumed they knew who we were, but I didn't have time for games.

"I'm Luca Marino. Scotty's expecting us," I said.

"You carrying?" one of Scotty's guys asked.

"Yes," Alessio said. "All of us." He paused and glanced at Lincoln. "Except for maybe him."

"We aren't here to hurt Scotty, and if we were, we obviously wouldn't have come in through the front door, on camera, and talked to you," I pointed out. "Besides, he'll want to see us. I have something for him."

I motioned to Alessio, who opened one, then the other, side of his jacket to show the man large rolls of cash.

"What's that?"

I remained stone-faced. "We'll save the full explanation for Mr. Lance."

He hesitated, then went to tell his boss. After several minutes, he returned and said only Alessio and I could enter. Fine by me.

Scotty's office was eerily similar to my own office at Rize. Except Scotty sat behind a cheap-looking particle board wood desk and watched security footage of the casino live on his desk.

I said hi and offered my hand. He declined, gesturing to his video monitor where the rest of our associates waited. "Is this supposed to intimidate me?"

"No. Times are hard. We gotta carpool," I said with a grin. "I assume you know who I am?"

Mr. Lance nodded.

"Great. And this is Alessio Rizzo. Anyway, a friend of ours, Ryan DelFino, owes you some money."

"Oh, so this is a shakedown?"

"No, we're actually here to pay you. He said his original debt was ten grand, right?"

"Naa, it's way more than that now."

I nodded to Alessio, who began withdrawing the cash from his various pockets.

"Here's nineteen thousand. That's the full amount."

"Do you think I'm scared of you? Why would I take your money?"

"I don't think you're scared of me, or much else in this world. But I think you'll take my money because you're obviously a smart businessman. You see that DelFino is never going to pay you on his own, and this is a way for you to get your money upfront, plus get into business with another savvy businessman."

"You want to do business with me?"

"I want to talk about it." I glanced down at my phone. Giada was calling for the third time in under an hour.

"Look, I'm in a rush today, so we can talk another time. But it makes sense for you and I to be friends. Seems we might be able to help each other out every once in a while. For now though, this is what DelFino owes you, so his debt is gone. And just between you and I, he's not worth the trouble, so don't loan him anymore."

I stood. "And this probably goes without saying, but if any of your men harass him or vandalize anything else on his property or have any contact whatsoever with him ever again, I'll have to kill them, and that'll really fuck with this friendship. Understood?"

His eyes narrowed at me for a moment, then he nodded.

"Good. We'll see ourselves out."

"Except his debt was up to twenty grand," he called just as we reached the door.

I leaned across his desk. "Is that how friends play each other?"

Scotty didn't budge.

I stood and reached into my pocket, not missing his flinch. I pulled out my wallet and tossed five hundred onto the desk. "Split the difference. And don't fuck with me again," I said. "Take care."

Alessio waved as we left. I dialed Giada before we even left the club. It would be the middle of the night by the time we'd get home, so this would be my only chance to talk to her before bed.

Giada

'd fallen asleep alone well past midnight, so I wasn't sure what time Luca had joined me. I knew he wouldn't mind if I woke him to talk before I left for the day, but he had to be exhausted. I crept out of bed, getting ready for the day silently, then blew a kiss to my sleeping prince before stepping out of the apartment.

I sipped my coffee as I drove, checking that GPS said I'd have enough time to stop by the church before meeting Gabriella and the other bridesmaids at the dress shop. The final touches were going onto their dresses that day, and I was so excited to see my entire ensemble dressed for my big day.

Aside from weekly mass, I'd hardly been to church over the past few weeks, and I still felt like I owed God more gratitude for bringing my husband back to me. Well, God and Adrian…but something told me God would be easier to thank for that feat than Mr. Patras.

The church was dimly lit, its sanctuary a stark contrast to the fiercely bright late summer day. Two or three other parishioners sat throughout the sanctuary, but I didn't notice anyone in the confessional. I made my way down the center aisle. I knelt near the altar to recite Our Father, then retreated to a pew. I prayed the rosary, having just reached the final prayer, when a clicking noise startled me.

I jerked to attention just as a man sat at the opposite end of my pew.

"Sorry," he mouthed, holding up what appeared to be an informational brochure about the church.

I smiled politely and started to turn away, not having the time or interest to welcome a new church member before meeting Gabby, but I wasn't quick enough. The man stood, walked down the row, then sat again only a few feet away.

I adjusted my hands so he'd see my engagement ring and be

dissuaded if he was coming to flirt, but apparently, that wasn't his intent.

"I'm sorry to bother you, miss, but I'm new here, and if you have a minute… I just have a couple questions."

I gazed around, wondering why he'd chosen me out of the few people in the sanctuary at this hour.

"I think the church office is probably open now. They'd be a much better resource. I'm afraid I haven't been here for long. I just started coming here after I got engaged."

He nodded. "Your husband is Luca, right?"

My stomach clenched. If he was new to the church, he shouldn't know that. I clutched my purse and started to stand.

"I'm sorry. I didn't mean to startle you." He reached into his pocket and then rested a badge on the pew between us.

I froze several inches above the pew, my eyes blurring as I read the lettering on his shiny badge. "You're an FBI agent?"

He nodded.

A thousand questions flooded my mind, but I knew what I needed to do. I straightened all the way, ignoring the way my legs trembled as I stood.

"Your husband is in trouble, and you can help him," he said before I'd even made it out of the pew.

"Fiancé," I whispered, boldly raising my eyes to meet his. He stared back in a way that left me unable to determine if he recognized the lie or not. I waited for him to say something else, and finally, he did.

"Sit down," he said.

I did.

"I just want to talk. You don't need to be frightened," he continued.

I gazed around the sanctuary, noting only one other person remained. "What do you mean he's in trouble? Is someone going to hurt him?"

The man chuckled. "That's not what I meant. Come on, Ms.

Conti. You know what kind of a man he is. You're not that naïve. What else are you here praying about?"

I clenched my teeth together, certain both Luca and I had been insulted. "Maybe you should worry about your own prayers. Luca's a good man, and I have nothing else to say to you."

"There's a coffee shop around the block if you're more comfortable talking there," he said.

I pushed to my feet again, this time more determined in my actions. I rounded the corner of the pew just as the man spoke again.

"We could chat about your father if you prefer. Or maybe your brother?"

My legs stopped moving. I knew I should keep walking, but something kept me frozen in place.

The man stood and caught up to me. "We could be persuaded to protect one man in your life if you give us info about another."

My heart pounded in my chest, instantly reminding me of the panic I'd felt when Luca had been arrested. I heard Alessio's voice in my ear, telling me never to say anything to the police.

I swallowed the lump in my throat and scurried out of the sanctuary. I walked until I reached my car, then started the engine and locked the doors. The man had followed me out, but thankfully, he made no attempt to approach my car. Instead, he walked to a beat-up blue sedan, climbed into the driver's seat, and drove off. I watched his car until it was out of sight, still too shaken to drive.

I debated calling Lorenzo and asking him to drive me to meet Gabriella and the others, then decided against it. He wasn't my savior anymore. I had Luca. Luca would know how to make sense of it all, and Luca would comfort me.

He answered on the first ring, soothing me with the first words out of his mouth.

"Baby, I woke up all alone in our bed. You know I hate that," Luca said with a groan.

"I'm sorry. You looked so peaceful sleeping."

"Are you headed to meet the girls to see the dresses? Do you bring home your dress today too?"

"No, my dress fitting is later this week. Today's just the bridesmaids," I said, bracing myself to tell him about the cop. Luca sounded so perky, and I hated knowing I was about to ruin his good mood.

"God, I have a lot to tell you about from yesterday. I met Alessio's cousin. He's an interesting guy. Complete opposite of Alessio. The business stuff went great, though, and I don't want to jinx it, but I think my papà might actually be proud of me. I'm about to see him now. We're meeting at his favorite restaurant, of course. Could he be more of a cliché? It's like a scene from the Godfather," he said, chuckling at his own comment.

I hesitated.

"Baby? Everything okay?"

"Yeah, I just…I don't know. Something weird happened at church. I can tell you about it later."

"We're already married, amore. Whatever happened, it's not a sign. And it's not bad luck. Nothing can ruin the big day because we've already made it official. Okay?"

"No, it's not that, I just…" I paused as the line clicked, signaling Luca had switched the call from his car speakers to his phone. "Are you at the restaurant now?"

"Si, but my papà can wait a few minutes if you need something. You sure you're okay?"

I smiled at the offer, but Salvatore Marino was not the type of man who could wait. No one made him wait. "It's fine. Good luck with your dad."

"Grazie. Send some selfies from the dressing room, okay? Love you!"

He clicked out of the call before I could even reply. I sighed and peered around me. There was no sign of any other FBI agents, and my legs had stopped trembling. Nothing had happened. I would just tell Luca later.

My phone buzzed, making me jump. Seeing it was Gabriella, I shifted the car into drive before answering.

"Are you almost here?" she said the moment I connected the call.

"Sorry, yes. I'll be there in five," I said, praying traffic cooperated.

Luca

My papà insisted on ordering lunch and eating the salad course before we spoke about business. I updated him about my dealings with DelFino and Lance, pleased to tell him we were progressing better than expected with the casino work.

I'd expected my papà's praise, but I was surprised when he said he was glad I'd gotten that taken care of before we returned to Italy.

"We'll leave tomorrow afternoon. If you're bringing any of your men with you, let me know because I didn't buy any extra tickets," my papà said, reaching for his phone as though we'd somehow finished the conversation.

"Wait, what? We? I'm not going to Italy."

He gazed up and scowled. "Yes, you are. I told you. I need you to handle some meetings there."

"I don't have time for meetings there. I'm up to my ears with meetings here. You stuck me with all these new guys and switched everything around, and now I'm too swamped for anything overseas."

My papà mumbled under his breath in Italian, essentially insulting me in every politically incorrect way possible. "You have men to handle that sort of thing. Do you not trust them?"

I opened my mouth, then shut it. "I'm getting married soon. Did you forget about that? I have to handle wedding plans too."

"Are you the bride?"

"I can't just—"

"Luca, I'm not inviting you on a vacation. This trip is not optional. Get to the airport by noon tomorrow."

My papà then nodded at Maximo, his head bodyguard, who reached for me as though he were actually going to escort me out. I stopped him in his tracks with my most menacing glare, then stormed out on my own. I was still fuming when I reached L'Occhio.

"Uh oh," Alessio mumbled when he saw me. "That bad?"

"Apparently, I'm going to Italy tomorrow."

"But—"

"Yeah, I know." I strode back to my office and slammed the door once Alessio had entered. "Shit. That man has the worst timing. I swear he does this crap just to fuck with me."

"You want me to come?"

I considered that but couldn't afford to have us both out of the city. "No, I need you to handle everything here."

I was so busy trying to squeeze everything in the rest of the day that I didn't make it home to Giada until after one o'clock in the morning. Not surprisingly, she was already asleep. I showered, curled up beside her, then passed out.

In the morning, I woke to the smell of coffee. Giada was already up, so I stumbled out of the bedroom to find her in the kitchen, wearing the sexiest lingerie I'd seen in months.

"How did I not notice you looked like that last night?" I asked, coming up behind her and wrapping my arms around her.

"I don't know, maybe when you stumble home in the middle of the night, you miss some key details," she replied, grinning.

"I'm sorry. I was working late, and I have bad news."

She stared expectantly.

"I have to go to Italy with my papà."

She pouted, but didn't seem as bummed as I'd expected.

"I would've told you sooner, but I just found out yesterday and that's why I had to stay out late, rushing around to finish things before I left. I'll come home as soon as I can, though. I promise."

"When are you leaving?"

I braced myself for a slap. "A couple hours."

"What?" She flung her hands in the air but didn't make contact with my face or arm. Maybe she was maturing. "Luca, you promised you'd go to the final dress fitting with me tomorrow."

"Baby, I know, and I'm so sorry. You know my papà. I don't have any say in the matter. Besides, shouldn't your mom be the one dress shopping with you? It's bad luck for the groom to see the dress."

"We are already married. You keep telling me nothing can bring us bad luck. Besides, I cannot handle another wedding errand with my mother. I will literally lose my mind."

"Tesoro…"

"The dress boutique is an hour out of town. If you're not coming, I'm going to have to drive myself way far away."

I chuckled. She must really be desperate if she was plying me into babysitting her. "I trust you."

"No, you don't! And I'm not going with one of your guys."

That was true. I couldn't spare anyone to keep an eye on her anyway. "What about Gabriella?"

She worked her bottom lip. "Maybe." She shook her head. "We seriously only have a couple hours?"

I glanced at the clock. "I have to be at the airport in three hours. And I still need to pack."

Giada groaned. "Then you don't have time for breakfast before you take me back to bed."

I growled and picked her up. She shrieked and giggled the whole way back to our bedroom.

~

Giada

I hated that Luca was traveling overseas without me so close to our wedding, but mostly I just felt bad for him. Ever since the whole arrest snafu, he'd been swamped with work stuff. And now that it seemed like he was almost caught up on things, he had to leave, and he'd probably get behind again. I wished there was something I could do to help, but of course, there wasn't.

So instead, I focused on what I could do...wedding plans. Luca hadn't wanted to be involved in the vast majority of it anyway, and while I'd still run everything by him, I could probably make most decisions quicker on my own. There wasn't much left to do.

One major benefit of no one knowing Luca and I had already married was that my father still paid Enzo to drive me around when I needed it. So, the day after Luca left, Enzo chauffeured Gabby and me all around town to shop for veils, finalize the reception menu, and visit the florist. I still hadn't found a veil, but we had fun, and I was confident we'd made the right choices on the centerpieces and appetizers.

Gabriella had to work the day of my dress fitting, so it was just Enzo and me.

"How long do you think you'll be?" Lorenzo asked, pulling

into a space in front of the shop. "Or do you just want to text me when you're finishing up?"

I made a face. "I'm not doing this alone. I need company and someone to give me feedback on the veils."

Now it was his turn to cringe. "My opinion is worthless."

"Lorenzo, please. I'm almost out of time to find a veil, and there is nothing more depressing than shopping all alone. Come on. It'll be fun!"

Enzo groaned. "It will not be fun," he insisted, but he pulled the car around to an actual parking spot.

"Thank you, thank you, thank you!" I shrieked, leaping out of the car without waiting. I introduced him to the shop owner as a friend and dragged him back to the dressing room. The clerks offered us both champagne, which I accepted, but Enzo of course declined.

"You know, a sip would actually improve your mood," I teased him as they laid out the selection of veils.

He shook his head. "I have a feeling I need to keep my wits about me today. You look like trouble."

I made a face then ducked into the oversized dressing room with the middle-aged clerk carrying my dress. Even the sight of the gown encased in plastic increased my heart rate with excitement. Of course, the problem with wedding dresses was that they took forever to get on, and in the case of this one, required an assistant's help. The woman hung the dress then stepped outside of the private stall so I could change into my wedding day lingerie.

While I hadn't needed specific undergarments to select my favorite gown from the hundreds I had tried on over the past year, we had now reached the stage where such details mattered. The dress needed to fit like a glove.

I folded my jeans around the panties and bra I'd worn that morning, oddly self-conscious about the woman who was about to help me get dressed seeing my discarded underwear. Then I carefully fastened the snow-white lingerie in place.

"What's Sara up to today?" I called through the curtain.

"Umm…" Enzo stalled, which told me either he was distracted by something on his phone or they'd broken up.

I yanked the curtain open partway to get clarification. I wasn't completely dressed, but the white strapless bra and half-slip covered more of me than the swim suits Enzo had seen me in many times, so I wasn't too concerned.

"Is she okay? Did you guys break up?"

Enzo glanced up at me from his phone and blinked several times as if unable to believe his eyes. "If that's your dress, Luca will hate it. You look like you're in your underwear."

"This is my underwear. So about Sara?"

He sighed and reached for my champagne, gulping half the glass in one sip. "She's fine. We did not break up."

Two salesladies crouched by my feet with the gown. I carefully stepped into the opening, then held my breath as they slowly inched it up my body. Once the dress was high enough that only one assistant could finish the job, she nudged me back into the dressing stall.

I inspected my fingernails as the lady finished buttoning me into the gown. I was overdue for a manicure, but my mom had read in a magazine that brides should let their nails rest in their natural state before a wedding to ensure they'd be healthy. I honestly didn't think anyone would notice my fingers at the event, but I wanted a cute picture of our hands displaying the new wedding bands.

"Is Sara coming to the wedding?" I asked Enzo.

"Is she invited?"

I flung open the curtain again, stepping out even though the gown's bustle wasn't yet completely adjusted correctly. "You already got the invitation. It was addressed to both of you!"

He shrugged sheepishly.

I turned to the mirror, looking at the dress as the clerk finished fastening all the buttons.

"Wow," Enzo said, his eyes lingering on me. "You look stunning."

I twirled side to side, grinning widely. "Thank you." I turned to the clerk as she started to place the first of ten or so veils I'd selected onto my head.

"Veto," Enzo said before I'd even glanced up at myself.

"What?" I didn't mean to snap, but his harsh judgment on the veil surprised me. He'd claimed he wouldn't offer any opinion, and this one wasn't that bad. "What's wrong with this one?"

"It's not right."

"I think you look beautiful," the sales lady said, glaring at Enzo.

He stood, circling me. "You'll look great in any veil, Giada, but this one... I don't know. It just isn't you."

Enzo was right. It was pretty, but the sight of it didn't cause me to instantly swoon. This was not the one.

I shook my head and waited for the next veil.

"So, things are going well with Sara?" I asked, twisting my hair up off my shoulders.

"Yeah, I guess so. I mean, she hasn't dumped me yet, so that seems like a good sign."

"Do you think you'll get married?"

Lorenzo took his time answering. "I don't know. I'm not really sure I'm the marrying type. And she's not... like you or me. I don't want to drag her into all of this."

"Enzo, she'd be lucky to have you. You're a great catch."

He glanced at the lady behind me, and I caught her annoyed grimace in the mirror as she tried to position the next veil on my head.

"I just think my life is a little more complicated than hers," he said, returning his gaze to me.

Suddenly, it occurred to me that I didn't even know what

Enzo would do once he was no longer tasked with keeping me safe. Would he be driving my dad? Working with Matteo? Angelo?

"What are you even going to do with your time when I'm no longer your problem?" I asked him before swiveling to get a full picture of myself in the mirror.

"I'm sure I'll stay busy," he replied.

I turned to the clerk. "I like the line of this one, but it needs more lace."

She frowned, then flipped through a book and held up a different one.

"No, delicate lace. I want simple yet elegant," I said.

"She needs to look like the princess," Enzo said, standing behind me and brushing a loose sequin off my bare shoulder. He left his hand resting on my arm and smiled at me in the mirror.

The sales lady scurried off to look for another veil.

"Luca's a lucky guy," Enzo said, our eyes meeting in the mirror.

Something about the way he said that made me feel even more emotional than I already was. I tried to focus on simple, easy subjects like butterflies and kittens, but I still felt my eyes tearing up. Enzo noticed instantly and swiveled me to face him.

"Giada," he whispered, pulling me close for a hug. "What's wrong?"

The truth was, I didn't know. I was so ridiculously happy, but also terrified. Less than three months ago, Luca had been arrested for murder. And even more recently, the FBI had approached me about him. The possibility of Luca being taken away from me for good was still much too real in my mind. We were just so happy now. Life was too perfect. Things could only get worse.

"Nothing," I finally said. "I'm just, I don't know. Scared?"

He gripped my arms, guiding me several inches away so he

could make eye contact. "Don't be. Luca's never going to let you get hurt. You are everything to him."

"He's on another continent."

"You have Alessio and the entire Marino family looking after you. You have your brothers, your dad. You have me."

"Only until the wedding," I reminded him.

Enzo shook his head. "I'll always look after you, Principessa." He wiped his thumb under my eye.

I gazed at him a moment longer, comforted by the familiarity of his olive skin, stubbled chin, and dark eyes. "I'm not worried about myself. I'm worried about Luca."

Enzo furrowed his brows. "Luca is invincible."

"He almost went to prison."

"But he didn't. And he won't. No one will let that happen."

"If it weren't for Adrian…" I shuddered at the thought.

"Luca is fine, Giada. It's over now," he said.

I shook my head, already guilt-ridden for what I was about to say before the words even left my mouth. I should be telling Luca this, or at least Alessio. But there hadn't been a good moment before he left, and I certainly didn't want to tell him over the phone. Besides, the FBI couldn't touch Luca in Italy.

"Someone from the FBI approached me at church with questions about Luca," I said, my voice lower than a whisper.

Enzo furrowed his brows, but appeared less surprised than I would've expected. "Who?"

The question caught me off guard. "I don't know his name. He had a badge."

"Did he give you a business card? Was he in uniform? What did he look like?"

My heart began to thud harder. "No, I don't know. He was… maybe thirty-something? And I guess like average build." I tried to recall more details but couldn't even picture the man's face or hair. *God*, how unobservant could I possibly be?

Enzo tilted his head to the side and gave my arms a quick

squeeze. "Don't worry about it, Giada. He's on their radar because of the arrest. Maybe he always will be. But that doesn't change anything."

"I didn't tell the guy anything," I said.

"Good."

"He called Luca my husband, though," I continued. But then I stopped myself, not able to explain that I wasn't sure if the agent somehow knew the truth or was just confused.

Enzo paused before speaking. "What did Luca say about it?"

I dropped my gaze to the ground. My feet—clad in the delicate white pumps I'd wear on my wedding day—were completely hidden beneath the beaded hem of the dress. "I didn't tell him. He was dealing with some stuff with his dad, and then—"

"Giada, you have to tell him things like that."

I could tell he wanted to lecture me further, but the sales lady returned then. She froze, clearly uncomfortable at the sight of Enzo and I standing together, with his hands on my arms. Enzo dropped his arms to his sides, and I backed up, offering a fake smile to the lady.

"We've got a few more veils for you to try. Go ahead and step onto that riser, and our seamstress can make some final adjustments while you try them on," the lady said.

Enzo offered me his hand as I climbed onto the riser. Elevated over a foot and facing three angled mirrors, I had no choice but to stare at myself in the gown. Luckily, I still adored the dress. Particularly now that it fit me perfectly, I couldn't help but smile at the sight. I couldn't wait to see Luca's face when he caught his first glimpse of me in this gorgeous dress. And I couldn't help but giggle at the image of him struggling to take it off.

This dress was the polar opposite of the gown I'd worn at our last wedding. This dress was over the top and complex where the other had been simple and straightforward. Silk, lace, and beads layered together on this gown to create a beautifully intricate design, in contrast with the single-fabric of my elopement dress.

I smiled and twirled around once the seamstress finished. "I love this dress," I admitted, gazing at myself for another minute. For once in my life, I felt like the princess everyone claimed I was destined to be. Everything about the gown fit my personality perfectly. It was elegant and sophisticated, sexy but sweet, and completely magical.

I gestured to my purse next to Enzo. "Grab my phone and take my picture please," I asked, telling him my passcode once he pulled the device from my bag.

I posed, letting him get a few shots from every side, then took back my phone. I scrolled through the photos, smiling, then stared back up at the mirror.

"I'm never certain about anything, but this dress is the one," I said. My voice sounded breathless, and my chest constricted as I pictured walking towards Luca in a church wearing that gown.

"It's perfect," Enzo agreed, his eyes locked on my reflection.

I bit my lip, feeling tears well in my eyes. "I swore I wouldn't be one of those girls who got all weepy when she found the dress, especially since..." I cut myself off before I blew the secret about my relationship with Luca.

Lorenzo stepped closer, reaching out a thumb and gently wiping the tears under my eyes. "Especially since what?" he asked. He actually looked suspicious, but surely I was just seeing things.

I dismissed the question with a nod of my head. "My mom is going to be so bummed she wasn't here to see the final look."

"She'll see it soon enough," he said.

I rejected each of the veils they offered me, dismissing the nervous unease rising in my stomach. My anxiety urged me to settle for one, certain I'd never find the perfect one this close to the big day.

"I'm going to end up with no veil," I mumbled as the saleslady removed the final option from my head.

"You'll find the perfect one soon enough," Enzo promised.

"And if you don't, you can grab one of the rejects then. You'll still be the prettiest bride anyone has seen."

I flashed him an appreciative smile in the mirror.

"I think we're done on the alterations, but let's get you out of the dress to clean up the stitching, and then we'll have it back to you in fifteen minutes. Okay?"

I nodded and started into the dressing room with her. "Have you spoken to Adrian lately?" I called through the curtain.

"Why would I?" Enzo replied quickly, his tone clipped.

"I don't know. I thought you two were sort of friends or something." I paused, remembering the secrets I'd told Adrian, the look of hatred and disgust in his eyes when he realized I knew everything about Luca and loved him regardless.

"Adrian and I got along. That doesn't make us friends," Enzo finally said.

I supposed he was right. "I'm not sure how we're ever going to repay Adrian. Besides, he hates me now."

"I'm sure Adrian doesn't hate you. He may hate Luca, but—"

I yanked the curtain open. "Do you hate Luca?"

Enzo laughed, shaking his head. "No, but I didn't love you the way Adrian did."

I supposed that was fair enough.

"Hey, your phone keeps buzzing. Want me to hand it to you?"

I wasn't quite out of the dress yet, and I worried the saleslady would kill me if I moved again before she finished with all of the teensy tiny buttons. "Can you just check it for me?" I asked.

There was a pause. "Looks like a couple of texts from Luca."

"Anything urgent?"

"Uh, no. He says…"

There was a lengthy silence, and then Enzo laughed uncomfortably.

"God, I'm not reading that aloud. Jesus, Giada. Does he kiss his mother with that mouth?"

I laughed, now eager to see what impossibly dirty things Luca had written. The saleslady handed the dress to the seamstress to clean up a few final stitches, so I changed back into my street clothes then sat beside Enzo. Someone had refilled my champagne flute, so I sipped happily.

"Bold move, not asking Julia to be in the wedding," Enzo said, seemingly out of the blue.

I cringed, but I didn't regret my decision. "For all I know, she and my brother will break up before the big day."

Enzo quirked a brow. "I don't think so. She's had a lot of questions about you and Luca lately. Gives me the impression she thinks she and Angelo will be next to walk down the aisle."

I wrinkled my nose, not bothering to hide my dislike for the woman. I couldn't actually pinpoint what I didn't like about her, but she'd always rubbed me the wrong way. "I loathe the idea of that skank becoming my sister-in-law," I admitted.

Enzo snickered. "Well, I'm not saying she's my favorite either, but I do think you might as well get used to her. And she really does seem to like you."

"What makes you think that?"

"I don't know, she just seems so curious about anything to do with you. Well, and Luca. She had so many questions about what happened with his arrest and how he got off."

"That's weird."

He shrugged. "Yeah, a little. But I think she's wondering if it could happen to Angelo. And really I think she's hanging around enough to have some questions about his work that she can't exactly ask."

"Something is off with her," I said.

He didn't disagree, and finally, my gown was ready. They packaged it in a giant box, but instructed me to hang it once we reached home. We'd already paid the deposit, but the balance for the dress was now due.

"Will your husband be paying for this?" Enzo asked.

I could've sworn he quirked a brow at the word "husband," but again, it could've been my imagination. I gazed at the price slip, shocked that the gown wasn't nearly as expensive as I'd assumed. Granted, the label was from an up-and-coming designer, not a big name, but that really only made it more special to me.

"No, my dad is paying," I said.

Enzo smirked, then made his way to the cash register. "I assume you take cash?" he asked the clerk.

She nodded, wide eyed.

"Uhh, tell me you have not been driving around with that kind of cash," I said, grimacing as he began unfolding hundred-dollar bills from a money clip.

"When you're shopping with the princess, you come prepared," he quipped.

I sighed, then turned to my phone. I skimmed through Luca's texts, feeling my cheeks burn as much as Enzo's had, then I replied with a kiss emoji and told him I was dress shopping. I sent the photos of me in the dress to my mother and Gabby, then sent a picture of the dress on its hanger to Luca.

Even if we were already married, I didn't think he should see me wearing my wedding gown until the ceremony.

Luca replied instantly, this time, with a picture. His photo was of a drawing I'd made, ages ago, of my dream wedding gown. In the picture, I'd included my fantasy veil and shoes.

My jaw dropped as I dialed Luca.

"Why do you have my drawing?" I asked the moment he answered.

"I took it with me in case I saw something you'd love here in Italy."

I smiled. It was a sweet sentiment, but the thought that he could pick out a wedding dress for me without even seeing it on me was ridiculous.

"I found something," he continued. "I was going to surprise you, but if you hate it—"

"What is it?"

"Hang on."

There was a rustling, then a moment later, my phone pinged with a text. It was a photograph of a gorgeous veil. It was my dream veil. "Oh my God. That's…it's as though someone had sewn the exact veil I'd drawn."

Luca chuckled. "They did," he admitted.

"What?"

"I gave the designer your drawing, and he brought it to life."

I was speechless. I gazed at the photo again.

"Think it'll go with the dress?"

"Yes. I love you," I said. "Hey, um, that last text you sent…um, Enzo may have read it."

Luca said something under his breath in Italian but then laughed.

Enzo rolled his eyes at me.

"Okay, well, I'll call you later when I'm home."

"Actually, I might be able to catch a flight later tonight, so if I don't answer, I'm on my way back to you."

Between the promise of Luca returning home soon and finally having my dress, I was ecstatic. I put the dress on hold and made plans to return later that day with my mother, then Enzo and I headed out. As we passed L'Occhio, I got an idea.

"Hey, can we stop here real quick?" I asked, gesturing up ahead.

Enzo eyed the club warily. "It's closed."

"I know, but Luca was really sweet to have a custom veil made for me, so I want to do something for him."

Enzo didn't answer, so I kept talking.

"I just want to leave him a few nice notes. It'll take like five minutes. Please?"

He groaned but pulled over and parked. There were only two cars in the lot aside from ours and a delivery truck, which seemed surprising. The delivery guys seemed to be unloading, so I just headed for that entrance.

"You can stay in the car if you want," I said.

He shook his head, then eyed the delivery guys warily. "Giada, wait!" He called as I hurried on ahead. "I don't think this is a good idea."

I ignored him and hurried on in.

I'd never before seen the guy working at the front, so I smiled politely and introduced myself. "I just wanted to leave something in Luca's office."

The guy hesitated, then looked past me. I turned to see José, one of the guys that almost always worked at the club, walking by. He smiled at me then turned to the new guy. "I can vouch for her. How are you Giada?"

"Good. You?"

"Can't complain. Have to run, though." He turned to the new guy. "Lock up when they're done with the delivery. I'll be back in an hour."

Enzo followed me back to Luca's office, sitting in the chair looking bored while I doodled on a few different notes.

"So, um, how is your Italian these days?" he asked.

"Terrible," I said with a snort. "Why?"

"Luca's text seemed to include some Italian. Did you just skip over that?"

I shrugged. "He's got a few lines he uses pretty regularly. I know what those mean."

He made a face, but didn't expound, and I was done anyway. I pushed away from the desk, sticking the last note right on his computer monitor.

As we reached the bar on our way out, the new guy seemed to be frustrated over something the delivery guys were telling him.

"That's not what the price is supposed to be," he said to them.

"Guess it went up," the taller guy replied.

Enzo sighed and gripped my elbow. "Giada, come on."

"Is there a problem?" I asked the new guy.

"No problem," the delivery man said. "We were just explaining to your friend here that we'll have to take all our products back with us if he's unable to pay the full invoice."

"The invoice is wrong. This isn't the price they'd agreed to," the new guy replied.

"Giada, come on. Luca can straighten this out when he gets back. You are not getting involved," Enzo said, tightening his grip on me.

"Are you kidding? Luca is a busy man. He doesn't have time to fix this shit." I threw my hands in the air and walked out into the bar where the men were starting to load up the booze.

"Giada!" Enzo cautioned me. I dismissed him with a shake of the head and approached the guys.

"Put the boxes down," I said, pleased as punch with how assertive I sounded.

The men froze, looked at each other, then looked back to me. One of them snickered. Another smiled. Perhaps I hadn't sounded so scary after all.

"You agreed to the terms of this arrangement, and you will abide by them. What's more, if you don't stop being dicks, we're knocking another ten percent off your payment for the next shipment."

The head guy stepped forward, still looking amused. "Listen sweetheart, it's cute of you to step in here and try to help, but why don't you leave the business matters to us big boys," he said, gently touching my arm.

I swatted his hand off me, shuddering. "I highly recommend you keep your hands off me. Do you have the slightest clue who I am?"

He glanced back at his friends then turned to me. "You're Marino's girl, right?"

I nodded. "Yes, and Luca doesn't share well, so trust me when

I say you should probably take a step back before someone sends him a picture and he gets the wrong idea."

The man stepped forward, causing me to straighten so quickly I nearly stumbled. Thankfully, I held my ground—and my breath—while he spoke. I reminded myself that Enzo could shoot both men in a matter of seconds if necessary.

"Like I said, it's best for you to stay out of this, darling. I'm sure you mean well, but I hear your man is halfway across the world right now and by the time he gets back, we'll be long gone."

"Maybe so, but I'm not sure you did your homework about me. I'm Giada Conti. Does that name ring a bell? Wanna guess how long it'll take Daddy to get here and sort this out?"

The man's expression changed noticeably, and he glanced back at his partners.

"Lorenzo, could you call my father please? I think he has some associates in the neighborhood." I said.

Enzo nodded and pulled out his cell phone.

The man in front of me set the box down. "You win," he said.

"No," I replied.

He looked at me with confusion.

"Set the boxes on the bar and unload them."

To my joy, the men did as I said. Enzo still looked like he might pass out at any moment, but personally, I was feeling like a badass.

"We'll see you here next month at the same time, but we'll be docking that ten percent. If you don't cause any more trouble, maybe my fiancé will bump your rate back up after that. If not, well, you'll have two of the most powerful families on the east coast hunting you down."

They finished unloading by the end of my speech.

"Thanks. Have a good day!"

The men stomped out, and Enzo immediately rushed to me.

"Damn it, Giada, you can't do that. Do you know what your

father or Luca would do to me if they knew I let you confront them?"

I couldn't conceal my smile. It was just too exhilarating. "Eeeee," I shrieked. "I totally see why you guys like this stuff now."

"Giada, I'm serious," Enzo said.

I made a pouty face.

He rolled his eyes. "For your sake, you better be as good in bed as I imagine, or Luca may make you wish those guys killed you."

I laughed, but felt oddly flattered.

Enzo turned to the new guy, watching in awe. "You go home. You're fired. You saw nothing, heard nothing."

"But I…you don't even work for Luca."

I shook my head. "No, really, it's best if you just listen to him. Luca isn't going to love your role in all this."

Frowning, he shuffled out. Enzo locked up the bar then handed me the keys.

CHAPTER 8

Luca

My trip to Italy was a complete waste. Nothing I did while on my native soil required my physical presence in the country. It was obvious that my papà dragged me overseas at the least convenient time simply to remind me of the control he still wielded, and that fact angered me far more than it should have. I'd known for a decade now that my papà was a manipulative, power-hungry prick, so I shouldn't be surprised when he behaved consistent with his persona.

Despite my annoyance, or perhaps because of it, I managed to finish all the bullshit tasks he'd asked of me quickly. I booked a return flight for myself less than a week after I'd arrived, and I was already cheerfully anticipating seeing my girl again when Lorenzo called and ruined my good mood.

I supposed I should have been grateful that he told me what had happened right away, saving me the mortification of hearing it after the fact from one of my guys. But then I also wondered if his confession was, in part, because he feared backlash from me over his role in the entire debacle. Maybe I deserved that based on how I'd responded to him fooling around with my girl years ago, but then again, those were very different circumstances.

Besides, now I'd matured. So, I simply thanked Lorenzo and then called Giada to lecture her. Almost comically, she thought I'd be grateful.

"But I saved you ten percent!" she insisted.

"Giada, I would pay double if it meant keeping you safe."

She had no response to that.

"I'm serious, Giada. You cannot get involved in this stuff. Ever! If you don't get yourself killed, you're going to get *me* killed when your father finds out."

"Oh please, I can handle him."

"Can you? You mean like how you handled my guy? Giada you can't fire my people. That's not how we do things."

"Technically, I didn't. Enzo did."

I gritted my teeth, annoyed that Lorenzo had been close enough to fire someone and still let Giada talk to those guys. "I guess I'll have to talk with him again about my expectations when he's watching you."

"Luca, I don't need a babysitter. And don't worry, he was ready to shoot them the whole time."

"That's not how I want to do business. I don't want to have to shoot people all the time just to keep you safe."

She didn't reply, and the overhead announcement told me my flight was boarding.

"I'll see you soon, amore. Don't do anything stupid before I get home, okay?"

Giada agreed, and I shifted my focus back to work I could do during the return flight.

Giada

I awoke suddenly, acutely aware that I was no longer alone in the darkened room. I heard rustling by the closet and saw a large, looming shadow figure, but I wasn't afraid.

"Luca?"

"Si, baby, it's me," he replied, his whispered tone matching my own.

A moment later, the bed shifted as he crawled beside me. As I always did when I fell asleep alone, I'd positioned myself in the middle of the large bed, leaving space on either side of my body for Luca to join me. Tonight, he scooted up behind me, his chest against my back. As I rolled to face him, his arm swung over my waist, pinning me on my side, facing the windows.

"You're still mad," I guessed based on his posture.

"I am," he said. His voice was calm, which made me think he wasn't too angry. But then again, he hadn't tried to seduce me yet, which wasn't a good sign.

"I've been a bad girl," I said, opting for a different approach to distract him from his annoyance. "You could punish me."

I felt him harden along my backside and smiled at the effectiveness of my plan.

"You want me to spank you?" His voice was deeper now.

I wiggled my ass against him harder in response.

Luca reached around and pulled my cotton shorts down just to mid-thigh. Had I known I'd have a visitor in the night, I would've chosen something sexier than shorts and a loose tank top, but at least it was dark.

He smoothed his hand along my bare skin, following the curves of my body as it led him in between my legs. He paused there, then withdrew his hand. "My papà taught me never to hit a woman. Probably the only good advice he ever gave me."

His hand disappeared entirely from my body, and when I felt it again, his finger was damp. This time, he moved up my shirt, pinching and rolling one nipple, then the other, until they formed stiff peaks. I moaned and shifted against him harder, suddenly desperate for some relief. Luca laughed, his voice sexy and gravelly.

"I could punish you like this, just do this for hours and see how long it takes to drive you mad," he mused.

He licked his finger again, then slid it down between my thighs, stroking the sensitive bud. I parted my legs slightly, offering him better access, so his finger slid back and dipped just into my entrance then dragged back out, spreading the moisture all along my slit. He continued the slow torture for a few more minutes, alternating his movements from my breast to my core and back again.

Finally, when I was certain I'd combust if he didn't hurry up and fuck me, I felt the broad head of his cock pressing against me. I moaned happily, and he firmly pinched my nipple as he thrust fully into me with one solid roll of his hips. His finger stayed at my breast for a moment as he drove in and out of me, the pressure quickly building inside of me. When he moved his finger back to my clit, rubbing directly against the burning bundle of nerves, I was gone, spasming wildly around him. His hips moved faster, letting my muscles milk him as they rhythmically tightened and released, and then he exploded into me with a loud cry.

Luca slowly withdrew and tugged my shorts back to my waist, apparently unconcerned with my now-pressing need to go clean up.

"Sleep," he whispered. "I can punish you in the morning."

I smiled, trying to imagine how he could ever top that as a punishment. I was certain I wouldn't fall asleep, my body still tingling with the aftermaths of my intense orgasm, but before I registered Luca's breathing slowing, my mind went blank.

~

Luca

*S*ince my papà planned to return to the States before all of the wedding festivities began, I didn't delay scheduling a time for Giada to meet my half-brother. Although my papà could easily have men watching me in his absence, I'd convinced myself I was safe to meet up with Carla and the kid as long as my old man was in Italy. I didn't bother telling Carla that Giada would be with me, but I hadn't anticipated any issues. Not wanting to visit Carla's crappy apartment, I offered to meet them at some indoor playground.

Carla smiled when she saw me, dipping her head forward and raising an eyebrow in what I suspected she thought was a seductive manner. I couldn't help but notice then that her too-tight denim shorts and dangerously low-cut top seemed inappropriate both for the weather and the venue. My stomach churned at the thought that this woman—who had fucked my papà—was trying to flirt with me.

I forced a polite smiled onto my face, but directed my attention to Jacob first. He wore an adorable little polo shirt that looked like it could have a matching adult version, but his socks were designed to look like zebras.

"Hey buddy," I said, not surprised when he didn't acknowledge me. I couldn't compete with the play kitchen, padded obstacle course set up, or dozens of books filling the oversized room.

"Hi Luca," Carla said, her tongue curling around my name in a way that made my skin crawl.

"Hey," I mumbled, not looking up.

"It's good to see you. Have you been working a lot?"

"Uh same as ever."

"You look like you've been working out," she said, her hand brushing against my bicep.

Barf. I shrugged away.

"Why is she here?" Carla asked, her tone quickly changing.

I gazed up, smiling at the sight of my beautiful wife approaching.

"They didn't have espresso," Giada whispered apologetically, handing me one of the tall paper cups in her hands.

"He's my son, Luca. You can't just bring whoever to see him," Carla continued, not even bothering to acknowledge Giada.

She was infuriating. I clenched my fist around my cup to keep from strangling her. "You should get used to seeing her. She's my…"

"Giada," Giada interrupted right before I blurted out 'wife.'

Giada extended her free hand towards Carla, who reluctantly shook it. "Giada Conti. I don't think we officially introduced ourselves before, but it's good to meet you. I've heard a lot about this little guy." Giada turned to Jacob and smiled.

Carla scowled at me. "It's a pleasure," she said, her tone not matching her words. "Luca, could we chat for a moment?"

Carla stepped to the side, motioning for me to follow. I turned to Giada, hoping she could read the look of desperation in my eyes.

"Be the bigger person, Luca," Giada said, her voice soft. Her hand reached forward, her delicate fingers stroking my knuckles in a way that slowed my heart rate.

I made a pouty face but turned to talk with Carla.

"I don't want a parade of random women spending time with my son, Luca."

I refrained from pointing out that given her career as a stripper, Jacob probably witnessed many parades of women in his own home. "I understand, and it's one woman. Giada and I will be married in a matter of weeks. She'll be a part of my life till the day I die, so she's going to be a part of Jacob's too."

Carla snorted. "You are not the marrying type. You'll never go through with it."

I wanted to scream that I already had, to shake her and tell her I'd marry Giada every single day if I had to, but instead, I chewed the inside of my lip. "Look, I could stand here and tell you about what a wonderful person she is and how lucky your son is to have her in his life, but that is all beside the point. As long as you want to continue this arrangement, I will bring Giada with me to see Jacob whenever I want, and you will treat her with respect. If you want to stick around whenever she's with us, that's fine, but you don't get to upend my life with your games and then tell me who can or can't come with me to see Jacob."

Carla's eyes narrowed, and she opened her mouth to speak, but I cut her off, reaching into my pocket and retrieving the envelope of cash I'd brought for her.

"Do you want this or not?" I asked, pausing while she glared for a moment before snatching it out of my hands and peeking inside. "I want what's best for Jacob, but let's not pretend like you have any choice in this matter. If you don't let me see him on my terms, I'm not giving you money. If you try anything stupid, you'll get to deal with my papà instead."

I swiveled abruptly and went back to Giada, wrapping my hand around her side and pressing a kiss to her forehead. I could tell from her expression that she'd caught the gist of our discussion, but she quickly calmed me down.

"I feel like I'm in a time machine watching toddler Luca stumble all around," she teased as Jacob tripped over the edge of the mat.

"I never stumbled," I retorted.

Her grin widened. She tensed briefly as Carla rejoined us, then quickly regained her cool.

"He's adorable," Giada said. "And I love those little socks. Do they make them with other animals?"

Carla nodded. "Yeah, they come in a pack of eight with all different animals on each pair."

"So cute."

None of us really talked much after that, or interacted with

Jacob a whole lot either. He seemed pretty content to toddle around the play area, exploring on his own while we watched and cooed over his every step. I caught Carla eying Giada a few times, noting she seemed particularly annoyed by her engagement ring.

On the drive home, I mentioned it to Giada.

"I noticed, too," she said. "It makes sense. She's jealous."

"Jealous of what?"

"Me. Because I have you."

"She hates me," I pointed out.

"No, she wants you to want her, and the fact that you don't is driving her crazy."

I wrinkled my nose. I had to agree with that, even if the thought of Carla being interested in me nauseated me.

CHAPTER 9

Giada

*A*fter I met Luca's half-brother, Luca deposited me at my parents' home for the night. He stayed for dinner, then lingered inside my childhood bedroom for an extended goodbye kiss before leaving. I hated the thought of spending another night away from him after just getting him back from Italy, but my bridal shower was the next afternoon. My aunts were coming in the morning, and my mom had planned an entire day of pampering for all the ladies in the family. I'd wanted a cute couple's wedding shower, but my mom yearned for a more traditional and formal event. As her only daughter, I felt compelled to indulge her wish for a girls' day.

Once Luca left, I opened the packages which had already arrived from out-of-town guests who wouldn't make it to the shower. There were a few random knickknacks, two items off our wedding registry, and a collection of slutty lingerie from a great aunt in Sicily.

I turned to a knock on the door, smiling as my mom poked

her head inside the room. She joined me by the bed where I surveyed the collection of gifts.

"You're staying on top of the thank you notes, right?" she asked.

I nodded. I hated writing, so I had been forcing myself to send the notes the same day the gifts arrived. That way, the chore didn't build up to the point of overwhelming me.

My mom lifted a silk teddy off the bed, her eyes going wide. I cringed, not even wanting to guess what thoughts might be flitting through her mind. Just as I prepared to yank it out of her hand, she laughed and dropped it.

"I still remember when you told me you were waiting until marriage for…" she paused and made an exaggerated face at the items. "You were so convincing. I actually believed you."

Even though the conversation she referenced had taken place over a decade earlier, I still remembered it. Awkward conversations with parents about sex tended to imprint themselves on my brain, I supposed. I'd been barely sixteen at the time, and Luca had just turned eighteen. My mom had wanted to put me on birth control after seeing a picture of Luca and me on the beach.

"I wasn't lying," I insisted, rather than dropping it.

My mom snorted.

"I'm serious. You know how important the Church was to me. Is," I quickly corrected. "I fully planned to wait till I was married."

She still looked skeptical. "If you expect me to believe you and Luca haven't—"

"Mom, stop. Omigod," I breathed, feeling heat rush to my cheeks. "I'm saying at the time, we hadn't. And we didn't, not for a long time."

"Wait, are you saying Adrian was your first?"

I regretted a thousand times over not ending this conversation before it started and just letting my mom think I had lied to her as a teen, but now I saw no way out but to finish the conversation. "No, it was Luca."

My mom raised an eyebrow, and I thought that was the end of the conversation. She made her way to my window and straightened the curtains. "I always assumed you and Adrian had—"

"Okay, Mom, this discussion is beyond awkward. I know I'm getting married in a week, and so apparently now is the time for us to have all these weird conversations, but enough. Luca was my first ages ago, but over a year after I told you I was waiting for marriage. And in my defense, the only reason I changed my mind was because I decided it didn't matter if we waited until after the actual wedding when I was so sure we were going to get married."

"Wait, so you finally slept with him, and then he dumped you and left the country?"

I nearly giggled at my mom's expression of outrage.

"That is not exactly what happened, but regardless, it all worked out. I have no regrets." I paused. "Except for letting you into my room to start with because I'm going to need years of therapy to forget this awkward conversation."

My mom tugged me to her in a hug. "Oh sweetie. I'm happy you're happy. It's just hard for me because you're still my baby. Now that you're getting married, I realize I have to let you grow up. I thought I'd have more time before I lost you."

I let her hold me for another minute, then I pushed back and spoke. "Mom, haven't you heard the expression? You're not losing a daughter. You're gaining a son."

She rolled her eyes. "Yeah, well no offense to Luca, but I already have two sons just like him."

Her words wound their way through my brain as I wondered if she truly understood how similar the three men were. After nearly three decades of marriage to my father, surely she must know more than she let on. I supposed at this point, her awareness didn't matter. But it might offer her some comfort to hear I wasn't oblivious to the life I was choosing.

"Mom," I began, keeping my voice soft. "I realize everyone

thinks I'm so naïve and innocent, but I'm aware of a lot more than you think. Luca is a good man. I know who he is and what he does, and I don't want you to worry that I'm going into this blindly. He's not perfect, and I'm not perfect, but together, we make each other better."

She sighed and smiled. "You can't save everyone Giada."

"Luca doesn't need me to save him. He's not the person the rest of the world sees."

"I just want you to be happy."

"I am, promise. Literally all of my childhood dreams are coming true."

We hugged again, and then she left me alone with my lingerie and thoughts.

~

Luca

While I managed to dodge mandatory attendance at the bridal shower due to my gender, my mom apparently thought that meant I had a surplus of free time. Well, either that or she was bored with my papà still in Italy. She summoned me to the house for brunch the day of Giada's shower, and even though I told her I was slammed with work, she wouldn't take no for an answer.

I supposed it didn't matter.

Alessio was meeting with Thomas and Giovanni about the new guys they were bringing on board. As per my papà's grand plan, I was supposed to stay out of the process. Thomas and Giovanni were each going to train a few of their current guys to take on some new duties, and then those men in turn could bring some new foot soldiers on board. Those men wouldn't be "made" men in the traditional sense. They'd never swear an oath of loyalty to myself or my papà, and ideally they'd never really know who stood at the head of the family they served.

Theoretically, that process would let the official Marino family achieve more work, dabble in more fields, and oversee more turf—all with less potential liability. I had doubts about the whole plan. But, if it meant I didn't have to worry about spending another night in jail, I was willing to cooperate.

"Ahhh, Lucasino," my mother cooed, greeting me at the door. "How are you my little topolino? You look skinny. Is Giada not feeding you enough?"

I sighed, certain I was far too old for the "little mouse" nickname. "I'm an adult, Mamma. It is not Giada's job to feed me." I inched my way into the house and closed the door behind me right as my mom's eyes widened.

"She's about to be your wife. Of course, that's her job."

I debated reminding my mom that she, like Giada, wasn't a big cook, but decided I was better off staying quiet. As a child, I'd mostly eaten food prepared by a cook or by my aunt, who came to live with us for a few years after her husband was killed. My mother also wasn't big on cleaning, but I figured she'd chastise Giada for hiring out that task, too.

"Giada's actually been doing really well at the interior design firm lately," I said finally. We reached the dining room where I saw the table was set for three. I stopped in my tracks. "Papà came back early?"

"No, he'll return in two days," she said, fussing over the floral arrangement in the middle of the table.

"Then who else is joining us?"

Her smile widened and she opened her mouth to answer, only to be interrupted by the doorbell. She scurried to the door without another word.

I filled my glass with sparkling water and sipped while I waited for my mom to return with our mystery guest. I expected my aunt, or perhaps another family friend, but nearly dropped my glass when I heard the familiar voice trilling through the entry.

"Chiara," I choked as she appeared in the room.

"Luca," she replied, rounding the table to greet me with a lingering kiss on either cheek. "You look positively scrumptious."

I cleared my throat and tried to regain my composure. "Oh? My mom was just saying I'm too skinny." I glared at my mother, but she simply smiled back, feigning ignorance as to the reason for my annoyance.

"Chiara, make yourself at home. I'm going to help my mom bring the food to the table," I said. I turned and stormed off to the kitchen, determined to wait as long as it took for my mom to catch up. Luckily, she came right away.

"Why is she here?" I asked.

My mom shrugged. "I always liked Chiara, and you know that. I haven't seen her for ages, so it'll be good for us to all catch up. It won't kill you to be nice for an hour."

"How did this sound like a good idea? You're headed to a shower for my bride later today."

"Exactly. If I'm going to have to spend the rest of the day with that girl who refuses to even learn your language, you can handle one meal with the woman I wanted you to marry."

"Jesus, Mamma." I blew out a sigh and turned to the wall. It was only ten a.m. and already I needed a stiff drink. The worst part was that I wouldn't even be able to vent to Giada. Normally, she'd be sympathetic, but it wasn't fair to make her even more self-conscious around my mom this close to the wedding. Besides, she was already sensitive over Chiara's sudden appearance in town.

Whatever.

I was a big boy. I could handle gangsters, manipulative strippers pretending I'd fathered their child, and the most judgmental and demanding boss in the world. Surely I could survive an hour with my ex-girlfriend and mother.

Giada

My bridal shower was everything I'd imagined, only amplified. I'd never seen so many flowers in one room my entire life, nor smelled so much perfume. Luca would've hated it, so I supposed I was grateful my mom had insisted on it being a girls-only event. Without him there, I could enjoy myself without feeling sorry for him.

My aunts had planned a handful of ridiculous games, then we'd all enjoyed a light lunch. I opened gifts after we ate, trying to focus on my gratitude for everyone's generosity and not think about the mountain of thank you notes I'd need to write later. Just when I felt certain I couldn't possibly untie another bow, my mom announced that it was time for dessert.

I downed a second mimosa and nibbled a miniature fruit tart while talking with Julia. She'd been dating my brother Angelo for over a year and seemed destined to join the family, but I still didn't like her. She hadn't ever done anything truly offensive, but there was something off about her entire demeanor.

"That was crazy about Luca's arrest," she said, licking a drop of cupcake frosting off her finger before selecting a lemon bar from a nearby dessert tray. "Thank goodness you found that alibi."

"Excuse me?" I said, my breath catching in my throat over the way she'd phrased it. As far as anyone outside of Luca's inner circle knew, his alibi was legit.

"Well, just think if Adrian hadn't stepped up," she continued, oblivious, as always.

"Yeah, I think about that a lot," I replied. "But Luca's attorney would've called Adrian to testify anyway, so there was never any real threat of conviction."

She furrowed her dark brows. "You really think he was innocent?"

The pastry I'd been chewing formed a lump in my throat, and I chugged my mimosa to help force it down. "I know he was innocent. People can't be in two places at once, and that's not the sort of thing Luca would've done anyway. I thought you knew him better than that."

I turned, not even bothering to excuse myself. I spotted Gabriella, and I rushed to her side.

My best friend's smile instantly calmed me. "You need another drink and one of those miniature strawberry custard things. They're exquisite." She guided me towards the main dessert table, forcing a tiny pink goblet and miniature spoon into my hands. "Go get some fresh air, and I'll bring your drink."

I stepped out the French doors of the ballroom into the decorated courtyard. Guests milled about happily, enjoying the sunshine and slight breeze. Gabby was back by my side before anyone else had a chance to accost me, so that was nice.

"Strawberry lemonade," she said.

I must have frowned, because she quickly added, "With vodka."

"Thank you," I whispered.

"Just doing my job as the maid of honor." She checked her phone and grimaced. "You still have an hour left. If anyone that you don't want to talk to gets in your way, just tell them you were on your way to find me to do some photos with the ribbon bouquet, okay?"

I nodded, having forgotten the wacky bouquet my bridesmaids had made from all of the ribbons I'd removed from gifts. Apparently the ribbon bouquet was a tradition, though I wasn't sure why.

"Okay. Go mingle," she said, taking the now-empty dessert goblet from my hands.

It really had been delicious, although every dessert I'd

sampled so far was fantastic. Maybe it was simply the adorable sizing, or maybe the caterer was a true expert with desserts. Either way, I'd never fit in my wedding gown if I kept eating like this.

I decided to head to the restroom before returning to the main ballroom, but I paused in the hallway outside the ballroom to chug the rest of my lemonade before abandoning the cup.

"Excuse me," a man said from behind me.

I turned, expecting to see a waiter, as no other men had attended the event. This man wore a suit, but it differed from those donned by the wait staff.

"It seems congratulations are in order," the man said. His smile was friendly and natural, not stiff or predatory like I'd come to expect from the people who were clearly not thrilled by the union.

"Thank you," I replied, ready to head into the bathroom.

"How much do you know about your fiancé?" he asked, stopping me in my tracks.

"I'm sorry, do we know each other?" I asked.

The man extended his hand as if to shake mine, but as I glanced down at it, I saw he was clutching an FBI badge. I froze.

"Give me thirty seconds, Giada, and then you can be back to your party," he began. "You are in danger, and we can protect you if…"

"Who is going to hurt me?" I asked.

His lips parted, and he frowned, clearly not having anticipated an interruption.

"Who would you protect me from?" I rephrased.

"Your fiancé, the entire Marino family is…"

"You're telling me you think my fiancé, Luca, might hurt me?" I interrupted again.

He hesitated, then nodded. "We can offer you complete protection in exchange for your cooperation. I know you're a good person, Giada—"

"Luca is a good person, so you're clearly very mistaken about something," I replied. "And I'm in the middle of my bridal shower. If you keep harassing me, I'll have you reported."

I scurried into the women's bathroom before he could say anything else. When I emerged a few minutes later, the man was gone.

I felt like I should've been shaken up by the encounter, but as I rejoined my guests, I realized I wasn't. Maybe it was the alcohol calming me, or maybe the excess sugar. But as I gazed around a room of more than fifty women, all willing to sacrifice their afternoon to celebrate my wedding, I couldn't help but feel invincible.

I was the princess, and I had a whole village ready to protect my crown.

CHAPTER 10

Adrian

Everything in my world had remained blissfully calm for several weeks, so I should've known shit was about to hit the metaphorical fan. Work had been going eerily well. Angelo hadn't dropped by my office or apartment unannounced, and everyone at the firm treated me like an actual employee. I wondered if Mr. Russo was the only one who knew my practice was limited to mafia cases, since the firm at large handled a variety of criminal matters wholly unrelated to organized crime. I could've forgotten I was even involved with Marco, aside from the fact that Mr. Russo often asked me to deliver my findings on various issues directly to Marco, in person.

Still, dropping by the house to meet with Mr. Conti about legal matters felt like the normal sort of thing a legal intern might do. There was nothing clearly nefarious about my work. I didn't feel like a criminal. I wasn't even doing anything wrong. Guilty or not, all individuals were entitled to a proper defense, and advising clients on the legality of certain activities was well within the bounds of professional responsibility.

My sister had decided to move to the area, which didn't completely surprise me after her recent visit. She found a room in a reasonably-priced, furnished apartment with two other young professionals. She planned to stay there for four months while scoping out alternate living arrangements. Annie had always been friendly and laid back, so I didn't doubt she'd do fine living with two other women, but I had thought it odd she didn't even attempt to find a place further from the city where she could've afforded a small place on her own, like me.

Regardless, I was excited to have family nearby, even if that meant my parents would now come visit more often. I would have liked to see them more, but I wasn't sure how my father—himself an attorney by trade—would respond to my choice of defense work. And with my sister in town, she agreed to come with me to Giada's wedding, sparing me the awkwardness of finding a date.

When Angelo called me to say he'd pick me up on his way to Luca's bachelor party, I thought he'd been kidding. I didn't even recall being invited to the event, but Angelo insisted I was. When I told him I already had other plans, his response had been clear. This wasn't the sort of event I could skip. It occurred to me that maybe Angelo was just being his usual dickish self, but it didn't matter. He barked orders; I followed. Apparently, that was how our arrangement worked.

He ignored me during the drive to the club where Luca's party was being held, but when Eddie parked the car, Angelo asked me to stay behind.

"Look, you don't have to like Luca," he said once we were alone. "I sure don't. But you can't be disrespectful. Our families have an arrangement, and if I have to go along with it, so do you."

"I can play nice, but it still doesn't make sense," I replied. "Luca is marrying your sister, so of course you should be here. But I don't see why he'd want her ex showing up to his bachelor party. Or the wedding, for that matter."

Angelo grinned. "Come on, Patras. You're a smart guy. I'm sure you can figure out his motivation." He paused, but not long enough for me to speak. "He wants to rub your nose in it, make sure you realize you lost. Well, and maybe confirm you're not still trying to get her back. You're not, are you?"

I wrinkled my nose. "No. God, no. If I could go back in time and never ask her out, I'd do it." That was a lie, of course, but it shouldn't have been. A rational man would have nothing but regrets over his time with a woman like Giada. But somehow, the good days with her made up for the heartache and shitshow that followed.

"Aw, but if you'd never dated my sister, you never would've met me," Angelo taunted.

"Exactly," I replied.

Angelo snorted, clearly not bothered by the insult. I followed him into the club, bracing myself for disaster.

The club wasn't too busy, and the men milling about didn't exactly resemble the usual clientele. Bikini-clad women in high heels carried trays of drinks around the room, and my gaze latched onto the closest waitress. She appeared to have a variety of shots on her tray, and I knew if anything could help me relax and get through the night, it would be copious amounts of liquor.

Angelo followed my stare to the woman and clapped me on the back proudly, clearly having misinterpreted my interest. "Have fun, Patras. Use protection."

I wrinkled my nose at the thought of hooking up with a random girl paid to entertain the seedy party guests, but made a beeline for the woman regardless. I accepted two shots from her tray, chugging them both in quick succession while trying to avert my eyes from the tassels dangling from her nipples. Then, I made my way to the bar for a bottled beer. I hoped having something in my hands would keep me entertained while stuck at this hellhole.

"Adrian."

I turned at the sound of my voice to see Luca. He smiled politely and raised his drink as though toasting me.

"Congratulations," I said, certain it sounded as awkward and forced as it felt.

He tipped his head. "Thanks. I didn't expect to see you tonight, but I'm glad you could join us."

"Angelo insisted."

Luca chuckled. "Sounds about right." He brought his drink to his lips then paused. "I heard you were doing some work for Marco now."

"Not exactly." I took a swig of my beer while I thought of something else to say. Since no one else was right by us, I decided to speak openly. "Isn't it a little late for a bachelor party?"

"When you own the club, every day is basically like a bachelor party anyway," he said with a wry grin. "Besides, we've still got a week until the wedding."

"Right."

"Giada was the one who wants to keep the secret, you know. Not me. I'd prefer the whole world know, but she's pretty happy that there are just four people on this continent who know the truth."

"Four?"

"You, me, her, and Alessio." He sipped his drink. "If we broaden the scope to Italy, there's a handful of people from the church there who know too."

I hadn't realized they'd kept the circle that small. But the rest of Luca's message was pretty damn clear—if I blew the secret, I'd be hurting Giada, not him.

Luca gently slapped my bicep then turned. "Well, enjoy the party. Highly recommend you give the girls some time if you're up for it. Sasha is a fan favorite."

I grimaced as he walked off. Nothing about strippers appealed to me. Maybe if my current dating drought continued, I'd change my tune, but for now, I just didn't get the thrill of hooking up with someone who lacked any genuine interest in me.

I gazed over to where Luca had rejoined his close group of friends. I'd noticed that he hadn't so much as glanced at any of the dancers on stage tonight, so maybe he shared my opinion on strippers. Or, maybe he was just a changed man now that he officially had Giada.

Or, maybe not.

Not knowing the majority of party guests, I'd taken a seat at a table with Angelo and some of the other guys I recognized from Marco's house. They were chatting about sports and didn't seem to mind my presence, but I couldn't focus. I kept watching Luca, still stumped as to what Giada saw in him. It couldn't have been more than ten minutes before I watched Luca walk off with a tall woman whose long hair appeared to be the only thing covering her breasts.

Angelo caught me staring and chuckled. "I'm sure he won't take too long, and you can still have a turn before the night is over," he said.

"Where are they going?"

"Private rooms are down that hall."

"But—"

"I assume you don't need me to explain what goes on in those rooms, right?" Angelo turned to the other guys standing with us, and they joined in his laughter.

"You're okay with that?" I asked him, gesturing to the hall. "He's married to your sister."

"Not yet," he clarified. "And this has nothing to do with her. Men have needs. I hear Sasha is the best." He paused and glanced at the rest of the guys a knowing grin. "Maybe I'll give her a try before the night is over."

The image of the guys all passing her around like an appetizer tray before they went home to their girlfriends, wives and fiancées nauseated me. "I need another drink," I mumbled, stalking off to the bar.

I slumped onto a barstool, but couldn't stop glancing towards the private hallway as I drank the club soda I'd ordered. No way was I risking getting drunk and losing my inhibitions in a room filled with mafiosos.

For all their talk of respect, I couldn't believe that these guys were okay with Luca cheating on Giada. Even if they didn't realize he'd already married her, it still wasn't right. She deserved to know what kind of a man Luca was. Not that it would do her any good anyway. The Giada I knew would never agree to a divorce, so maybe I should be the bigger person and just let her go on a little longer thinking Luca was a decent husband and not a complete jackass.

I sipped the rest of the drink and placed the glass of ice on the bar. Maybe it wasn't a terrible idea to get proof of Luca's misdeeds, even if I wasn't ready to rain on Giada's parade quite yet. It wouldn't hurt to have an ace in my pocket for a rainy day. Right now, Luca still owed me for my testimony, but surely that goodwill wouldn't last forever.

Emboldened, I stood and headed towards the private hallway. I slid my phone out of my pocket and opened the camera. I wasn't sure what I'd expected—maybe picture windows or something, but of course there was no way to see in the room without opening the door. I told myself maybe he'd be too distracted to notice me and that if he wasn't, I could pretend I was drunk and looking for a bathroom. It would only take a second to capture the evidence I needed anyway.

Two of the doors in the hallway were shut, so I pressed my ear against the first one. I heard nothing, so I tried the other door. Luckily, I could make out the sound of a man talking in that room, and the man didn't sound like Luca. I took a deep breath, confirmed my camera was ready to shoot, then opened the door of the first room.

At first glance, I wasn't surprised at all. The girl was on her knees in front of Luca, her back to me.

But it took less than a second for me to realize she wasn't doing what I thought she was at all. Nor was Luca.

He'd been scrolling through something on his phone, which he dropped onto his lap as he looked up at me. His glare was all too familiar except, I realized, this time it was possibly warranted.

Luca was fully dressed aside from his shoes, which were lined up on the floor beside him. He didn't look aroused or even remotely interested in what Sasha was doing. And actually, I wasn't sure what she was doing, really. Her hands were on his foot, but…

"Jesus Christ, Adrian. Do you not know never to walk into one of these rooms when the door is shut?"

"I was looking for the bathroom," I stammered. But even as I said it, I realized my phone in my hand was a dead giveaway. "What are you doing anyway?" I needed to shift the focus back to him. I wasn't the one doing anything wrong here.

Luca slowly dragged his eyes away from me and back to the girl. "Thank you, Sasha," he said, slipping his foot off her lap. "Can you give us a minute?"

She eyed me like I was a kid who'd gotten caught sneaking treats from the cookie jar. Luca reached into his pocket and pulled out a folded bill. I couldn't tell how much it was, but she seemed happy enough with the tip. She stood and started towards the door when Luca's voice stopped her.

"Shirt," he called out.

She laughed as she tugged the long tee shirt up over her head, revealing round perky breasts far too large for her small frame. As she shoved the shirt into a small cupboard in the corner, I couldn't help but notice small metallic barbells piercing her nipples.

"She said it didn't hurt much," Luca said, reading my mind.

I couldn't help but wince.

"A little bit of pain is worth it for a whole lot of fun," Sasha said in a raspy, seductive voice. She finger combed her hair then sauntered out of the room, closing the door behind her.

"Sit," Luca commanded.

"I'd rather stand," I replied, unwilling to even consider all of the fluids that may have spilled on the furniture in this room.

Luca chuckled as he slid his feet into his shoes and began tying.

"What were you doing?" I asked.

He raised his gaze to meet mine. "Clearly not what you were hoping to catch me doing."

"I wasn't—"

"You weren't looking for the bathroom," he interrupted. "And you aren't so stupid that you didn't know what goes on back here. So the question is why you thought it was a good idea to try to catch me in the act. You said you were done fighting me for her."

"I am."

"Right. So you don't want her back, you just don't want her to be happy with me, either?"

"She deserves to know what kind of man you are."

"And what kind of a man is that?"

I wanted to say that he was the kind of man who screwed strippers in the back room of his club even though he was married. But thanks to my shitty timing, I had no proof of that.

"You really expect me to believe you were just back here for… what? A foot rub?"

"I don't care what you believe, Adrian."

"Why would you come back here with her if you didn't intend to sleep with her?"

Luca made a sour face. "Look, not that I need to justify my actions to you—or anyone else—but Sasha is like a sister to me. I came back here with her because my papà told her to show me a good time. I don't want to get her in trouble, and frankly, I didn't mind the chance to get some peace and quiet."

"You let her rub your feet."

"They were killing me, and she offered." He shrugged. "You of all people should be able to imagine how little I need other women. I assure you Giada is satisfying my every desire, so you don't need to worry about my faithfulness."

I swallowed the lump rising in my throat. I knew I should just leave, but I couldn't. He'd already won the only battle between us that mattered, so I wasn't about to let him silence me too. "People don't change," I said. "You may be playing the part of the loyal husband now, but I know the type of person you really are, and I'll be watching."

"Yeah? Giada knows too. I'll tell her you said hi when I go home to her tonight." He shook his head, now visibly annoyed. "You think you're untouchable because of your history with Giada, but how do you think she'd feel if I told her you tried to come between us?"

"Tell her whatever you want. I moved on, and I'm never going back. But just because I'm not interested in her romantically doesn't mean I'm going to sit back and let you treat her like crap."

Luca took his time answering. "I'm fine with that. And as long as you're still running in Marco's crowd, we're going to have to be cordial around each other. I can handle that, and I hope you can too. Because if you ever come between me and Giada, or if you ever do something to hurt her, I will kill you. Alibi or not."

"Enjoy your party," I mumbled, backing out of the room.

Giada

I lingered peacefully in the drowsy state halfway between sleep and awake for several minutes before the hairs on my arms prickled and I got the distinct feeling that someone was watching me. I slid my arm across the bed to feel for Luca, tugging up my sleep mask when I found his side of the bed empty. My eyes popped open, and I flipped quickly to my side, adrenaline flowing, ready to react to whatever I found.

"Luca," I exhaled with relief.

His eyebrows dipped as he breathed a laugh and rose to his feet. "Were you expecting someone else?"

I gazed at my gorgeous husband. Standing beside me, he looked tall. Much taller than his actual 6'1 inches. His thick dark hair looked dry, but I could tell he had showered recently. He smelled fresh, the scent of his manly aftershave permeating my nostrils as he neared. Thin sweatpants clung to his hips, framing his muscular torso perfectly.

Suddenly, the adrenaline had transformed into something else. I reached out and stroked the smooth skin along his abdomen.

"I thought you were sleeping at Alessio's," I said, remembering he'd asked a question.

"We couldn't decide who got to be the big spoon," he teased, a hint of a dimple poking through his freshly shaved olive-toned cheeks.

I frowned, trying to decide if that meant he hadn't slept at all.

"I slept in the guestroom," he said, answering my unasked question.

"You should've joined me."

"I didn't want to wake you. They tell me you have a pretty big event in a week and need to be well rested."

"So do you," I reminded him. "Anyways, it's creepy when you watch me sleep. Freaked me out."

"Yeah, you look terrified," he said, sliding my sleep mask completely off my forehead and gently stroking my hair.

"Oh, shut up," I tugged on his pants till he took the hint and stretched out over me. I sighed happily as his weight settled over me. I squeezed his firm butt as my eyes drifted shut again.

"I'm getting mixed signals here. Are you trying to seduce me or sleep?"

"Can't I do both?"

"If you fall asleep, I'm not as good as I think I am," he replied, ducking under the covers.

Knowing exactly where he was headed, I parted my legs in anticipation, but the first stroke of his warm tongue against my sensitive flesh still made me squeal. I let him work his magic a little longer, letting my body fully rouse in every way possible, then reached for his hands and pulled him higher.

Luca cooperated, sliding his pants below his butt as he climbed over me. He was gifted with his tongue for sure, but the moment his hardened length filled me, I had no regrets about skipping to the main course.

We both moved slowly, but with purpose, like a finely rehearsed waltz. Luca knew I was close before I fully realized it, and he shifted his lips from my mouth to my breast, stroking my nipple with his powerful tongue until I couldn't withstand the growing tension any longer. I imploded around him, gripping his hips with my hands as though I feared he'd stop, but instead he simply sped up, thrusting faster and faster for another minute before he, too, found his release.

Neither of us spoke for a moment, then Luca groaned contentedly.

"You are way better than any of those strippers last night," he said.

"Asshole," I replied as he crawled off of me.

He returned a moment later, handed me a few tissues, and rejoined me in bed.

"So, did you have fun last night?"

"Sure," he said, in the least convincing tone possible.

My chest tightened. I'd wanted him to actually enjoy his bachelor party, but I'd known that would be a challenge since I was keeping him from telling any of his close friends that we were actually already married.

"I guess having it after the wedding kills the fun," I said.

"It wasn't that. It's just, I'm not sure it was that different from any other night. You know, me and the guys hanging out at the club I own."

"At least all the attention was on you for the night."

"The attention is on me every night," he reminded me.

Luca and I had that in common.

"My papà treated me to an entire half hour with Sasha," he said.

I rolled my eyes. *Of course,* my shithead father-in-law would do that. "He must not realize you don't need a half hour."

He grinned, and we both fell silent again.

After a moment, Luca again broke the silence. "Your brother brought Adrian."

I winced. Leave it to my stupid brother to drag my ex-boyfriend to my fiancé's bachelor party. "Sorry."

"It's fine. We are both completely capable of being cordial, and I suppose technically we do have some of the same friends."

"Adrian always hated Angelo."

"Yeah, well…I don't know. Maybe the circumstances have changed. I think we might…keep…seeing Adrian." Luca chose his words so carefully that I wasn't sure what he meant.

I sighed.

Seeing Adrian always filled me with guilt. I'd been terrible to him, and still he'd helped Luca. Granted, my mistreatment hadn't been intentional. I truly hadn't known what I wanted. But it wasn't like my good intentions resulted in Adrian hurting any less.

As I snuggled closer against Luca, it hit me. Luca had voluntarily told me about seeing Adrian. I'd never have known if he hadn't said something, and the Luca of a year ago would've simply kept the information to himself in hopes of keeping me calm.

"Thank you for telling me that you saw him," I said, gazing up at him. "I like when you're honest with me." My words came out more patronizing than I'd intended, but Luca didn't seem offended.

"You're mine," he said, squeezing my hip for emphasis. "Now that it's official, I'm not keeping anything from you. And I expect the same from you."

"I have always been an open book," I insisted. But the moment the words left my mouth, I remembered something else. "But you can't seriously tell me you're not still keeping secrets." I pressed up to my elbows to challenge him with eye contact.

He furrowed his brows. "I'm not. I told you everything. Adrian, sex with strippers, spooning with Alessio..." his voice trailed off as he flashed me a wicked grin.

"I'm not talking about your bachelor party. I'm talking about your little brunch with your mom. She came to my shower, you know?"

Luca's groan interrupted me. "No! Tell me she didn't say what I think she did."

"Depends if you're thinking she ratted you out about a little breakfast date with a certain gorgeous Italian girl."

He smacked his palm to his head. "God, I can't believe she brought that up at your shower. I still can't believe she invited Chiara at all, but why did she have to tell you?"

"So you weren't planning to tell me," I confirmed.

He shrugged. "I don't know. If I'd seen you yesterday, I would've griped about how awkward it was. But once I had time to get over it, it didn't seem so pressing. You're already uncomfortable around my mom. I didn't want to make it worse by telling you something that would lead you to believe she—"

"Likes another woman better than me?" I supplied.

"She only likes that Chiara speaks Italian. That's literally the only thing Chiara has going for her."

"Do you want me to learn Italian?"

Luca snickered. "No! I love that Alessio and I can talk about work right in front of you without you following at all. If you learned Italian, we'd have to pick up pig Latin or something."

I giggled.

He roped his arms around me and rolled us over until he was on top of me. "Baby, you are perfect just the way you are."

I gazed into his deep brown eyes before pressing a light kiss to his full lips. "I love you," I said, pulling away and climbing out of bed.

He flung his hands up. "If you love me, why are you leaving the bed?"

"I'm leaving because I have a trillion thank you notes to write before my bachelorette party tonight."

He groaned. "I thought the shower yesterday was your party."

We both knew that was a lie, but I smiled anyway. My brides-maids and I were heading to dinner, then dancing that night. Luca had already confirmed that Matteo and Enzo both would be chaperoning, and I didn't think any of the guests would try to surprise me with male strippers. So Luca really had nothing to worry about.

He settled back under the covers, probably desperate for a nap, while I went to shower. It wasn't until the hot water pelted my skin that I remembered the FBI agent. Somehow, I'd just chastised Luca for keeping secrets, when I was the one with-holding information.

CHAPTER 11

Luca

Somehow, I blinked and it was already the day of our rehearsal dinner. I hadn't slept great, mostly thanks to Giada's incessant tossing and turning. She hadn't turned into a bridezilla, but she had definitely been more stressed the last two days than I'd ever before seen her. I offered to relax her the best way I knew how, but she was too frazzled to even let me try. She'd finally fallen into a deep sleep in the early hours of the morning, which meant we both clocked a couple of hours before the brutal screeching of the alarm woke us.

I stroked my fingers along Giada's hair, trying to recall everything I needed to do that day. Since we were leaving town right after the wedding, I assumed there was a lot. And yet all I could focus on was the warmth of my bride's breath as it hit my bare chest. She groaned against my skin and snuggled closer to my side, swinging her thigh over mine.

"Can we just stay in bed all day?" she asked.

"I'm okay with that plan."

She groaned louder. "I have a spa appointment."

"Didn't you do that yesterday?" I had no clue what all was involved in the "facial" treatment or "detoxifying seaweed wrap" that her mom forced her into, but I'd fully explored the Brazilian bikini wax she'd received and approved.

"Today is mani-pedi day. Nails," she clarified.

I didn't answer, but it occurred to me that being male seemed much easier. I'd gotten a haircut the previous week, and I planned to shower and shave before our wedding, but that was the extent of it.

"And I'm supposed to go to the gym."

"I could give you a workout here," I offered.

"Mmm. Tempting, but pretty sure I'll get plenty of your kind of workout during the honeymoon."

"What time are we meeting up today for the practice? Six o'clock?"

Her head flew off my chest, and those beautiful big brown eyes locked on mine. "Oh my God, Luca. Five. It's five o'clock. And you can't be late to your own rehearsal dinner."

"Five seems early for dinner."

"It is. We eat at seven thirty. We need time to practice all the wedding stuff at the church. If you leave me alone for even one minute with your whole family there and my whole family there…"

She didn't have to finish the sentence. I knew what could happen, but I was equally aware that it wouldn't. Both families would be on their best behavior tonight.

"I need to pack," she said.

"For the honeymoon?"

"Well yes, but also for tonight."

"Where are we going tonight? I mean, after the dinner at five o'clock."

Giada sighed. "My mom is insisting that I spend the night at home tonight."

"This is your home."

She ignored me. "She says it's bad luck and bad taste for the bride and groom to share a bed the night before the wedding."

"You could move to the guestroom."

She swatted me. "I told her I wanted to stay with you tonight, and she asked if I was worried you'd leave me at the altar."

I laughed. That didn't surprise me at all. Martina Conti had always shown very little faith in my ability to show up when it mattered. In this instance though, there was zero risk of Tina's concern actually coming to fruition.

"I'll be happy to finally see your ring on your finger," she continued.

I gazed at my hands. "I already have rings on my fingers," I teased, wiggling my fingers to show her the signet ring and ring from my mother that already adorned my hands.

"Luca, I am in no mood for jokes today. I am stressed enough about dealing with all of the people this weekend," she snapped, starting out of bed.

I yanked her back to the mattress by the hand. "Baby, you are so tightly wound, you aren't going to make it to dinner at this rate." I nudged her backwards, keeping my palm on her abdomen to hold her in place then ducked my head between her thighs. "Now hold still, because I'm not stopping until you come at least twice."

"Luca," she groaned. But once my tongue reached her damp apex, soft sighs replaced her protests. My fingers spread her tender folds so I could delve into her warmth, and within minutes, she was squirming against me. And when she thrust her hand into my hair, gripping me like she thought anything could tear me away from that sweet pussy of hers, I knew she was close. I grinned against her softness, wondering if there would ever be a better way to start the day than with Giada falling apart against my tongue, the taste of her fresh on my lips.

"Oh fuck, Luca," she panted as I pulled away.

"Not done yet," I reminded her. I'd promised her two orgasms, and I intended to deliver. Still limp from her release, Giada didn't protest as I rolled her onto her stomach. I stood on the side of the bed and tugged her closer until feet rested on the ground and her upper body still lay on the bed. I traced my fingers along her slit, using her moisture to coat my cock before positioning it at her entrance.

She gasped when I pushed into her, filling her fully on the first thrust. I started to move, determined to stave off my own orgasm until I'd brought her to the brink again. I reached around, stroking her clit with one finger while stretching the other hand up to pinch her nipple. A low moan escaped her lips, and I picked up the pace. Right as I knew I couldn't hold off any longer, Giada began grinding back against me harder. I let myself explode into her right as she cried out with the force of her own release.

I pulled out and made my way to the bathroom, but by the time I returned, she'd already left the bed and started coffee. I smirked to myself but refrained from pointing out how right I'd been about her need to relax.

We both left the apartment an hour later. I hadn't told Giada, but I was meeting her father, brothers, and my own papà for lunch that day. Alessio drove me to the restaurant and offered to join us inside, but I declined, hopeful the men in my family could get along for once.

I was careful to arrive late, not wanting to risk any time alone with my papà. I relaxed the moment I entered the restaurant, seeing the men were all seated and enjoying their drinks. They all greeted me jovially, and managed to keep the conversation purely social until after we'd ordered.

Part of me hoped to dodge shop talk altogether, but I knew that wasn't likely, so it was better to get it over with sooner rather than later. The waiter refilled our drinks, then I turned to Marco.

"You asked for this meeting. So what can I do for you?" I asked.

He cocked his head at my directness, but smiled. "I like the way you think, but I thought we'd focus more on what I can do for you. Afterall, you're already taking my daughter off my hands. That's a pretty big favor."

Everyone at the table chuckled, except for me.

My papà turned to me. "Luca, Sal, and I have already discussed the business side of things. You know our families have always cooperated and helped each other out, but with this union, it's a good time for us to reaffirm that unofficial partnership."

"What does that mean?" Angelo asked, panic flooding his face. "Partnership?"

Marco shook his head. "Nothing you need to worry about now. Your men are all still loyal to our family. But we will never do anything that could hurt the Marino family business, either. And as opportunities present, we can pool our resources and manpower."

I quirked an eyebrow at the vague statements, but wasn't about to question any of it. I'd been treading the fine line between serving one boss and two for years. I didn't anticipate the balance becoming any simpler in the near future, but I had already learned to appreciate the benefits. Afterall, it seemed the man who stepped up to free me from jail was now aligned with the Conti family. Who was I to say the family wouldn't continue to be helpful?

Two waiters brought food to the table, and we all fell silent for several minutes. Once we'd begun working on our entrees, Marco turned to me again.

"Giada expressed some concerns about not having Lorenzo drive her after the wedding," he began. "If it's okay with you, I can see that that remains part of his job duties, at least for a few months while you find someone new that she trusts."

I hated that I hadn't known Giada was worried about that, but I hid my surprise by nodding. "Sure, if that's what she wants, I'd appreciate that. I'm happy to pay for—"

"No, no," Marco cut me off. "Consider it a wedding present."

I thanked him, and the discussion turned towards the plans for the reception in Italy. Not wanting to force our entire family to travel abroad for the wedding, my parents had convinced Giada and me to allow them to plan a second reception back home. Giada's immediate family planned to attend, but other than that, I assumed most guests would be business associates of my papà.

We finished the meal without drama, and I started out towards the car where Alessio waited. As I reached the edge of the sidewalk, Marco stopped me.

"I'm sure you've heard that Mr. Patras is doing some work for our family now," he began, his voice low even though no one else was within earshot. "I hope there's no ill will about that."

I shook my head. "Of course not. He seems like a hard worker, so I'm sure he'll be helpful. And, um, I'm still grateful he stepped up when he did."

"Right, yes," Marco agreed. "Well, I just wanted you to know that despite that, as far as my daughter goes, I always hoped it would be you."

My lips parted, but the compliment was so unexpected that I took my time answering. "I appreciate that, Mr. Conti. I'm looking forward to joining the family."

He patted me on the back, and I made my way to the car.

Giada

Starting my morning with Luca's tongue all over my body set the tone for the entire day. He'd been right that I was too tense, and he'd known the fastest way to calm me. I'd finished packing for the honeymoon, then met up with Gabriella at the gym. We'd done a light workout, then showered before meeting up with the rest of the bridal party at the salon. We'd rented out the facility for a solid two hours, which gave my friends and I plenty of time to catch up and sip champagne while being pampered. Having already endured the painful spa services —including having my eyebrows done and a Brazilian wax before my facial the previous day, I could now truly relax.

I rest my eyes while my feet soaked in the bubbling water, happy to just focus on the pleasant sensations for a moment.

"You okay?" Gabriella asked from her chair to my left.

I opened my eyes and smiled. "I'm good. You?"

She nodded. "I thought you'd be more frazzled today. You seem calm."

I shrugged. "Yeah, I was a hot mess this morning, but then Luca…" I paused, not wanting to get too graphic with so many girls in the room, even if we were all friends. "He took care of it. Twice."

Gabriella's eyes widened. "Nice. So I definitely don't have to worry about you sneaking out of the chapel with Adrian?"

I could tell she was teasing, but the implication annoyed me nonetheless. I took a moment to formulate a mature response. "Adrian is coming to the wedding. He's bringing his sister, actually. I wish he'd bring a real date. He's a good guy. He deserves to be happy. He's just not right for me."

Gabby reached over and squeezed my hand. "I know. And I honestly don't blame you for being confused about them early on. I'm glad you're happy about your decision," she said.

We kept the conversation lighter while the technicians finished our pedicures, but I already felt the tension begin to creep back into my shoulders. I excused myself from the main room, stepping outside to call Luca. I walked to the end of the strip mall housing the salon, finally spotting a bench on the side of the building. The sun shone brightly, and the fresh air alone started to calm me... which was a good thing, since Luca didn't answer my call.

I didn't move for a moment in case Luca texted, and he didn't disappoint.

"Sorry, baby, with my papà and can't answer. You okay?"

I started to type a reply just as someone approached. Every muscle in my body tensed as I realized it was the man from the bridal shower. Possibly the same man at the church, though I hadn't gotten a good look at him then. Either way, he was FBI. There was no one else outside with us, and no way anyone inside the salon would hear me scream. I reminded myself I didn't need to be scared. This man was a police officer. He wouldn't hurt me. But the whole scenario felt wrong.

"Are you following me?" I asked, clutching the edge of the bench.

He nodded and thrust his hands into his pockets.

"Why?"

"You're about to marry the future head of an organized crime cartel spanning two continents. You have more access to Luca Marino than anyone else, aside from his employees. Our sources tell us you're a good person, that you would never do anything to hurt others. So we figure you're our best chance at getting useful intel on Mr. Marino."

He paused. "You could make the world a better place, Giada. We will protect you."

His honesty surprised me. A thousand different responses flitted into my brain. I wanted to tell him that he was wrong about Luca, wrong about me. I wanted to make him understand that Luca made the world a better place. I needed him to see that removing Luca from the equation would have no impact on anything in the greater scheme, but it would kill me.

But I remembered what I'd been told. Alessio, Lorenzo, and even Luca had hammered it home to me. *Don't say anything to police. Even if you think your words are harmless, stay quiet. Silence is safest.*

I gazed up at the agent, trying to note the details I hadn't before. In my defense, there was nothing terribly unique about the man. He was average height and build with a medium-light complexion. Light brown stubble dotted his face and matched the hair on top of his head. He wore dark slacks and a short-sleeved polo.

"What's your name?" I asked.

"Grady O'Keefe."

I thought about the other things he'd told me, then another question came to mind. "What sources do you have? You said they told you I'm a good person."

"You've been on our radar for years, Giada. The agency's compiled notes about people close to targets for years. We see you going to church a lot more than the rest of the family."

I considered that and resisted the urge to ask more questions about the targets he mentioned. "So you don't have people, like witnesses who aren't in the FBI, that tell you stuff about me and Luca?"

The man furrowed his brow. "You mean, like informants?"

I nodded.

"We've had a lot of informants over the years."

"I'm asking about right now. You want me to give you information about Luca, right? Well, I want to know if anyone else is already doing that."

He shuffled his feet back and forth for a moment, then sat on the opposite end of the bench and gazed out at the parking lot.

"We protect our informants' identities," he said.

I mulled over his words, focusing on what he wasn't saying.

Clearly, they must have someone feeding them information, or he'd just give me a straightforward answer.

"I have no reason to trust you if you won't be honest with me," I said, shifting forward to stand.

The man made no move to follow me, but his words stopped me. "We have someone on the inside, and they'll get us the information we need eventually. I'm giving you a choice to help the right side of this war. If you keep teaming up with the bad guys, we can't help you. You'll go down when they do. But if you cooperate, we can keep you safe."

I clenched my jaw, ready to walk back into the salon, when my phone rang. It was Luca.

Shit. I made a split-second decision to answer the call, to let that stupid agent know he couldn't rattle me.

"Luca," I purred into the phone.

"Are you okay?" he asked, his tone frantic.

Suddenly, I remembered that I hadn't answered his text. "Yes, sorry. I just wanted to hear your voice earlier. Gabby was stressing me out and…" I blew out a sigh. "I didn't mean to interrupt you. I'm good."

"Two more days and then I'm all yours for a month."

I couldn't help but smile at the thought. "Can't wait."

"Love you," he said.

"I love you too," I replied, disconnecting the call and turning to confirm Agent Grady was still watching me. He was, and he had a big grin on his face.

"Why are you smiling?" I asked.

He rose to his feet, starting towards the parking lot. "Because you just confirmed my hunch about you."

"What?"

"You didn't tell your fiancé about me."

I opened my mouth to protest, to tell him I would later, but he had already jogged off towards his car.

"Giada?"

I turned back to the salon at the sound of Gabby's voice calling me.

Later that day, Enzo drove me home from the salon. He lugged my overnight bag up to my room, then left me alone with my mom to change for the rehearsal. Instead of buying a new dress for the event, I'd opted to wear the gown Luca had bought me in Italy…the one I'd worn the day we'd actually tied the knot. My second cousin, a hair stylist in NYC, styled my hair in loose waves, securing small sections from each side on top of my head with beaded clips.

I did my own makeup and jewelry, then stepped into my shoes. I'd already been told to carry the ribbon bouquet from my shower at the rehearsal, so there didn't seem to be much else to do. I rode to the church with my nuclear family, my father behind the wheel, and it felt like the most normal, family activity we'd done in years. I spent the entire drive trying to recall the last time I'd ridden in a car with my parents, brothers, and no one else.

When we arrived, Gabby and I snuck off to the bathroom to touch up my makeup. I emerged from the bathroom to find Luca standing in the hall, looking positively dapper in his dark suit. His jaw dropped when he saw me, and he swore under his breath in Italian.

"Could you give me a moment alone with my bride?" he asked Gabriella, not taking his eyes off me.

"Sure, but you guys don't have enough time for the way you're looking at each other. The Father said we're starting in five minutes."

I giggled then approached Luca. I twirled in my dress and smiled. "Like?"

His eyes scanned up and down my body like they were taking x-rays. Luca reached for my hands, entwining our fingers and tugging me closer. "There are no words to describe how happy it makes me to see you in this dress again," he whispered, his breath tickling the sensitive spot behind my ear.

"Good. My mom was pushing me to wear something you hadn't seen before."

"This is perfect. You are perfect. And you're mine." He pulled back as if to kiss me, then wrinkled his nose. "Fucking lipstick," he murmured, burying his nose into my hair and kissing my neck until I squealed.

"Hey!" a voice behind us called. "No sampling the goods until after the ceremony."

Luca's stare turned dark, but he regained his composure before turning to greet my oldest brother. "Good to see you again, Angelo," he mumbled.

"The priest is ready to start. You two head to the back," Angelo instructed.

We all took our places, and after a few hiccups, we made it through the full rehearsal.

Luca and I rode together in the backseat of a limo from the church to the restaurant, but the drive was too short for us to catch up. Once we stepped into the restaurant for the rehearsal, we were both swarmed by various family members and guests and dragged apart until the meal.

When it was time to eat, we were seated together, but we barely had ten minutes to chew our food before Salvatore Marino stood. The room quieted instantly, before he even dinged his spoon against the champagne flute. Luca squeezed my hand under the table, and I hoped his dad wouldn't embarrass us too much.

Salvatore began by thanking everyone for coming. He made a few light jokes, then his tone became more serious.

"Every once in a while there is a couple that is truly destined to be together," he said. "That is certainly the case with Luca and Giada. Fate has brought them together, has brought all of us together here tonight. This is not only a union between two people, two souls, but also a union of two families, and even two businesses."

He paused and gazed at us both, his eyes practically twinkling as he smiled. "I dare say these two young lovebirds may have even united two countries. So it is with great honor that I welcome Giada—and the entire Conti famiglia into the Marino family."

I started to relax, assuming he was done, but his gaze pierced into me as he continued. "Giada, from this moment forward, I promise you the protection, respect, and honor that I would offer to a daughter of my own blood."

Heat rushed to my cheeks as Salvatore spoke, then intensified within the moments that followed. One by one, all of the men I'd seen working for Salvatore rose to their feet. Alessio, Thomas, and Giovanni did, too. They all stared straight at me, bowed their heads in unison, then recited something in Italian. Their serious tones and somber expressions sent chills up my spine.

As they spoke, I gazed around the room, confirming my hunch. Only the men from Luca's side of the "family" standing. None of my cousins, uncles, or other relatives, biological or otherwise, had risen to their feet. They also didn't seem the slightest bit surprised by the odd ritual.

When they all finished speaking, they still didn't sit. Instead, Luca stood to join them. He lifted his wine glass and turned to my father.

"Thank you for trusting me with your greatest tressure Mr. Conti. We won't let you down." Luca turned back to me, winked, then faced his guys. "Alla principessa," he said.

Murmurs of "salute" filled the room, then everyone seemingly accepted the toast and went on with their meals.

Luca was snatched away in conversation before he could sit back down, but Alessio soon filled his seat.

"What was that?" I asked, still flushed.

Alessio grinned. "That was an entire family pledging their

loyalty to you. It's official, Princess. You're in." He snatched a grape tomato off my plate, then wandered off to chat with someone across the room.

~

Adrian

Angelo acted like I'd drawn the short straw when Marco asked me to keep an eye on the house during the rehearsal dinner, but I didn't feel that way. I would've given anything to have dodged that event. Marco had a couple real security guards holding down the fort, so I wasn't sure exactly what my purpose was. I simply settled in on the back patio.

The temperature had dropped considerably, but the massive house sheltered me from any wind, so I opted to remain outside as long as I could handle it. I was just about to head inside when I heard footsteps rounding the side of the house. I turned to see Enzo approaching, a giant box in his arms.

I stood to open the door for him, then spent the next several minutes helping him unload more boxes from his trunk. Additional wedding presents, he explained.

"Does that mean the dinner's over?" I asked.

He shrugged. "They'll probably head back soon."

"Well, you're welcome to join me for a drink. I don't think I'm supposed to leave until Marco returns."

Enzo eyed me warily for a moment before speaking. "You know, a lot of us thought you gave up sooner than we would've bet."

"Gave up?"

"Giada. A couple guys were sure you'd fight for her right up until their wedding."

I rolled my eyes. "She made her choice. And they're perfect for each other. They deserve each other."

Enzo clicked his tongue, clearly catching the bitterness behind my words. "I agree. But I don't think that's why you gave up."

I shrugged. What he did or didn't think wasn't my concern.

He continued, unswayed by my pretend nonchalance. "I think you know Giada doesn't believe in divorce, and once she's married, it's game over."

I did think that, but I wasn't sure why he was bringing that up now. As far as he or anyone else knew, she wasn't yet married. *Unless…*

I turned to make eye contact with him. "What's your point?"

Enzo cocked his head to the side. "Luca uses all these cutesy Italian nicknames with Giada. Have you noticed that?" He paused, then continued when I made no attempt to answer. "I don't think Giada knows what half of them mean, but when he called her amata moglie, his beloved wife, that seemed pretty different from the word fidanzata, or fiancée. Funny thing, this was weeks ago. She was still getting her wedding dress fixed up, and he was already texting her and calling her his wife."

I figured there were several ways I could play my hand, but it all boiled down to whether Enzo was fishing or whether he already knew. I was willing to bet it was the latter, but I'd kept my mouth shut this long and wasn't about to blow the secret now. Although, given the way Enzo was staring at me, I supposed he'd already read my mind anyway. I wondered when Marco would sign me up for the training to become a human lie detector. All his other guys seemed to have that skill mastered.

"Look, I get what you're hinting at, but um, I'm not saying a thing. Sorry," I finally said.

Enzo nodded slowly, finally breaking eye contact. "Understood. You're a good man, Patras. And your ability to keep your mouth shut, that'll serve you well in this world."

He resumed packing the boxes, but I couldn't resist but ask my next question.

"Am I in, though? Because I'm pretty sure I'm still an outsider, maybe an errand boy, but definitely not in."

Enzo chuckled, and he looked like a teenager when he smiled. "I'd say you have your foot in the door."

"What does that mean?"

He shrugged. "Eh, once your foot is in the door, if you want out, you maybe lose that foot. But once you're all the way in, you're gonna lose a lot more if you try to get back out."

He balanced the full box on his hip and started in the house.

CHAPTER 12

Luca

I'd awoken alone on my wedding day. Well, Alessio was in my apartment, but passed out on the guest bed. I downed a cappuccino before heading to the gym for a quick but intense workout. After, I managed to shower and make myself a second coffee before Alessio stumbled out of the guest room, still rubbing his eyes.

"You're up early," he said. "Couldn't sleep without the princess?"

"Something like that," I replied, scooting to the side so he could help himself to coffee. I sat on the couch, catching up on my email and then scanning the daily news for anything relevant to my business. When the clock reached ten a.m., I decided it was late enough to call Giovanni. He'd taken the late shift at the clubs, which meant overseeing not just the clubs themselves, but really all of our business. In our line of work, a lot tended to happen in the wee hours of the morning, so someone was almost always on duty.

He gave me a quick update, and then I dialed Thomas, who'd

promised to check in at the docks that morning. All was well on that front, too, so I dropped my phone and peered up at Alessio.

"I'd offer to drive the getaway car to Atlantic City so you could escape this whole debacle, but since you're already hitched, you're kind of stuck," Alessio said, a cheeky grin on his face.

I kicked my feet up on the coffee table and chuckled. We were due at the church by noon, so it was probably time for me to start getting ready.

"Remind me again what we're doing for three hours," Alessio said, reaching for the framed wedding invitation resting on an accent table. "This says the ceremony is at three and reception at five."

"Were you not paying attention during the rehearsal?" I teased. "We have hours of photos."

"And then a full mass?"

"Yes." Giada had insisted on that detail. "And then we'll take a limo to the reception." I pulled up the note file on my phone where Giada had given me the full itinerary. "Guests start hors d'oevres at 5, we make some grand entrance at 5:30, then dinner's at 7. Toasts are 7:30, then all the traditional dances—"

"What?" Alessio interrupted.

"We do our first dance as a married couple," I explained.

"That ship sailed."

I ignored him. "Then she dances with her dad, I dance with my mom, and so forth. American traditions." I paused. "The dance floor opens to everyone once that's done, then we cut the cake at 8:30, do the garter and bouquet toss an hour after that, and Giada and I get to leave at eleven. We've got the DJ till midnight though, so you're welcome to stay and dance longer."

"I might need a nap before all that," he said.

I shot him a look, and we both got ready to go.

Much to my frustration, I didn't even see Giada until after one thirty. For the first hour, the photographer snapped pictures of me with my groomsmen, my parents, and even some solo shots. We enjoyed the catered lunch buffet during breaks between photos, and finally, the wedding planner assured me they were nearly done with the photos of the ladies. Since I still hadn't seen my bride in her wedding dress, they wanted to do some grand "first look" photo shoot. I didn't love the idea of someone recording our most private moments, but today was about Giada. If she wanted photographic evidence of the moment, so be it.

They sent me to the courtyard behind the church to wait for my bride, then directed me to look awestruck as she made an appearance. That instruction was unnecessary.

The moment Giada stepped through the French doors, delicately clutching part of her dress in one hand and her bouquet in another, my heart stopped. Giada's gown suited her perfectly, reflecting her upbeat personality with its sparkling gemstones, her delicate nature with the intricate lace patterns, and her elegance with the neat layers of beads. The outer layer was sheer, revealing a fitted bodice showcasing her rounded butt and hips and narrow waist. The top of the dress dipped low enough to show off her cleavage without triggering my possessive side.

The veil—which I'd ordered based off of Giada's drawing, matched the style of the dress perfectly. The gown cut low on her hips, leaving her back mostly bare, and the sheer fabric of the veil offered a teasing view of the naked flesh beneath. Her hair had been pulled up aside from a few curled tendrils framing her face, and delicate pearl earrings showcased the elegance of her long neck. A sparkling tiara secured the veil to her head.

Giada stepped closer, and I realized I hadn't yet said a word. Truthfully, I wasn't sure what to say. She looked gorgeous every day, but this, this was an entirely new level. When I'd pictured our official wedding day, I had assumed Giada would look different, like some Stepford bride, in a stuffy, overly-formal gown and accessories fitting for a granny. But the angel standing before me personified everything I loved about Giada. This beauty was my Giada, only amplified.

I reached for her hand right as she stumbled, clearly not accustomed to walking in such an intricate dress. She released the hold on her gown and gently tapped her tiara, confirming it hadn't shifted out of place.

"My princess finally got her crown," I said, my voice as soft as a whisper.

Her smile widened, and she blushed as though we hadn't known each other for most of our lives.

"This was worth waiting for," I said, referring to the image of her in the formal dress. She interpreted my words differently, though.

"You didn't exactly wait, though, Husband."

Her adorable wink made me laugh out loud.

"I pictured this moment in high school," I said. "Did you know that?"

"You always were a romantic," she replied.

"I'm glad you insisted on all this formal crap."

She quirked a brow. "We'll see if you still feel that way in ten hours."

My heart thudded at the thought that she was all mine in a matter of hours. No one would disturb us after the wedding. We'd have a day alone together in a NYC hotel, then we'd fly to Sicily, just the two of us, where we'd have a few days to relax before the reception there. Once that was over, we'd have nearly three full weeks alone together.

I leaned forward, unable to resist the lure of her full, rosy lips any longer.

"Stop!" shrieked a voice behind us.

We both froze.

"No kissing! Lipstick!" the assistant to the photographer shouted.

I sighed, but angled my lips upward, planting one soft,

lingering kiss on her forehead, then repeating the gesture with her hand. The photographer came closer then, and spent an ungodly amount of time posing the two of us for photos outside, then repeated the process inside the church. Once that was done, she gave us a quick break for hair and makeup touchups, then launched into photographs of the entire group.

The photos didn't stop until a half hour before the ceremony. Already I was exhausted and my feet ached, but as the wedding planner led Giada and I back into our separate dressing rooms to make final preparations for the ceremony, I was excited.

~

Giada

My wedding day was a chaotic blur of photos, hugs, makeup, and of course, Luca. I loved the happy anticipation filling the dressing room as my bridesmaids and female relatives laughed, ate, and drank together while fixing our hair and makeup in between photos. Every conversation felt more poignant, more significant, while I wore my wedding gown. Every joke seemed funnier, and every moment, more memorable.

I thought back to all the times I'd had doubts, not so much about my feelings for Luca but about his feelings for me. And I prayed I would always remember the look on his face when he first saw me that day. Gazing into his deep brown eyes, there was not a doubt in my mind that this man would love and cherish me with every ounce of his being for the rest of his life.

As I walked down the aisle, my father's strong arm guiding me down the flower-lined path, my gaze broadened. I stared not just at Luca, who was positively mouthwatering in his crisp black tuxedo, but also at the men beside him. Not too long ago, I'd been wary of Alessio, Thomas, and Giovanni. Now, I'd come to trust them, to consider them friends, really. And after the way they'd all pledged their loyalty to me, I started to understand that I wasn't just walking towards a future with Luca alone. I was walking into a life where Luca and I would be forever supported by the men standing beside him.

The ceremony was beautifully unique. Father Ben had tweaked his usual spiel to suit our particular needs, already being wed in the eyes of God. The adjustments were subtle enough though that my parents wouldn't suspect a thing. During the mass, Luca clutched my hand tightly, squeezing it at such regular intervals that I wondered if he were sending messages in Morse code. Whenever I gazed at him though, he simply grinned.

At the end of the ceremony, when the priest granted Luca permission to kiss his bride, I leaned in, anticipating the mature, chaste kiss we'd practiced at the rehearsal. Instead, Luca gripped my waist, dipped me backwards, and kissed me like he was headed off to war. The entire sanctuary whooped and cheered, flooding my cheeks with heat.

When Luca returned me to my feet, he simply smirked and whispered, "Sorry baby, couldn't resist." Then he kissed me again.

We walked down the aisle hand in hand, then ducked into the room Luca and the men had used as a changing room earlier in the day.

"That was not what we rehearsed," I said, sinking onto a plush leather chair.

"I know. It was so much better, right?" he replied, dropping to his knees in front of me.

I grasped his hand, kissing the thick platinum wedding band finally in its rightful place. "Finally, the whole world can see you're mine," I said.

He smiled, stroking my hand with his thumb, then laying his head on my lap.

There was a short rap on the door, and then it flew open. The wedding planner stepped inside, then covered her eyes and jerked around. "Guys!" she said. "There is not time for that!"

Luca and I both laughed, and he rose to his feet, showing her that our positions were completely innocent.

She sighed, then plastered her overly enthusiastic smile back in place. "Just wanted to tell you guys you have five minutes, and then we'll do more photos before heading to the reception hall."

"Thank you, Mindy," I said, grateful she couldn't see Luca's annoyed scowl.

Luca sat on the couch across the room, then motioned for me to join him. I sat beside him, and he lifted my legs onto his lap. He nudged off my shoes, and began massaging my tender feet.

I groaned with pleasure. The shoes weren't terrible, and I'd broken them in a little over the past few weeks, but it had been a long day with a lot of standing.

"I have cute tennis shoes to wear later," I confessed.

"You can't change into those now?"

"No! I want to look tall for the pictures."

Luca laughed, then moments later, Mindy returned for us.

The wedding reception was a blast. I'd always enjoyed black tie affairs, and ever since my first formal dance with Luca back in high school, I'd been looking forward to the time when we could throw our own grown-up prom, but with all eyes on us. Tonight was that night, and every last detail, from the flowers to the food to the music, was crafted to my tastes.

My mom insisted that I speak with all of the guests, so I didn't get as many dances with Luca as I would've preferred, but that was okay. We'd have the rest of our lives to dance together. Whenever I felt like we'd been apart for too long, Luca had magically appeared at my side, usually carrying a small plate of food to force into my mouth. He didn't smear the cake all over my face after we cut it, instead simply licking my finger clean in a gesture that left my core aching for a few minutes alone with him. He danced with me whenever I asked, and he smiled for every photo.

In short, Luca was the perfect groom.

Adrian

I survived Giada's fake wedding, mostly thanks to my sister's presence. And for a whole week after the wedding, I didn't see anyone in the Conti family since they'd traveled overseas for some wedding reception in Italy. Life had settled down and started to feel normal to me.

The next week, I invited my sister over for dinner after work. I'd planned to leave work by five, but got delayed. I texted and told her to let herself into my apartment with the spare key I'd given her. She agreed and promised to mix up some cocktails for us to enjoy when I got home.

I whistled as I approached my apartment, then stopped abruptly at the door. I could've sworn I heard a man's voice. I listened for a moment, and caught my sister's carefree laugh. I let myself in, half expecting to see she'd brought a new boyfriend to meet me.

Instead, it was Angelo.

I gazed from him to my sister, then back to him.

"What are you doing here?" I asked. "How did you get in?"

My sister rose to her feet and brushed past me, retrieving a tall glass with a pinkish liquid. She forced it into my hands and smiled. "I let him in."

"You shouldn't let strangers in my apartment."

"We met at the bar when I was visiting, remember? And at the wedding."

I knew that, but that still didn't mean I thought she should be alone with the creep.

"Your sister makes a mean cocktail," Angelo said. "I'll get out of your hair in a few, but can we chat business first?"

I glanced over at my sister then back to Angelo. It was a small apartment, so there was really no place for privacy. "We could step into the hall for a minute," I said.

My sister flung her hands up. "I'm not kicking you out of your own apartment. I'll walk your dumb dog and be back in fifteen minutes."

I thanked her, then she left.

"I think we have a rat," Angelo said once we were alone.

My eyes darted across the room where I kept my gun. Surely he didn't think I was the rat, but…

"I can't tell if they're after us, or the Marinos, but someone tipped off the cops about a shipment we had coming into the docks a couple days after the wedding. Whoever it was knew that we'd all be out of town then, so I'm worried if might be someone close to the family."

"Do you have any leads?"

"Not really. You don't think there's any chance Giada would be talking to the cops, do you?"

If there was one thing I'd learned from my relationship with Giada, it was that I had no clue what she would and wouldn't do. I simply shrugged. "Why don't you test her? When she gets back, tell her some made up top secret thing, and then see if she tells someone?"

He considered that. "Yeah, I guess that could work. Or maybe I'll just take her with me on some runs and remind her she doesn't want to mess with me."

"She's your sister. Not to mention the wife of your rival. Or partner, or whatever you two are now. You can't do anything to hurt her."

Angelo rolled his eyes. "Yeah, I know. The princess is untouchable." He sighed and stood. "I'd watch your back when you're out and about. Keep your Glock with you at all times."

I nodded, then showed him to the door. I immediately went to the kitchen and climbed on the counter to reach the back corner of the fridge where I stored my gun, despite having purchased an overpriced safe for that precise purpose. Just then, the door clicked open.

My sister stared right at me as I stood on the chair, gun in hand. "What have you gotten yourself into?" she asked.

I swore under my breath then stowed the gun in a drawer. It was still out of sight, but at least it would be closer if I needed it. Surely I wasn't at risk inside my own apartment, though.

"Nothing, it's fine. Angelo just runs with a rough crowd. He said some things that made me nervous." I paused. "Come on, help me prep the chicken."

Annie reluctantly joined me by the stove, and together we made dinner. We didn't talk about Angelo or my gun the rest of the evening.

CHAPTER 13

Giada

Exhausted from the wedding festivities, I'd slept the entire flight to Rome. I decided to be productive during the short connecting flight to Naples, penning two dozen thank you notes before my hand cramped up. By the time we collected our luggage and climbed into the sleek SUV driving us to the dock, fatigue had overcome me again. I knew from experience that I'd perk up once the brisk wind hit my face aboard the ferry, and I did.

Luca had arranged for us to take a private ferry, which meant we didn't have to wait to depart for Capri. He stood behind me as we cruised, roping his arms around my waist while I gazed out at the Mediterranean.

"Will I ever get sick of these views?" I asked.

"No," he replied, pressing a kiss to the top of my head.

"Then why aren't we taking the ferry to Palermo later this week?"

"Because the ferry takes the entire day, and a flight is only a couple of hours."

I swiveled in his arms. "Have you ever heard the expression, life is about the journey, not the destination?"

Luca wrinkled his nose.

"By the time you factor in the lines for security, baggage check, and all that, it's really about the same," I pointed out.

My husband shook his head. "It really isn't, but if that's what you want, I'll switch the tickets as long as the weather cooperates."

I hugged him.

We only spent three nights in Capri, but that was perfect. We explored the island, shopping and eating. We lounged at the beach where the early fall temperatures rivaled a Manhattan summer, and we fully exhausted ourselves in bed. By the time we traveled to Palermo—by ferry—to meet the rest of the family, I felt rejuvenated and closer to Luca than ever before.

Due to the language barrier, I hadn't been involved in the planning of the reception in Palermo. And while I'd appreciated having every moment of our "official" wedding reception catered to my precise specifications, I felt more relaxed at the event that I hadn't planned. I experienced the Italian reception almost as a guest, simply taking each element as it came.

A surprising number of Luca's distant relatives and family friends spoke no English, so I spent a fair portion of the evening smiling and nodding with no awareness of what was being said. Luca tried to rescue me when he could, but his mother kept him occupied, dragging him from guest to guest.

After enduring yet another exceptionally wet kiss on the cheek from Luca's great uncle, I sunk into a chair at the center table, grateful for a moment of peace to enjoy my prosecco. Unfortunately, I'd barely swallowed my first sip when Julia sat beside me.

"It's so pretty here," she said.

I wasn't sure if she meant the specific reception locale—a courtyard a few blocks from the center of town—or Palermo in general, but it didn't really matter. "Is this your first trip to Sici-ly?" I asked.

"Yep. How come you and Luca don't live here?"

The abruptness of the question gave me pause. "I don't speak Italian. And my family and friends all live back in Connecticut."

She shrugged. "But aren't you worried Luca will get arrested again? Seems like he's safer here."

I selected a macaron from the tray in the center of the table, determined to ignore her annoying questions.

"Plus, then you don't have to worry about any of Luca's work jeopardizing any of your own family's business. Or your family's safety," she added in a know-it-all tone.

"What?" I turned to face the witch. "What exactly do you think Luca does for a living?" I shook my head, sucking in a deep breath. "Look, I'm not sure what Angelo has been telling you, but you seem very confused about some pretty big things. Maybe you should shut your mouth until you get a clue."

I rose to my feet and sauntered off, only making it a few feet before Luca popped out of nowhere, grabbed my hand, and tugged me towards him.

"Did you not hear the announcement?" he asked. "We're supposed to encourage everyone to dance now."

I couldn't help but smile at the adorable twinkle in his eye. Of course, he knew I hadn't understood any of the announcements. But unlike his mom, Luca didn't care.

We danced, drank, and ate the night away, partying until nearly one o'clock in the morning. The next day, we'd share a brunch with family, and then they'd leave us to enjoy the rest of our time in Palermo alone. Surely I could tolerate Julia for a few more hours.

Luca

I'd never felt more indebted to Alessio than I did the week Giada and I spent in Palermo. He'd saved my ass countless times over the years, but when my wife said she wanted a full week of me to herself, Alessio made it happen. I checked in with him daily, typically calling in the evening when Giada had fallen asleep.

For any project or issue I asked Alessio about, his answer was the same. "It's under control."

If I pressed him further, he might elaborate to say "I've handled it," or even "Everything is going well," but simply hearing that someone else was managing the chaos lightened my mental load.

"I feel like Alessio could handle things just fine without you," Giada said at breakfast on our last day in Palermo.

Late that afternoon, we'd fly to Rome, where we'd spend another week at my family's home. My parents were staying in Palermo, so we wouldn't have to share the house with them, but a few of my papà's guys would be at the house. I figured it would be a nice transition back to the real world, mixing a little bit of work with a whole lot of pleasure.

"Are you trying to kill me off?" I asked my bride.

"Luca!" she scolded. "I only meant that you could retire or move away, and the world wouldn't stop spinning. Alessio has proven himself more than capable of filling your shoes."

I grinned at the expression, which didn't translate exactly into Italian, then smoothed my palm along her thigh. She knew there was no such thing as retirement in my line of work. I didn't need to remind her.

"So what is going on with work?" she asked after a few more bites of fruit.

I quirked a brow, debating how much she wanted to know. "Everything at the docks is going well, the clubs are doing great, and once we get back home, Alessio and I are going to finalize the contracts with the casinos."

"What exactly are you doing with the casinos?" she asked.

"For starters, we're just helping with security. But once we get the hang of things, we'd love to break into the New York City casino market."

"There aren't casinos in New York," she said.

"Not yet. But they've legalized them now and are offering huge incentives to bring them to the City. We want to get a bid in to help with a casino inside one of the larger hotels."

"Hmm," Giada mused, sipping her coffee. "Anything else new?"

I cringed, realizing there was one other project I hadn't really mentioned. "Not really. Still doing some construction crap with your brother, but not very involved in that. Or at least I'd like to not be very involved. Angelo seems determined to branch out and take over a few more companies. I don't have time for it, and I really don't have an interest in more ties to him, but your father won't give him the green light on the project unless I'm involved." I shook my head. "He's really determined to merge our families."

"That's nice in theory, but I don't blame you for not wanting more time with Angelo. How exactly do you have time for all of these different projects?" she asked.

I grinned, certain what she actually wanted to know was how I'd have time for all of that plus her. "My papà encouraged us to bring in some new guys to help. It's weird though, because I'm really not involved. They don't know me, and I don't know them. These guys only know whoever is directly above them. They don't even know who their boss reports to."

"What's the point of that?"

"Less liability for me. Plausible deniability, you know?"

She wrinkled her brow. "Isn't that risky, though? Like, what if they do something you don't want them to do?"

Giada was right, and my controlling nature hated that I

couldn't have my hands in every single deal we brokered. But this system only worked if I trusted my guys. "Giovanni and Thomas are handling training for the guys that'll supervise the new guys. And they're not giving them big projects at first. They'll handle day-to-day menial crap like security at the docks until they prove themselves."

Giada sighed, slipping from her chair to mine, roping her arms around my neck. "I'm not ready to go back to the real world," she confessed.

"We're not."

"You said some of your dad's guys will be at the house in Rome. If we aren't alone, how am I supposed to ravish you at the breakfast table?"

"I suspect they'll give us privacy."

"Not reassuring," she said, slipping her hands from my neck down my torso, landing squarely on my lap. She reached beneath the band of my sweatpants, softly stroking my length until it reached its full potential. Giada dropped to her knees in front of me, tugging my pants down. "I need more of a guarantee."

I sucked in a ragged breath as the tip of her tongue traced the head of my cock. She paused and gazed up at me, clearly confident she had me right where she wanted me.

"You will be my priority in Rome," I promised. "Any time you want me for anything at all, just say the word, and I'm yours."

"Promise?" she asked, the vibration of her word causing my pulse to skyrocket as her mouth already returned to my cock.

"Yes, God yes," I panted.

Giada

*A*s Luca and I settled into the villa in Rome, we started to spend more time apart. I was eager to peruse all the shops, hoping to find items for several of our clients at the design firm. And Luca was clearly itching to get back into the groove of things with work. Still, we managed to hold on to the honeymoon phase of life in little ways, like meeting up for lunch at the same restaurant where we'd had our first real date as adults. We explored the Coliseum and other ancient sites like boring tourists and made out at the art museum. We strolled the cobblestone neighborhood streets hand in hand after late dinners at cozy cafes, and we woke up snuggled in each other's arms late each morning.

Well, most mornings. On our second to last full day, I woke to find Luca's side of the bed empty. The suite we shared was generous, but not so large that he could've been hiding. I was alone.

I yawned, stretched, then headed to the bathroom, hoping my husband would return with coffee by the time I finished brushing my teeth. When I emerged to find him still missing, I reluctantly pulled on the silky, striped, pale pink pajama shorts and button down that I'd set out to sleep in…but hadn't actually worn yet this week. I started down the stairs, headed straight for the sitting room.

I wasn't surprised when I saw three other men in the sitting room with Luca. I'd heard their voices. They spoke Italian, and judging from their volume, either they weren't discussing something sensitive enough to require discretion, or they were confident I couldn't understand the language.

Either way, I couldn't bring myself to care whether they thought their discussion topic was important. Luca had promised he was mine on this trip, and I'd woken up alone.

I stared directly at Luca as I approached, avoiding eye contact with any of the other men. Luca's eyes darted to me, then back again to the other men as I approached, but a sly grin appeared on his beautiful face, telling me my interruption was not unwelcome.

I cut through the circle formed by the room's furnishings and climbed onto the side of Luca's lap, curling my legs beneath me. I started to wobble backwards, apparently not having launched myself far enough onto his lap. Luca caught me, his arms pressing into my lower back and holding me close. I realized the other men had stopped talking, but I didn't care what they were thinking.

Luca smelled delicious, reminding me of the woods after a rainfall, with a hint of mint as he opened his mouth. Certain he was about to say something I wouldn't like, I pressed my lips to his before he could speak.

I half expected Luca to pull away, but he didn't. He kissed me back like we were all alone, his tongue teasing the seam between my lips until they parted for him, welcoming him into the warmth of my mouth. My tongue clashed against his, and I lost myself in the wash of delicious sensations until a deep voice spoke behind me. I froze, having forgotten the men were even there, or maybe having hoped they'd left us alone.

"We were discussing something," Luca said, his voice low. I shivered as his warm breath tickled my ear. Behind me, another man spoke—still in Italian—then they all chuckled.

"I figured as much," I whispered in reply to Luca, pulling back just enough to gaze at his perfect face. My fingers gravitated to his chin, stroking the familiar, rough stubble. "But I didn't care. You said you were mine this trip, and then I woke up alone. You should still be in bed with me."

Luca gazed back at me for a moment, his silence offering no hint as to how he planned to respond. The other men were still speaking, and I wondered if Luca was still listening to their discussion. "I can remedy that," Luca finally said, having delayed so long that I almost forgot what he was offering to fix. He nudged me to the side of the chair, scooting out from under me to stand partway before gripping me harder and lifting me with him. I roped my arms around his neck, clasped my feet behind his waist, and pressed my lips together to keep from squealing as he precariously shifted me in his arms.

He cleared his throat, then angled his head around me. "Gentlemen, we can continue this discussion later," he replied, adding something else in Italian. I didn't even notice if they responded as Luca carried me down the hallway towards the bedroom. He struggled with the door, finally angling us so I could twist the knob, then he kicked the door shut behind us and dropped me on the bed, toppling over me.

I squealed then pulled him to me, clutching his face while kissing him. He rolled to the side, unbuttoning his shirt. I thought he was just eager to undress, but as he pulled away to neatly drape the garment across the chair beside the bed, I realized he simply didn't want wrinkles.

"If you didn't want to mess up your fancy clothes, you should've stayed in pajamas," I said.

"Oh, like you?" he replied, his palm swatting my butt cheek. I yelped at the slight sting, then climbed over him.

"Yes."

My husband gazed up at me, his smile wide. "But neither of us slept in pajamas."

"That alone should've told you that you weren't supposed to leave the bedroom." I unfastened the three oversized buttons securing my top.

Luca reached up, cupping my newly freed breasts. "We were discussing something," he said, his fingers pinching my nipples just hard enough to make my vision go white.

"Something important?" I asked, my voice breathy.

"Very." His hands left my breasts, but just long enough for him to lick his fingers then resume stroking my sensitive flesh.

I bit back a moan and reached for his zipper, unfastening his pants as quickly as I could. "I guess I could let you go finish your meeting," I teased. "This could wait till later."

"This cannot wait another minute," he insisted. He lifted his hips, helping me drag his pants down his legs, then reached for my waist.

I let him position me over him, but didn't lower myself onto him. "But you have a whole lifetime to do this with me. If you need to go talk with those guys first…" I began.

"What I need is you. Always." He tugged my hips, and I moaned as he sunk into me, filling and stretching me as if we hadn't joined together mere hours before.

"You have me," I replied as I began to move.

CHAPTER 14

Luca

*L*ife as an officially married man was good. Well, to be honest, the relationship part really wasn't any different. But everything with work felt easier now that I'd seen firsthand that Alessio could keep everything running smoothly in my absence. He was taking the lead on the casinos, too, which meant I didn't have to trek to Atlantic City every few days like he was.

The only negative I've noticed since the wedding was that Marco seemed to think I was now at his beck and call. I'd woken to a text that he'd love to chat with me before lunch. Giada offered to come with me and catch up with her mom, but when I'd replied to Marco and said we'd both be there, he asked me to leave Giada at home.

That stressed me out. Giada offered to relax me, but I needed to get ready. I'd showered the night before, so I decided just to shave. Giada stood at the sink beside me, using her fingertips to spread a thick greenish goo across her face.

"Didn't get your fill of Halloween?" I teased. "Dressing as a witch today?"

"It's a purifying mask," she said, poking her pink tongue out at me through the green mask. "My skin's still all stressed from the honeymoon."

I started to ask a follow up question, but my phone rang.

Giada retrieved it from the bedroom, handing it to me and mouthing, "It's your boyfriend."

I grinned and answered the call. "Pronto."

"Hey, so wanted to run something by you about the casino project," Alessio said.

"You are on speaker," I informed him as I rinsed my razor in the sink. I assumed he'd just switch to Italian. He didn't.

"It's fine, I just was wondering if you had any objection if I, uh, mixed a little pleasure in with business."

I chuckled. "You gambling now? Need some fast cash?"

He laughed back. "Not that kind of pleasure. I met someone."

My grin widened, making it hard to keep shaving. Alessio's love life had been fascinating over the years, but it had run a little dry lately. He didn't always make the best romantic decisions, but I trusted his judgment when it came to ensuring his sex life didn't interfere with business.

"You don't have to run that by me. Have fun. Be safe."

Alessio cleared his throat. "It's not the kind of someone your father would approve of, so…"

I paused. That explained why he was mentioning it. Still, I wasn't going to let my papà's prejudice ruin Alessio's good time. "Which casino?" I asked.

He paused, probably trying to recall the code names we'd given each. And as I thought about it, the casino didn't matter.

"Nevermind. Does your uh special someone work there?"

"Yeah. Bartending. The Sprite casino."

That was definitely harmless, maybe even helpful. "Have fun, amico."

We disconnected as Giada came back in, prancing around me and leaning against the counter. I grinned and lifted her onto the counter next to the sink. "Almost done," I promised, resuming my shaving.

"So Alessio met a girl?" she asked.

"Something like that," I replied. Alessio's love life was none of her concern. "Are you going to wash this off so I can kiss you before I leave?"

In lieu of answering, she leaned forward and kissed me, smearing green crap all over my smooth cheeks.

An hour later, I found myself at the Conti's front door. Now that I was technically family, I never knew if I should ring the bell or just trudge right in, so I was grateful when the door swung open as I approached.

"Morning, Angelo," I said.

He quirked a brow instead of replying. "You got here fast."

"I have work to do today. Figured I'd come here first."

Angelo nodded, then motioned for me to follow him into Marco's office.

"Luca, how are you?" My father-in-law greeted me, standing to wrap one giant arm around my shoulder and pat my back.

"Good, thanks. You?"

"No complaints," he said. "Can I get you coffee?"

"No thanks."

Marco motioned for me to sit. I took the chair next to Angelo.

"I've heard some concerning reports about Giada lately," Marco began.

I frowned and leaned in, already feeling my pulse quicken.

"For one, her mom says she's still working..."

I waited in case Marco was going to add something to that. When he paused and looked at me though, I nodded.

"Money tight?" he joked, a peculiar expression on his face.

"It keeps her occupied," I replied, not willing to justify his taunt. I was confident he knew I wasn't experiencing any financial difficulties now. "And she likes it," I added, annoyed.

"What about the driving? Is there a reason she doesn't have someone driving her lately? I told her Lorenzo could keep up the job for a while."

I had no response for this. Yes, she liked driving herself, but frankly I agreed with her father on this one. Especially in NYC, there was no reason for her to drive herself.

"You bought her the car," I said finally.

Marco's mouth curved upwards. "Yes, and I let her drive it herself only because I assumed you would pull the plug on that practice pretty quickly."

"I didn't realize that," I admitted. "I hadn't wanted to step on your toes by changing her driving privileges." Also, I didn't want to rely too much on Lorenzo, and I had no one on my team to drive her. The men I trusted most were the ones I relied on to handle the actual business matters with me.

I didn't want just anyone chauffeuring my wife. For Marco, it had been an easy decision. He trusted Lorenzo like a son, but didn't want him eligible for leadership roles since he wasn't technically family. The fact that Lorenzo was a skilled sharpshooter and respected in the community meant Giada was safe with him. Plus, Giada liked Lorenzo, so she didn't resist having a driver. Of course, after she fooled around with him in the car…

"I was told that she's been seen at one of your clubs," Marco continued.

Again, I had no response for him. Giada had been to all of my clubs, on countless occasions. Without knowing exactly which instance he referred to, I couldn't risk saying something to alert him to more.

Marco stared at me, signaling he wouldn't move on until I said something.

"Well, yeah, I think she might have dropped by one sometime. I'm there a lot, so…"

"Gentleman's clubs aren't a suitable place for women."

"Right."

"Did your mother spend a lot of time at these types of places when you were younger?" Marco barely paused, clearly intending it as a rhetorical question. I assumed he knew as well as I did that the answer was no. "Tina certainly isn't involved with the shipyard," he continued. "And why would she be? It's business. *My* business. Not hers."

I nodded awkwardly, casting a sideways glance to Angelo. Why was he even here anyway? Unfortunately, he interpreted my look as an invitation for him to join in the discussion.

"I think my father is simply recommending you keep the Princess on a tighter leash. It's okay if you walk her, just shorten the lead," Angelo said, snickering along with his father at the analogy.

If he thought comparing my wife to a dog was the way to get on my good side, Angelo was mistaken.

"Right, maybe I should see if the salon is hiring. Surely she could help Julia wax unibrows." I said.

"Gentlemen," Marco chided, breathing a laugh. "We all have the same goal here. We're on the same team."

"Is there something specific you're concerned about with your daughter?" I asked, quickly growing impatient.

Marco's expression shifted. He was uncharacteristically quiet for a moment before speaking. "Giada is no fool. If you do not take precautions to…preserve her innocence, we will all pay the price. Do you understand what I'm saying?"

"Yes." I paused. "But now that Giada and I are married, you don't need to worry about any of this. That's my responsibility now. She's my responsibility now."

"True." Marco swirled the ice around in his glass thoughtfully. Finally, he spoke. "But it's like when you sell a business. That business is the owner's baby. When the original owner sells a fine-tuned, well-oiled machine, it pains him to watch the new owner mishandle the business."

He paused long enough for me to ascertain he was now comparing his child to a business.

"Even though it's no longer my business, I have a vested interest in its success."

"As do I, sir." I slowly rose to my feet, not missing the flash of annoyance on Angelo's face that I dared to instigate the end to the meeting. "I assure you I have Giada's best interests at heart, and I do appreciate the fine job you did raising her. I won't ruin your hard work," I said. "But I probably should get on my way. I've got several different business matters to check on today."

A sharp knock on the door accented what would have been my dramatic exit.

The door opened a crack, and Matteo peered inside.

"You're back," Marco said jovially. "Come in. We gentlemen were just discussing your sister. She seems to have gotten a little out of control lately, don't you think?"

Matteo turned to me, eyebrow raised. I averted my eyes.

"All of you?" he asked, goading me to jump to his sister's defense.

"Yeah, I think we're all on the same page," Angelo said. "We covered her driving, working, showing up at Luca's business... maybe we should talk about her clothing for a minute. I'm not sure the way she dresses is really appropriate now that she's married—"

Matteo cut him off. "So you are all just sitting in here discussing Giada like it's the nineteen fifties," he summarized. "You don't think she'd like to be involved in this conversation?" Matteo asked, glancing at me for support.

Clearly, he'd never learn.

"Giada doesn't always know what's best for her," I said, tilting my head conspiratorially towards Marco. Angelo's lips curved upwards into a smile that he tried to hide.

Matteo's eyes widened. "Jesus," he mumbled. "You're right about that." He walked forward and dropped a set of car keys and a thick roll of bills on his father's desk. "I'm heading out again. I'll be at the office by noon tomorrow unless you need something sooner."

He cut out of the room quickly, avoiding eye contact.

"I should go also," I said, eager to clarify to Matteo that I wasn't the asshole he thought I was. "It was nice seeing you," I said, offering a firm handshake to Marco, then Angelo.

I walked slowly out of the house, then once I hit the front steps, I jogged to catch up to Matteo.

"Matteo!" I called as he opened the door to his Navigator.

He paused, still scowling at me.

I waited until I was at his side to speak. "Look, I think you misunderstood in there. I'm on Giada's side."

Matteo snorted and shook his head. "Whatever, Luca. Have a good day."

I gripped his wrist as he reached for the doorknob. "You don't get it. I can't just piss off your father. I have to consider—"

He shook free of my hand. "You are the one who doesn't get it, Luca. You are literally the only person who could stand up to them with zero consequences. You are untouchable, and you know it. But despite that, you're still too much of a coward to defend Giada despite the fact that you just took vows in a church to do exactly that." Matteo tugged the door open. "She trusts you. She thinks you're different than they are."

"I am," I said, hating that my voice sounded less certain now.

"Then prove it." He climbed in his car and drove off before I even thought up a response.

Giada

I met Gabriella for an early lunch that day. We'd barely ordered drinks when she lunged for my phone.

"Show me the pictures!" she shrieked.

I was just as eager to show her the proofs of my wedding photos as she was to see them…but I couldn't resist making her wait a little. "First, I want to hear about this new boyfriend. You've been on, what, five dates already, and I still haven't met him?"

"You were out of the country, and stop changing the subject. I've already told you everything there is to tell about Dan."

She surely hadn't, but I'd taunted her long enough. I slid my iPad from my bag and navigated to the wedding photo site. I entered my password, then scooted closer to Gabby so we could admire the pictures together. I'd already looked through them all three times since the photographer sent the link—a mere two days before. First, by myself, then with Luca, and then with my mom and aunt Sofia. But Gabby would pick up on all sorts of details my mom and Luca had missed.

"Ahhhh," she groaned. "Giada, you look so beautiful. I mean, it's ridiculous."

The waiter deposited our drinks, and Gabby waved the iPad in his face.

"Doesn't she look stunning?" she asked the poor guy.

He smiled like a good sport. "Yes, congratulations. Have you had a chance to check out the menu?"

We ordered two separate salads, planning to split both, then focused on the photos the moment the waiter left us. We made it through the first look photos of Luca and me before I decided to hit the bathroom before our food came.

"Be right back," I promised. I was quick in the bathroom, eager to get back to my gorgeous pictures, but as I stepped out into the back hallway, the bathroom door slammed into someone.

"Sorry! I didn't see you…" my apology trailed off as I recognized the person I'd hit with the door. It was the FBI agent. The one who'd been stalking me. Agent Grady O'Keefe.

"Are you following me?" I made no effort to keep my voice down. This situation had gotten way out of control. Besides, why were they still after me? I was already married. "Aren't you going to congratulate me? I'm a married woman now. And you can't compel me to tell you anything about my husband."

"Giada, it's not too late for you to do the right thing," he said. "Give us information on your husband, and we'll stop looking into you."

I felt my face blanch. He hadn't said that before. "Why would you…" I stammered. "I've done nothing wrong."

"Accessory to theft, embezzlement," he paused and caught my eye, "Murder."

I shook my head, reminding myself he was just trying to scare me. "Luca is a wonderful man, and I'm saying that as the person who knows him better than anyone else in the world,"

Grady's disapproval was all over his face. "Giada, we already know what your husband has done, so we just need verification. If you're not going to cooperate—"

"If you agree to leave Luca alone, I can give you information about someone else."

I watched his chest rise and fall as he considered this.

"Who?"

It didn't take me long to decide who to throw under the bus. "My brother, Angelo Conti."

He considered that for a moment, his face expressionless. I rapped my nails along the Formica counter lining the back hall to drown out the sound of the blood whooshing through my ears as I awaited his response.

"Giada, this isn't some generic manhunt. I'm not out to get one random person. I'm after the specific person who has been causing harm to this community. You and I are on the same side here."

"I'm telling you that you have the wrong man. The things you think Luca has done, he didn't. Angelo did, plus more. And I can give you details."

He clasped his hands together on top of the table. "Did Luca put you up to this?"

"No! I wouldn't even tell Luca I'm talking to you!" I replied without thinking of the ramifications.

"Why? Because he'd have me killed?"

I felt my eyes widen. "No, because he's already busy and has enough other things to worry about."

"Like his business managing the strip clubs and importing Italian drugs?"

I pushed to my feet. "Nevermind. You clearly have no interest learning the truth about anything." I turned and started out when his hand gripped my arm. The sensation of someone outside of my intimate circle grabbing me only angered me more.

"If you really knew anything about my family, you would not touch me against my will," I spit.

He dropped my arm, raising his hands to signal he was backing off. "I apologize. Please sit down."

I didn't move. "I have wedding photos to order. I don't have time to waste listening to your dumb conspiracy theories about my husband."

Grady lowered his voice. "Tell me about your brother. Give me something, anything I can verify."

I gazed around, surprised to see none of the other patrons seemed to care at all about our little spat. "I'll think about it," I said. I blew out a breath and returned to my friend before she started to worry.

∾

Luca

Giada seemed off when I got home that night, making me wonder if Matteo had called her. Instead of worrying about it, I decided to be upfront. I kissed her on the head and asked how her day was, pouring us each a glass of crisp white wine.

"I need to talk to you about something," she blurted out before we'd even sat down.

I grimaced. "No, let me go first," I said. I detailed the entire conversation with her dad as best I could, gauging her reaction from her expression.

"Is that what you're stressed about?" she asked.

"Yes. Well, and the fact that I have to see them again on Thursday." I sighed. "I just don't think I can handle any more drama this week."

Her lips parted, but then she sipped the rest of her wine instead of speaking. "Don't worry about my dad or brothers. And Thanksgiving will be great. There'll be so many people at my house, you won't even have to see my immediate family."

I grinned. "Promise?"

She pressed a kiss to my forehead then shuffled off to the couch with her laptop to finish ordering our wedding photos.

When we reached her house on Thursday, I soon realized she was right. The Conti family holiday was a big deal, not some intimate family affair. Everyone we greeted wished us a happy Thanksgiving, asked about the honeymoon, then more or less left us alone.

"Do you remember your first Thanksgiving with me?" Giada asked. "You were so overwhelmed."

"Still am, and of course I remember." We'd been in high school, and when Giada had realized that my parents planned to fly back to Italy before Thanksgiving Day, leaving me home alone, she'd insisted I join her family. "I had the biggest crush on you then but was still fooling myself into thinking I could ignore it."

"Um, no. If I remember correctly, the only thing you ignored that weekend was me. You spend all of your time with my brothers."

"Only because I didn't trust myself to be alone with you."

"Probably wise," she teased. She started to lean forward for a kiss, but I snatched her hand and dragged her towards the patio. Fires roared in the fire pit and the woodburning fireplace, but I still shivered without my jacket. A couple of Giada's cousins stood around the cooler housing the beer, but no one really paid us much attention.

I positioned Giada in front of one of the wood posts supporting the pergola, hoping she knew what I was showing her. Even though time and weather had warped the wood, I could still make out the crudely scrawled "LM + GC."

Giada smiled, leaning back into my arms. "You didn't carve this on Thanksgiving," she reminded me.

"No, but I believe I told you I'd bring you back here and show you this on our wedding day, and I didn't quite get around to it."

"It was a busy day," she said.

"Yes," I agreed.

Giada rose to her toes, wrapped her arms around my neck, and kissed me like we were high schoolers without a care in the world.

A moment later, an empty beer can grazed the side of my Gucci jacket.

"Get a room!" Giada's cousin shouted.

I gritted my teeth and escorted my wife inside before I succumbed to the temptation to shoot her relatives.

CHAPTER 15

Giada

*L*ife as a married woman moved fast. Between my perfect husband and my dream job, I kept busy. Well, and the holidays made everything fly by. Somehow, I blinked and already it was springtime. I was promoted to an actual associate at work, and Gabby threw me a party to celebrate. Luca and I returned to Italy over Easter. He was pretty busy with whatever crap his dad made him do, but I didn't feel lonely. I spent my days shopping for various clients and redecorating our apartment in Rome.

I flew back home on a Friday after ten days, but Luca had to stay for the weekend. As it was our first time apart overnight since the wedding, I planned to spend Saturday with my family to preempt any feelings of loneliness. Catching up with my mom was wonderful, but when it came time for me to leave, neither Enzo nor Matteo was available to drive me home. And since Lorenzo had picked me up that morning, I didn't have my car.

"I'll call for an Uber," I told my mom, keeping my voice casual as if I did normal things like that all the time.

Angelo breezed into the kitchen just then, shaking his head. "I have some errands to run in the area. I'll take you," he promised.

Mom seemed thrilled at the idea of two of her children spending time together, so I didn't protest. As much as I didn't enjoy alone time with Angelo, I figured nothing too terrible could happen during a forty-five minute drive.

I was wrong.

We'd only driven for about fifteen minutes when Angelo pulled into a shady-looking strip mall. "I need to make a quick stop. Wait in the car," he said.

I groaned audibly as he shifted the car into park. He was over the line, but few other cars remained, so no one would complain.

I started to pull out my phone to text Gabby, but I gazed up just as Angelo pulled a gun out of his jacket, kicked a door in, and burst into one of the darkened stores.

Horrified, I watched, but couldn't see anything inside the store thanks to the lack of lighting. Suddenly, there was a gunshot. I screamed, then covered my mouth, acutely aware I probably shouldn't scream.

I barely had time to consider running or locking the doors or anything before Angelo was back and shifted into reverse.

He seemed perfectly calm as he steered back onto the main road.

"What the fuck, Angelo?" I yelled as soon as I caught my breath.

"What? Guy owed me money. I remembered as we drove past. I'll take you home now."

I punched his thigh as hard as I could. "What is wrong with you?"

"Ow," he rubbed his leg and cast an annoyed grimace at me. "What's wrong with you? You shouldn't hit someone when they're driving a car."

"Did you seriously just shoot someone?"

"He'll be fine," my brother insisted.

We pulled up to a red light, and I jiggled the doorknob. "Let me out."

He shook his head. "I'll drop you off at home. Geez."

I was so angry that I was actively shaking, but I couldn't even look at Angelo. I just stared out the window instead.

"I don't get why you're making this out to be such a big deal," he said. "Don't even pretend like you didn't already know your precious husband shoots people all the time."

"I don't know what you're talking about," I snapped. "You're insane."

"Sure."

We didn't talk for the next several minutes. When Angelo pulled up in front of my apartment, he disengaged the child locks, and I flew out of the car. He rolled down the window and called after me.

"Probably best if you don't tell Luca about our little errand tonight. I mean, if you're serious that he's nothing like me," he said.

I flipped him the finger and scurried inside.

Once inside, I turned on every single light in the apartment. A chill had soaked into my bones, so I grabbed a blanket and sat on the couch. I glanced at the time on my phone and decided it was probably about three a.m. in Rome, maybe four. Luca wouldn't be upset if I woke him, but he couldn't exactly do anything to comfort me from across the Atlantic anyway.

And calling him would only reinforce his opinion that I couldn't take care of myself.

I scrolled through my contacts and dialed Alessio. He answered on the first ring.

"Giada?"

"Yeah, it's me. I'm um, sorry if I'm interrupting something."

"Are you okay?"

I knew to say yes, but the words didn't come as quickly as I wanted.

"Giada?"

"I'm, yes. I just…well, I'm scared."

"Where are you?"

I heard rustling noises in the background and then another voice. I winced, certain I had interrupted something.

"I'm at home," I finally said. "I'm okay. I'm sorry I disturbed you. I'll be fine."

"What happened?"

"I was with Angelo, and…" I paused, hearing music blast as a car door slammed. I assumed that meant he was already in his car. "He just did something I don't think he should have, and it freaked me out. I'm safe now. Don't wake up Luca."

"I'll be there in five minutes," he said.

Unsure of what else to do while I waited, I huddled under my blanket on the couch.

I'd barely gotten comfy when there was a knock on the door.

"It's Alessio," he said.

I recognized his voice, but checked the peephole anyway. Then I unlocked the door and let him in. His hair was messy, and he had a leather jacket thrown on over an undershirt and sweatpants. If I'd had any doubt that I interrupted something before, now I was certain.

"Are you alone? Angelo isn't here?" he asked, peering around.

"He dropped me off and left. I'm sorry I called you. I'm totally fine. I just panicked, and I was freaking myself out, and—"

"Hey," he interrupted, reaching his hand out to my shoulder. "It's fine. You did the right thing, calling."

I nodded and planned to thank him for coming over, but instead I burst into tears. Alessio stepped forward and wrapped me in a hug. When I finally calmed down, he asked me what happened with Angelo. I told him the whole story, answering a million questions for him as he constantly interrupted. Then, he made me tell him again.

He blew out a sigh as I finished talking.

"So, now you see I'm completely fine, and I ruined your evening for nothing," I said, mortified.

Alessio chuckled and stood up, making his way to the kitchen. "Where's Luca keep the good stuff these days?"

I followed, not sure what he meant. Luca kept several weapons around the apartment, but I had no clue what classified as good.

Alessio turned around with two highball glasses in his hand. "Whiskey or bourbon preferably?"

I pointed to the cabinet.

"Want some?" he offered, even though technically we were in my apartment, so it was my alcohol.

I started to say no, then realized I really did want a drink. "Vodka and cranberry."

Alessio already knew the vodka was in the freezer, so he mixed my drink and handed it to me before pouring his own.

"Saluti," he said, clinking his glass against mine.

He took a long sip and then exhaled.

"You didn't interrupt anything," he said suddenly. "We had finished the good part. Honestly you just saved me from that awkward moment where I have to find an excuse to kick 'em out. I don't like hosting sleepovers."

I nodded, unsure of what else to say.

We were both silent for several minutes. I finished my drink, and Alessio mixed me another, handing me a bottle of water along with this one. He poured himself another drink as well.

"Your brother is a dick," he said after he tasted his drink.

I waited for him to elaborate, which he did.

"He's been wanting to meet with Luca, and Luca has been avoiding him. He did this just to force Luca's hand."

"What do you mean?" I asked.

"Luca is going to have to meet with him now. Luca won't just let this go."

"Angelo told me not to tell him."

"He knew you would, and he knew Luca's a hothead and would barge in to see him the second he's back in the country."

I frowned. "Then don't tell Luca. I don't want to put him in any danger. I can just avoid Angelo from now on. He didn't actually hurt me, or—"

"Luca isn't in any danger. Your brother doesn't want to hurt him; he wants to work with him."

"But if Luca gets in Angelo's face over this, Angelo might react badly. They both have tempers."

Alessio didn't seem to disagree with my last statement, but he shrugged. "They're both professionals. No one will get hurt. Especially not Luca."

He finished his drink, then rubbed his eyes.

"Are you planning to stay here tonight?"

"I'm guessing Luca would want me to stay with you until he gets back. If you'd rather I call him and ask…" His voice trailed off.

"No, you can stay. The guest room is all made up."

Alessio smiled but made no attempt to move off the couch. I wasn't actually tired yet anyway.

"Were you with a girlfriend tonight?"

His face blanched. "Uhh, no. Nothing, um, serious like that."

I nodded, realizing I probably shouldn't pry. But then somehow I heard myself asking about his mother and sister and all sorts of other personal questions. We talked for more than an hour, until I was finally calm enough to head to bed.

I actually slept well that night, despite my anxiety. I assumed it was a combination of the alcohol and Alessio's comforting presence. When I awoke, I saw a missed call from Luca and two text messages. I clicked on them both.

"I hear you had a sleepover with another man last night. I'm glad you called him. Boarding a flight soon. Will be home by evening. Stay w Alessio today."

The second one was shorter, reading "Bought you something XXX at the airport. Miss you. Ti amo tanto."

I laughed at that one. I wasn't sure if the XXX was a typo or some translation issue or if he literally meant he bought me a dirty gift at the airport. Regardless, I felt better. I wondered how early Alessio had called him, and what they'd decided. Or how much he'd even told him over the phone.

I tried calling Luca, but wasn't surprised when it went to voice mail. I left him a message telling him I loved him, then texted the same thing. I figured it couldn't hurt to have him in a good mood before he went to kill my brother.

~

Luca

I replayed Giada's message as Thomas drove Giovanni and me to Angelo's office, smiling at the sound of her voice. I'd spoken to Alessio and already knew exactly what Angelo had done, and I didn't want to talk to my wife until I'd dealt with her brother. I knew I was playing right into his hand, but he'd given me no choice at this point.

I burst into Angelo's office, making no attempt to hide my fury.

A few of his guys hopped up at the sudden intrusion. I knew them all, but even if I hadn't, I was certain they knew me.

"I'm sure he's expecting me," I said, making my way directly back to his private office.

I pounded on the door. "Open up, Angelo."

I heard a hearty laugh on the other side. "Come on in, Marino," he said.

I shoved open the door, then slammed it behind me before yanking my gun out of the holster on my back hip.

I shot a plant on the desk, enjoying Angelo's startled look. "Is this what we do now? Barge into places and shoot things?" I dropped my gun on his desk right as a slew of his men rushed in.

Angelo raised his hand, effectively calling off his dogs. "Leave us," he said.

They glared at me. Giada's cousin, Eddie, was the last to leave.

"It slipped," I said with a shrug.

Angelo rolled his eyes. "Get that thing off my desk, Marino," he said.

I complied, positioning it back into the holster. "Well, you wanted to talk, and here I am, so fucking talk."

The smug bastard still had that obnoxious grin on his face. "I wasn't sure she'd tell you, to be honest. She seems convinced that you're different from me, somehow." He paused. "Honestly, I'm shocked she hasn't dumped you, with as much as she clearly knows about you."

"Angelo, if you keep talking about your sister, I'm getting the gun out again and this time, I won't shoot a fucking plant."

"It was fake anyway," he said. "I can't keep anything alive it seems."

I sunk into the chair facing his desk, worried I would strangle him if I continued to stand. "You know that isn't what your father meant, about keeping your sister on a tighter leash? Pretty sure he wouldn't be happy if he knew you were involving her in your…drama."

Angelo smirked. "Lucky for me, you won't tell him."

I clenched my abs. "Look, I don't think we make a good team, you and I. We have different methods, different lines of business, and we don't get along."

"But we're family."

"You need to stay away from Giada. Don't talk to her, don't go near her," I cautioned. "And definitely keep all your goons away from her."

"My 'goons' are her cousins and uncles. You really want to isolate her from her entire family?"

I shook my head. "Angelo, this is a war no one can win. Let it go." I left before he could cause any more drama.

I went straight back to my apartment after meeting with Angelo. I was starting to feel the time change, and since I'd been too angry to sleep on the plane, I knew I'd crash soon.

I unlocked the door with my key, then smiled as I took in the sight before me. I hadn't realized how much I'd missed being home, even after such a short trip.

Giada flew up from the table where she appeared to have been working on some designs. Alessio was sprawled across the couch texting someone. He offered a casual wave in my direction as my wife launched herself onto me.

"No more traveling without me," she said, planting a firm kiss on my lips.

I chuckled and set her down, nudging her all the way into the apartment so I could shut the door behind me.

Alessio stood slowly and stretched.

"We should talk," I said to him, my arms still wrapped around Giada. I gently pried her off of me.

"I know your priorities," Alessio said, glancing at Giada. "And you look tired. We'll talk tomorrow morning."

That plan made sense. It wasn't quite dinner time locally, but Alessio was right. I'd never make it late tonight.

~

Giada

After I spent an hour in bed welcoming my husband home from Italy, we snuggled up against the headboard.

"I'm glad you called Alessio after what happened with Angelo," Luca said suddenly, brushing my hair off my forehead.

"I felt silly. I wasn't in danger..."

"Giada, you did exactly what I'm always asking you to do. I

don't want you to ever be scared, and knowing you'll actually call him when you're worried, that takes a lot of pressure off me."

"You don't mind that I let another man sleep over?"

"Any other man? I'd mind. Alessio, no."

"Because he's seeing someone? Or I'm just not his type?"

Luca chuckled. "Even if you were his exact type, I'd still trust him. He's my right-hand guy. If I can't be there for you, he can, and he'll do anything I would to take care of you."

"Anything?" I repeated, eyebrow raised, lifting my head off his chest to make eye contact.

Luca breathed a laugh as he caught my implication. "Okay, no. Not that."

He kissed my forehead, then yawned, his eyes drifting shut.

I realized it had to be the middle of the night in Italy already. "Get some sleep, Luca. I'm going to grab a snack and binge a show. Maybe drool over our wedding album."

"Again?" he asked with a sleepy yawn.

"I will never get sick of those photos." I kissed him again, then tiptoed from the room. I closed the door behind me and made myself comfy on the couch. I pulled a blanket over my lap and turned on the latest episode of my favorite home renovation show, but I couldn't concentrate. I waited a few more minutes, then grabbed my cell phone and tiptoed into the guest room.

I dialed the number I'd programmed into my phone as "Gabby's brother," even though that wasn't at all his real identity.

Despite the relatively late hour on a Sunday, the man answered.

"Officer Grady? I have some information about Angelo for you. When can we meet?" I asked, already feeling better about it all.

CHAPTER 16

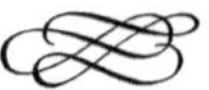

Adrian

My phone jolted me from a deep sleep. I cursed before answering, not even bothering to check the caller ID. The number would be blocked regardless. The caller was either Angelo or one of his cohorts. They'd been ruthless with their demands lately, seeking me out for one ridiculous favor after another. None of the tasks were illegal or even nefarious, per se, but they also weren't all jobs that required a lawyer.

Sometimes they'd ask me to check on the status of a case, but more often they'd tell me to pick up their food order from some fast food dive near the courthouse. I wasn't sure if they were testing me or just hazing me, but I was sick of typing, "I don't work for DoorDash" in response to their texts.

"What?" I growled, rubbing my eyes and peering at the clock. It was just after one o'clock, so I actually hadn't been asleep long at all.

"Hi. Is this Adrian?" The caller had a vaguely familiar but clearly feminine voice.

"Yeah, who is this?"

"It's Jade. Look, sorry to wake you, but can you come down to the hospital?"

"Jade?" I gazed at the phone, confirming it was in fact my sister's overly friendly roommate and not the world's most annoying mobster disturbing my sleep.

"Everyone is okay, but I need you to come to the hospital. Can you do that? Your sister is here, and—"

"My sister is in the hospital?" I flew out of bed and had my jeans up to my waist before Jade even confirmed that fact. She reiterated that Annie was going to be okay, and then she hung up.

Thanks to the hour, there was no traffic to fight, but still too much time passed between the phone call and my arrival at the Emergency Room. When I asked at the desk for my sister, a nurse told me that Dr. Burton wanted to talk to me first.

I opened my mouth to ask who that was, when Jade appeared at the end of the hallway. She wore a white coat, and only then did I remember. Jade Burton was doing her medical residency in Emergency Room medicine.

"You can see your sister in a minute, but we need to talk first," Jade said, guiding me into a miniscule conference room.

"What happened? Was she in a car accident? Is she awake?"

"Adrian," her eyes pleaded with me to stop talking. "Your sister is okay. She will be discharged soon. I need you to calm down and listen to me." She pulled me in for a hug, which did relax me some, even as she released me and gestured for me to take a seat.

"The police are here to take your sister's statement. I thought it would be helpful for you to be with her then, and maybe to talk with her before, just because of your legal experience."

I nodded, urging her to continue.

"Annie asked me to tell you what happened. It's actually not uncommon in cases like this for the victim to feel more comfortable telling a stranger than her own family and friends."

Bile inched up my throat at the word "victim." A sick sense of dread told me I already knew what had happened to my sister, but I prayed I was wrong. "What do you mean, cases like this?"

Jade's face tensed, confirming the worst. "Annie was sexually assaulted tonight, Adrian."

I was on my feet in an instant. I turned to the wall, desperate to punch it. I'd never in my life wanted so badly to cause some serious damage. I settled for leaning into it, pressing my palms against the chipped grey paint and pushing with all my might. When that didn't make me feel any better, I dragged a hand through my hair and swiveled to face Jade.

"She says the assailant didn't rape her. He tried, but I guess he was interrupted, and—"

"Wait, she wasn't?" Relief washed over me. "Why didn't you lead with that?"

She ignored the question. "Your sister has been through a lot. She is scared and embarrassed and traumatized. She needs your support. She does not need to see you acting angry or sad right now. Do you understand?"

I was so angry I couldn't even nod my agreement. *Fuck.*

Jade slowly rose, placing one hand delicately on my forearm. "Your sister is strong, and she has an amazing support system. She will get through this."

I took a few deep breaths, then followed her down the hall. Annie sat at the edge of a hospital bed in a small room. I tapped on the doorframe, then let myself in, only them noticing the nurse seated on a chair in the corner.

"It's my brother," Annie said to the nurse before even addressing me.

The nurse forced a tight smile and left us alone. I swallowed the lump in my throat as I gazed up at my sister, confused by how small and fragile she looked sitting there.

"Apparently, if you get attacked by a big scary monster, they send a petite nurse to babysit you," Annie said, cracking an awkward smile.

"Annie," I breathed. "Are you…okay?" It was a stupid question, and we both knew it, but I had to ask. Her lip was busted open and already turning purple, thick bandages covered her wrist, and her makeup was smudged to the point that she resembled a zombie prom queen. A green patterned hospital gown covered her petite frame, preventing me from observing any other external injuries.

"I've been better," she said. "But at the moment, I'm…I don't know, relieved?"

I frowned and inched closer. I was about to place my hand on her knee when I stopped myself. I would understand if she didn't feel like being touched right now.

Annie bit her lip, then winced in pain. Her face crumpled into tears as she reached for me. I wrapped my arms around her, holding her tight.

"I thought he was going to kill me," she said. "He had a knife, and I was just so sure that was it for me. All I could think about was how sad mom was going to be." She choked out another sob, pulling herself together enough to squeak out a few more words. "I've taken six or seven self-defense classes, and I didn't remember any of it. I didn't fight back at all. I just lay there and—"

"Shh," I said, feeling my stomach churn at the thought of what could have happened. "You might not be here now if you'd fought back. He might have killed you. You were smart, and you're alive. You will recover."

I startled at a sound at the door, turning to see Jade.

"The police want to take your statement now," she said.

Annie gazed up at me. "Do I need a lawyer for this?"

"Sure, I'll stay with you the whole time."

Annie glanced from me to Jade then back to me. "I mean, will it be okay if you're not here? I appreciate the offer, but I…" her voice trailed off, but the pink in her cheeks told me what she couldn't. She was embarrassed for me to hear the gory details.

As much as I hated to admit it, I was relieved. Listening to the details of what she'd experienced sounded like torture that should be reserved for the ninth circle of hell.

"You'll be fine without a lawyer, Anne," I told her. "Just be honest, and take your time answering. If you don't remember something, tell them you're in pain and need to give them the full story once you're discharged. All they need now are the basic points so they can go catch the creep."

She nodded, and I made my way to the hall.

The night dragged on, and the sun had risen by the time Annie and I left the hospital. Her clothes had been taken into evidence, but Jade loaned her an outfit. I encouraged Annie to come stay with me, but she insisted she wanted to go home. I walked Annie inside, made her an omelet while she showered, then stretched out on her couch while she tried to rest. Jade wasn't yet home from her shift at the hospital, and their other roommate had already left for work. I wasn't about to leave Annie alone, but I also didn't anticipate sleeping a lot after the night we'd had.

I hadn't told Annie, but when I spoke with the police after they left her room, they hadn't seemed optimistic about making an arrest. I knew she was safe now, but I couldn't stop thinking what would've happened if some stranger hadn't happened upon them when he had.

I had nearly drifted off when my phone buzzed. Only then did I realize I'd silenced my phone. I had multiple missed calls and texts from Angelo. The most recent message read: "I'm not the type of man who appreciates being ignored."

I swore under my breath and clicked to answer the call before it stopped ringing. I pushed off the couch and moved to the furthest corner of the apartment from my sister, before speaking.

"Angelo, I'll explain later, but I can't talk now."

"The fuck you will," he snapped back.

"Look, I haven't been home since last night. I was at the

hospital with my sister and then we had to talk with the police, and—"

"You talked with the police?" His already cold tone turned even scarier.

"No." I gritted my teeth. "My sister was attacked. The hospital called the police. They did a…" I stopped, unable to speak the phrase "rape kit." "They took some evidence and talked to her to try and find the guy, and…"

"Jesus. Is she alright?"

"Yeah. I mean, she will be. I didn't want to leave her alone, so I'm at her apartment now." As I spoke, I realized it was nearly lunchtime on a weekday. I hadn't told anyone at the office I'd be out.

"No, you should stay with her. Uh, I'll have Eddie call Russo and tell him you'll be out for a couple days. Just touch base with him when you're ready."

"Um, okay. Thanks." I was so unaccustomed to Angelo acting human, let alone kind, that the entire conversation was unsettling.

"Do you need anything else?" he paused. "Like, we could send a gift basket or something. A fruit bouquet?"

I winced at the image of the card on a gift basket. What would they say, sorry about the sexual assault? "Yeah, thanks for the offer, but I think she'd be mortified if she knew I told you."

"Right. Okay. Well, bye."

Angelo ended the call without ever telling me what he wanted.

Giada

*A*fter a late breakfast with Luca, I spent an hour at the office. At exactly five past twelve, I told Cami I was heading out for a walk. I headed one block south of the office, then sat on a bench.

Grady O'Keefe was already there waiting.

I told him what Angelo had done, surprised at how little guilt I felt. Although, in my defense, Luca was still all stressed out and cranky over Angelo's antics. If I had to pick between the two, it would be Luca, every time.

I was about to head back to work when my phone rang. I glanced down, assuming it was either Gabby or my mom, since I'd just seen Luca and no one else really called. Instead, it was Angelo.

The FBI agent glared at me as though I'd somehow set him up. Without thinking, I clicked to accept the call, leaving it on speaker.

"Angelo?" I asked, wondering if maybe someone had stolen his phone since he so rarely called me.

"Hey, I just talked to Adrian, and he said his sister was attacked last night. Just thought you should know so you don't fuck with him today or anything."

I rolled my eyes at his crude terminology. "Fuck with him? Jesus Angelo, I hardly ever see Adrian, and it's not like I'm toying with him every chance I get." Then I paused, and realized what he'd said. "Wait, did you say Annie was attacked?"

"Yeah, last night."

I flew to my feet, as if ready to race off to help her. "Is she okay? Is Adrian? God, what happened?"

"I don't know details yet. Some guy attacked her. She's resting at her apartment now. Adrian says she doesn't want people to know, so maybe don't mention it."

"Oh, poor Annie. Poor Adrian." I pressed my hand to my head, then switched the call off of speaker, realizing the topic was much too personal for speaker phone. "You really don't know any more details?"

"Nope. We'll figure it out though, and we'll take care of the guy. Don't worry. I got to go." He hung up without another word, leaving me standing in the middle of a sidewalk, breathless and teary.

After a moment, I realized Grady was still there.

"I, um, need to go," I mumbled.

"I'll verify what you told me and be in touch. Can I call this afternoon?" he asked.

I considered my plans for the rest of the day. There was no way I could return to work, not after what I'd learned. The only place that could offer me the comfort and peace I needed now was the church.

"Yeah, that's fine." I scurried back to my office to grab my things then walked the two miles to the church.

I skipped the confessional and went straight to a seat in the sanctuary in silence for some time before praying the rosary twice. My stomach growled, alerting me that nearly six hours had passed since my last meal, but before I could decide if I wanted to call Enzo or Alessio to pick me up, my phone rang. I silenced it quickly, then gazed around, determining I was completely alone in the cavernous room.

The caller ID told me that it was Grady. Somehow, he'd already confirmed my story, and suddenly, I couldn't wait another minute before hearing my brother's fate. A slight twinge of guilt over betraying him flitted over me as I answered the call.

"Hello?" I whispered.

"Giada?"

"Yes, I'm in a church, so I have to be quiet," I said, standing to move to a hallway.

Grady cleared his throat. "I just wanted to let you know that we sent an officer to the strip mall. No one at any of the shops admitted to any dealings with your brother. No one admitted being shot. No one even reported hearing a shooting that night."

"But I was there," I protested.

"I believe you. I'm not saying you're lying. This is what we're up against all the time with organized crime. If we don't have solid proof, it may as well never have happened." The agent paused. "Keep an eye on your brother, get me some firm details, and we'll talk. Otherwise, I'm still willing to listen to what you have to say about Luca."

I punched my phone to end the call, resisting the urge to chuck my phone across the building.

CHAPTER 17

Giada

News traveled fast in the family about Adrian's sister. Luca already knew by the time I got home, and he was now too rattled to leave me home alone for the weekend. He had avoided traveling to the casinos so far, but apparently their contacts there were insistent he come. I didn't want to make him cancel his business plans, or make him worry about me the entire weekend, so I agreed to tag along.

I figured it would be almost like a mini vacation, but of course that wasn't how it started. Alessio and Luca chatted business—in Italian—the entire drive there. Once we arrived, Alessio gave us a tour of the property. I resisted the urge to try my hand at the slots, instead settling for a delicious cosmopolitan at the bar followed by an indulgent steak dinner with the guys.

After dinner, we all returned to the suite. The luxurious space had two bedrooms connected by a small sitting room with its own kitchenette. Each bedroom had a private bathroom, both with a gorgeous oversized jacuzzi tub. I perched on the edge of the marble counter while Luca got ready for whatever business he and Alessio had to take care of that night.

"Will you be back in time to join me in that tub?" I asked, nodding across the room.

Luca smiled. "I wish, but no. I'll be late. Alessio and I need to talk with some guys over a poker game, and those run late. Enjoy the bath without me, then have a snack and watch some TV or something and get some sleep. I'll be quiet when I come back."

I groaned. He made it seem like he was going to be really late. "If I'm going to be alone all night, you should've just left me home."

His face fell. "Don't open the door while we're gone. It won't be all night. And I'll send Alessio back as soon as I can."

"I don't want Alessio back early. I want you."

"I'll be back before you wake," Luca promised. "And I hear this place has a ridiculously good brunch."

"I'm still stuffed from dinner."

Luca leaned in and kissed me, lingering just long enough to make me really wish he could join me in the tub. I pouted for a moment after he left, then filled the tub for myself. I relaxed in the water until my skin was pruny, then dried off and snuggled under the covers in bed. I propped myself up in the very center of the plush king-sized mattress and began watching reruns of a design show.

At some point, I must have dozed off. When I woke, the television was still on. I rubbed my eyes, confirmed there was no sign of Luca, and groaned. I reached for my phone and texted my husband. I didn't want to be a nag, but it was nearing two o'clock in the morning.

"I'm awake and you're not back. ETA?" I wrote.

A second after I sent the message, I heard the familiar bing of Luca's phone from across the room. Relief flooded me. Luca never went anywhere without his phone, so he had to be back. I wrapped a robe around myself, confirmed the bathroom was empty, then opened the door to check the living room.

That space, too, was quiet, and as far as I could tell in the dark, it was also empty. I crept over to the couch in case Luca had moved there to sleep, but it was bare aside from a jacket. I paused, then realized Alessio's door was open a crack. I heard a low mumble that sounded like Alessio talking, and I sighed, realizing I'd gotten myself all panicked when Luca was just talking with his friend.

Luca would've taken his phone if he'd gone anywhere. Knowing that, it was dumb for me to even have considered any other possibilities. Although, now that I was wide awake, I'd rather have Luca back in the room with me instead of hanging out with his bestie. Besides, he needed sleep just as much as I did.

I lifted my hand to Alessio's door, using my knuckles to half knock, half push the door open. "Hey Luca," I began, poking my head in.

I stared ahead, expecting to see my husband and his best friend lounging in the chairs or maybe side by side on the bed, discussing some ridiculous business matter that could always wait till morning. But that wasn't what I saw at all.

Instead, my eyes took in a tangle of arms and legs, a flash of Alessio's dark brown hair mixing with someone else's dirty blond strands. The sheets covered the critical parts, but as the couple in bed shifted, I yelped with surprise. The blond on top of Alessio—the very muscular, very masculine blond—was most definitely a man. And they were most definitely not talking or fighting or wrestling, not in the traditional sense of the sport anyway.

I should've turned the second I saw what was going on, but the scene before me was so unexpected that I literally froze in place for a moment.

"Omigod, I'm so sorry," I said, regaining control of my muscles. I turned abruptly, slammed into the side of the door, mumbled a quick "ouch," then rushed back to my room.

I sat on the bed, panting like I'd just run a race, pretty sure I was going to hyperventilate before I could block out the visions of what I'd just seen. I gazed at Luca's phone again, realizing my initial concerns about him being out and about without his phone were also well grounded. Probably, he wouldn't have gone far. Also, Alessio probably knew where he'd gone…except I wasn't about to bother Alessio to ask. I'd already mortified us both and interrupted him once-too-many times for the night.

I then considered the possibility that Luca hadn't left willingly. Maybe he'd gone into the common room for something and someone took him. Alessio was clearly distracted, so maybe…

I jumped nearly a foot off the bed when there was knocking on my door.

I squeezed my eyes shut, already pained by the awkwardness of this encounter.

"Come in," I said, taking a deep breath for strength.

I didn't dare make eye contact above ankle level, but based on the bare feet and worn sweatpants, I was certain my visitor was Alessio.

"Giada," he said softly. "You okay?"

"I, um. I am sorry. So, so sorry. I didn't mean to interrupt. I just woke up and Luca was gone and I realized he left his phone, so I started to worry, and then I heard voices in your room and your door was cracked and I just assumed he was in your room and you guys were talking and…" I paused, desperately in need of a breath.

"Hey, it's okay. I should learn to shut the door," he said.

I couldn't have agreed more.

Alessio breathed a laugh. "Wow, you can't even look at me, can you?"

My cheeks flushed more, which was truly an impressive feat since they already burned like they were on fire. I told myself it wasn't a big deal. I'd seen Alessio without his shirt before, and really, that was all I'd seen now. Just a shirtless man. Well, except when I'd seen him before without his shirt, he wasn't kissing another man, thrashing around under the sheets like…

I bit the insides of my cheeks to chase the intrusive thoughts away and focus on the issue. "I'm sorry," I repeated. I forced my eyes upward, to his face. "Do you know where Luca is?"

Alessio nodded. "He's still playing cards, and he wasn't sure if they'd confiscate his phone during the game, so he took a burner phone. He should be back soon."

That was a relief. "You're sure he's okay?"

"Yeah."

"Okay. Thanks. And sorry, again. Please tell…" I paused, wondering why I'd even begun this sentence when I obviously had no idea who the guy in his bed was. "Tell your friend I said sorry too."

"Jack," Alessio said.

"Huh?"

"His name is Jack. You met him earlier, actually."

I had no recollection of this.

"The bartender?" he continued. "You said he made the best cosmo you'd ever tasted."

"Oh, of course," I said, still not really willing to focus enough on the scene I'd walked in on to decipher if it was the same guy. I cleared my throat and glanced away. "Well, I don't mean to keep you from…that, so…"

Alessio chuckled. "Luca never told you, did he?"

"Told me?" I dared to look up at his face again.

"That I like guys."

As the implication of his words hit me, I was speechless. Luca had known? For how long? How? Had he walked in on Alessio? Why hadn't he told me? I had so many questions, but then quizzically what left my mouth first wasn't even a question at all. "But I've seen you go out with girls," I said. Sure, I hadn't seen him with a girl in the same way I'd just seen him and Jack, but I was aware of at least five girls he'd dated in the past couple of years. And the way he talked about women…

"I like women, too," he said. "I'm bisexual."

I felt like a total moron, staring at him slackjawed, but it was the middle of the night and I had been completely caught off guard earlier. "And Luca knows this?"

Alessio nodded. "I just assumed he'd told you."

I shook my head and a lengthy silence ensued.

"You and Luca never…" I began, regretting the words as soon as I heard them aloud.

Alessio made a face. "Eww, no. Being bisexual doesn't mean I'm attracted to everyone of both sexes."

"Right, of course not," I said, the heat rushing to my cheeks again.

"And I've never gotten the impression that Luca was into that, but I guess you would know better than me."

"Yes," I said, although I was questioning if I knew anything about anything at that moment. "Well, sorry again, and um, you should get back to Jake."

"Jack," he corrected.

"Right. God." I covered my eyes with my hand. "Sorry."

Alessio laughed again, clearly not even close to as mortified by all of this as I was. "I'll send him home," he offered.

I shook my head. "Don't feel like you need to on my account. As long as you're sure Luca is safe, I'm just fine and you can do what you want." I paused. "Maybe close the door all the way, though,"

"Good night, Giada. Knock on the door if you need me. Or text."

"Night," I said, dropping backwards onto my bed and covering my face with a pillow.

~

Luca

I lost at poker, but that was expected. I was there to make connections and show them I was trustworthy, not take their money. The game seemingly went on forever, and it was closer to morning than night by the time I headed back to the room.

As I stepped off the elevator onto my floor, a man walked onto the elevator. He smiled happily and I thought I recognized him, but couldn't think of where I'd seen him before until I reached the room. As I started to unlock the door, it swung open.

"Did you forget…" Alessio began, stopping midsentence when he saw it was me.

I laughed. "Expecting someone else?"

Alessio walked over to the mini fridge and helped himself to a tiny bottle of vodka. "Yeah, and there's probably something I should tell you about that, but first, I want to hear how the game went."

I gave him the basic rundown. We talked briefly about it, but I was exhausted. The adrenaline that had kept me going the past few hours was quickly wearing off.

But just as I was about to excuse myself to go to sleep, I connected the dots—Alessio still awake, the man I'd passed in the hall, and I had seen him before.

"The bartender was here, wasn't he?"

"Yeah. About that…" Alessio began.

I shook my head. "I don't need details, dude. I'm tired."

"I sorta screwed up," he said, catching my attention before I made it to my room.

I turned back to face him.

"Apparently, we didn't close the door all the way, and Giada kind of walked in on us."

"Kind of?" I repeated with a grimace.

He shrugged. "Well, completely. Pretty sure she saw everything. Well, not everything, just enough to know what was going on."

I closed my eyes, certain I did not have the energy for this talk now. Or the talk I was going to have to endure with Giada.

"I hadn't realized you never told her I'm bi."

"I never told anyone," I said.

Alessio nodded. "Well, thanks for that. That is actually very sweet, and mostly unexpected. Anyway, she, uh, she knows now."

I chuckled, able to picture the shitshow that must have followed that surprising discovery.

"Good night," I said, again starting towards my room.

"Hey Luca?" Alessio waited until I turned back to him to continue. "She asked if you and I had ever fooled around."

"Gross."

Alessio laughed. "That's what I said. But anyway, thought you should know."

I walked to bed, shaking my head the whole way. There was just too much in that statement to unpack in one night.

My beautiful wife was sound asleep, so I stripped and showered in silence, then joined her in bed. She sighed and snuggled closer to me, but didn't open her eyes. Within minutes, sleep overtook me.

The next morning, we both slept in. When I opened my eyes, Giada was staring at me.

"Why did you never tell me?" she asked.

I yawned, but already knew what she was asking about. "It wasn't my secret to tell. And I didn't think you cared what Alessio did in the bedroom or who he did it with."

"I don't. It was just surprising." She shook her head. "He's just so crass in the comments he makes about women sometimes. I never considered..."

"He's that way when he sees a guy he likes too," I said, shifting to pull her onto my chest. "Now that you know, though, you can't tell anyone."

"Of course."

"I mean, like absolutely no one can know," I said, wanting to make sure she understood the ramifications of this information getting out. "My papà doesn't approve of that lifestyle. He thinks it's a sin."

Giada propped her head up to stare at me. "Your father cheats on his wife with prostitutes, sells drugs, steals, and rarely goes to church. But he thinks a consensual relationship between two men is a sin?"

"Yep."

She rolled her eyes. Honestly, I was a tad surprised Giada was okay with it all. She'd never been the judgiest person, but she was pretty big on the tenets of her faith, and I was certain being gay was probably still a big no-no in the catholic church.

"Does Alessio know your father feels that way?"

"Yeah."

"And it doesn't bother him?"

"I'm sure it does. Hell, it bothers me. But I don't think he's about to pick that fight with my papà."

"Maybe you could talk some sense into your father."

"There's a very real possibility my papà would kill Alessio if he knew. I'm not willing to take that risk just to try to cure his bigotry."

Giada made a face, and we were both quiet for several minutes.

"So how long have you known Alessio was bi?" she asked.

I tried to count the years, then gave up and explained a different way. "Remember that dickhead roommate I had my freshman year of high school?" Giada was younger, so she hadn't actually been at the school that year, but I knew I'd introduced her to him later on.

"Vaguely."

"Well, Alessio used to hook up with him," I continued. "So I actually knew Alessio liked guys before I learned he also liked girls."

"You didn't learn by walking in on him, did you?"

That made me chuckle. "No." I left out the fact that, since then, I had actually seen him in bed with women. Alessio lacked the discretion with his personal life that he maintained so well with his professional one.

"Hmm. I'd always wondered how you guys met in high school since I'd never seen him, and he wasn't from your hometown."

"We bonded over the whole Italian thing. He lived a few miles from the school. He went to public school but spent a ton of time on our campus. I'm surprised you don't remember more about him. You must have met him over a dozen times in high school."

"I had a lot on my mind back then," she began. "Hair, makeup, nails, shoes, accessories, clothes…"

I tickled her in response. When she finally stopped giggling, I decided to raise the other point that had been on my mind since I'd talked with Alessio.

"Alessio told me you asked if he and I had ever—"

"Oh god. I'm sorry. I didn't really think… I just." She shook her head, her cheeks flushed. "I mean, I guess hearing that he was bisexual when I'd had absolutely no clue whatsoever made me realize how naïve and oblivious I can be and so then I thought, well if he's bisexual, who else in my life is too that I just haven't noticed."

I nearly giggled at her logic, but instead I kissed her to shut her up. "Just to set the record straight, I am not bisexual. I've never fooled around with Alessio or any other man. Got it?"

She nodded sheepishly.

"Why don't we get brunch just the two of us? Leave Alessio to catch up on his sleep," I suggested.

Not surprisingly, Giada agreed.

CHAPTER 18

Adrian

I was terrified to leave my sister alone for days after her attack, but her roommates were sick of me hanging around the apartment. Besides, I still had my own life to manage. I'd skipped a fair amount of work without consequence, but I had a hearing in the superior court that I couldn't miss.

I'd called the detective assigned to Annie's case every single day, but the police had made no progress. They didn't seem optimistic that they ever would, either. When they asked me to stop calling and promised they'd let us know as soon as they had any updates, I assumed that was the last we'd ever hear from them.

I was wrong.

The next morning, Detective Ardagh called as I was headed into work. He said they'd just gotten off the phone with my sister and wanted us both to come into the station. I texted Angelo, in part so he could vouch for me having a good reason to miss work, but also to ensure he wouldn't have his goons punish me for visiting the police precinct without explanation.

I picked up Annie, instantly launching into my questions

about what the police had told her. But apparently, they hadn't given her any indication why they wanted to talk with us, either. No matter. My Jag got us to the station in record time, where we both paced the lobby restlessly.

"You okay?" I asked for the millionth time.

Annie shook my hand off of her arm. "No, but you can stop asking me. I just need to hear that they caught the guy and that this is over until the trial."

My stomach clenched at the thought of a trial. I wanted the guy caught too, obviously, but forcing my sister to relive the awful night over and over again at trial was going to be a nightmare in and of itself. "Hopefully, he'll just confess or take a plea deal," I told her.

A female officer I recognized from the hospital came to greet us, introduced herself as Officer Clinton, then led us into a small, windowless interrogation room. It seemed an odd choice for the conversation, but I wasn't about to complain. I just wanted answers.

Detective Ardagh waltzed into the room, sipping coffee from a Styrofoam cup, then suppressing a yawn. We exchanged the requisite pleasantries while he sat, then he opened a file.

"Miss Patras, can you tell us where you were between ten a.m. and one p.m. two days ago?"

My sister frowned and then glanced at me, as confused as I was.

My patience had officially run out. "What is going on? I thought you wanted her here for a line up. I thought you caught the guy. I am here as my sister's brother, not her attorney, but if you're about to blame the victim here or some other harassment bullshit, you should know we will sue you and this department for—"

"Mr. Patras," Detective Ardagh interrupted. "Sit down, and I'll explain."

I hesitated, not having realized I'd even stood up. I lowered myself into my seat but kept glaring.

Officer Clinton turned to my sister. "If I show you a picture, do you think you can identify whether or not it is the man who attacked you?"

My sister nodded confidently, but I shook my head. "No! You need to follow the proper protocols. I don't want this asshole getting away on some loophole. I want him to rot in jail. Do a lineup."

"No one is rotting in jail Mr. Patras. He's dead," Detective Ardagh shouted back.

I struggled to process his words, then turned to my sister. Officer Clinton slid a photo across the table.

"Can you confirm this is the man who attacked you?"

My sister stared at the photo, her lip trembling. After a moment, she jerked her head to the side, sniffling loudly. "Yes. That is him."

The officers exchanged a glance and then flipped through the photos.

"I apologize for the gruesome nature of this picture, but if you're willing to view a full-body picture, we have some questions." Officer Jones said.

My sister looked disgusted but nodded her agreement.

Officer Jones flipped the photo over. The word "RAPIST" had been carved into the man's torso, and his genitalia had been removed and shoved into his mouth.

My sister flew out of her chair so quickly that the chair clamored to the ground. I turned my gaze to her, less nauseated by the site of her vomiting into a lidless trash can than I was by the picture itself.

"Put it away," I said. I grabbed a tissue and walked it over to my sister, still huddled over the trash can. "Why did we need to see that?"

"It seems to suggest that this man's killing was in revenge for a rape. As your sister has confirmed that this is the man who attacked her, we need to know where she was during the time in question. We'd also like to know if she has a boyfriend or close male friend in town."

"Why? What is the relevance of that?"

"Mr. Patras, your sister had motive to kill this guy, and she has produced no alibi. But given the nature of the crime, I'm not convinced she would be physically capable of doing it. So we are hoping to find another suspect to take the heat off her. But we just don't know of any other enemies he has."

The absurdity of the entire situation infuriated me. "He was a rapist. For all you know, he'd attacked hundreds of women before Annie. And I'm willing to bet such an upstanding citizen as that managed to make a lot of other enemies outside his hobby of attacking women. Maybe instead of wasting tax dollars looking into it, just be grateful the man is dead and won't keep creating new victims."

Officer Clinton nodded. "You know as well as I do that no one will be losing sleep looking for whoever did this, but a crime was committed, and we are obligated to investigate."

I flung my hands in the air. "I had motive. Do you want to interrogate me?"

The officers exchanged a glance. "You were our first suspect, but your alibi is air tight."

I frowned, trying to recall the times they were asking about, and then it hit me. I'd been in court that entire time. My hearing was scheduled to begin at eleven, and I'd gone into court an hour early.

"I don't have a boyfriend. I don't have any male friends or other relatives in town either, and I didn't tell anyone other than my brother and my roommates about the attack," my sister spoke up, her voice surprisingly even-keeled. "So, I don't see any possibility that this had anything to do with me."

"Thank you Miss Patras."

The officers had my sister sign a statement confirming the guy was the one who had attacked her, and then they released us. As soon as we got home, Annie ducked in the bathroom, and I stepped outside and dialed Angelo.

"We need to talk," I said.

"I thought you might be reaching out. I can swing by your place in an hour," he replied.

An hour later, I paced in front of my building, watched for Angelo's Escalade. I scurried over the moment it rolled up in front of the curb. To my surprise, Angelo was in the driver's seat. I climbed in next to him, and he took off. Even with an hour to rehearse what I'd say to him, I was stumped. Luckily, he started first.

"How's your sister?"

That was a loaded question. She was a mess. She'd gone through a horrific experience and now, instead of getting to see justice through to the end, she had to see a grotesque picture of her attacker and hear police refer to him as a victim.

"How do you think she is?" I snapped.

Angelo's expression was serious, and I appreciated that, for once, he seemed to have empathy. "Sorry," he mumbled.

"For what part? That it happened, or that you had to get involved."

He cast a glance to me. "I didn't personally do anything, Adrian. You should know that by now. But I would've if I'd had to and frankly, I'd expect you to do the same if it were my sister." He turned back to the road and shook his head with annoyance. "I expected gratitude."

"Seriously? I'm supposed to thank you? Jesus Angelo, they thought I did it."

"Your alibi was airtight."

I should've known Angelo would have ensured that. "They questioned Annie."

"They don't think she did it. No one will get in trouble. It's over. You're welcome."

I blew out a sigh. "They made her look at pictures of the guy, Angelo."

His lips widened despite his obvious attempts to hide his grin.

"God, you are a sociopath. You do realize that normal people actually don't like seeing others suffer, right?"

"I don't believe that for a second."

"Yeah, well, you know I'm a lawyer, right? That should tell you I'm a big fan of justice. So is Annie. I was looking forward to this monster having to face his crimes in a court of law and then rot in jail."

Angelo rolled his eyes. "He would've spent a couple years in prison, max, and you wouldn't have seen him suffer. And that's if they caught him and if he got convicted. You're romanticizing the whole process. This whole justice system you champion? It's broken. The sooner you figure that out, the better."

I bit back my snarky comment and turned to the window. Angelo had nearly completed a wide loop around my neighborhood and was approaching my apartment.

"Is that all you needed?" he asked.

I hesitated, unsure of the protocol. "I don't know. Do I…like owe you something now? Or how does this work?"

Angelo cut in front of a small sedan to park in front of my unit. "You don't owe me a damn thing, Patras. I didn't do it for you."

"Well, Annie sure isn't repaying some favor she didn't ask for."

"Jesus Christ. Can't you ever just say thank you and shut up? I don't expect anything from Annie or anyone else. It wasn't a fucking favor. She's your family, which means we take care of her. People don't fuck with Conti associates or their families and live to brag about it. That's just how it is."

I inhaled slowly, then exhaled, trying not to overthink the implication of his words. "Fine. Thank you, Angelo."

He shook his head and frowned, so I started out of the car.

"Adrian!" Angelo called after me. "She should talk to a therapist. I hear they work wonders."

I nodded slowly, then slammed the door.

❧

Giada

*L*uca, Alessio, and I survived the rest of our time in Atlantic City without any more "surprises," and the guys seemed pleased with the progress they made on their mysterious business deal. Before the weekend, I had hoped I'd have an opportunity to talk with Luca about the FBI guy who'd been stalking me, but between the late-night card games and everything with Alessio, the timing sucked.

I spent my morning scrolling through some design sites on the web, then ordered groceries to be delivered to the apartment that afternoon. I wasn't the most versatile chef, but I could make a tasty pasta sauce. Luca and I could enjoy a cozy, romantic dinner together, then I could crush him by admitting not only that I'd been talking with the FBI, but also that I still hadn't managed to tell him.

Just as I shut my laptop, the doorbell rang. As always, Enzo was right on time. Ever since Luca learned that Annie had been attacked, he'd insisted I never leave the house alone. His concerns were silly, since Annie had been attacked late at night and nowhere near our apartment, but I also wouldn't pretend the city was crime free. Anyway, I'd learned it was futile to try to convince Luca he was being overprotective.

The last few items I'd purchased in Italy for my latest projects still hadn't arrived, but I couldn't exactly complain to the shipping company since, well, I wasn't paying Luca for his services. So, I planned to shop for alternate furnishings. I'd found a few different local shops that seemed to have potential for selling unique furnishings and accent pieces.

Enzo was a trooper as always, chauffeuring me from shop to shop, even keeping his opinions to himself when I emerged from one store with a new scarf and a handbag Gabby would just love. We had one final stop to make when Enzo's phone rang.

"Yeah, I'm in the area, but the princess is with me," he said to the caller after a brief silence.

"I have a name," I chimed in.

Enzo turned and stuck out his tongue, then ended the call. "Sorry Princess, but we've got a brief detour. I just need to pick something up."

I sighed, but when he pulled into a parking spot a few minutes later, I perked up. There was a coffee shop right across the street from the hardware store he needed to visit. I gazed longingly at the promise of caffeine, then turned back to Enzo.

"Please? My treat," I said.

He gazed around, then apparently deciding I couldn't get into much trouble in this quiet suburban area, he nodded. "I'll meet you back here on this bench when I'm done."

I skipped off as if I were a kid who'd just been granted an extra recess. I pushed through the thick wooden door of the place and inhaled deeply, relishing the aroma of fresh ground coffee. Still smiling, I weaved my way between tables to reach the counter. A few customers formed a line ahead of me, so I gazed around the café while I waited. I'd never been inside the place, actually never been in this neighborhood before, so that wasn't surprising. But judging by the crowd levels, the coffee must be tasty.

The cutesy names of custom handcrafted recipes were scrawled on a chalkboard in the back. I squinted to read the bottom drink name, but the last few letters were blocked by a woman's high ponytail. Just as I was about to give up on reading it all, the woman shifted. I forgot all about the coffee as I realized who I'd been staring at.

The woman was Julia, Angelo's obnoxious girlfriend. I grimaced, certain it would be rude not to say hello now that I'd recognized her. But surely I could get my coffee first. I gazed up to the front of the line, then back to Julia. She wasn't alone, but I couldn't see the person she was sitting with until the men from another table stood to leave.

My breath caught in my throat right as the customer behind me tapped my shoulder. I couldn't turn, though. My eyes were locked on the familiar dirty blond swath of hair across from Julia. She was sitting with Agent Grady. I was sure of it.

"Miss," the man behind me said. "It's your turn."

I snapped out of my daze, and turned abruptly before Grady or Julia saw me. "I, um, uh, thanks. I'm not thirsty anymore."

Keeping my head down, I dashed out of the café as quick as I could. I practically sprinted back to the bench where I'd agreed to meet Lorenzo, and even then, I still didn't feel like stopping.

Grady O'Keefe had told me he was talking to someone else. And now? It all made sense.

I'd known Julia didn't like Luca, and she'd had so many crazy questions about his arrest and his guilt, but…

"Hey," Enzo's tone was casual, but I still leapt into the air like a clown had jumped out at me.

"Jesus. You okay Giada?" he asked.

I nodded and made a beeline for his car. "Yep. Totally good. Just in a hurry is all. Let's go."

He followed behind and opened the car door for me. "Where is our coffee?"

Shit. Totally forgot that. "I, um, I'm already jittery. Figured neither of us needed more caffeine."

"Gee thanks," he mumbled.

I told him to forget the last stop and just take me home, but that might have been a mistake, as it left me simply pacing the apartment, unsure of what to say or do. I'd been about to tell Luca the truth, and now it seemed more urgent than ever. Well, except it was also more complicated. If my family had been involved in Luca's arrest, well, that was huge. I could be launching a true mafia war if I spoke up.

I thought back to Angelo shooting that guy in front of me. Maybe that hadn't been just a ploy to get Luca's attention. Maybe, he'd been setting me up. He intentionally did something to see if I'd rat him out, then Julia would pass on the intel.

God, I was such a fool.

I wanted to call Angelo and to scream and yell. Or maybe even to call Luca and beg him to get rid of Angelo once and for all. But I knew the responsible thing to do was to gather more information. Angelo wasn't going to admit anything, so that left Julia. And I could approach her subtly.

I dialed her number, surprised it was even programmed into my phone since we weren't exactly besties. She answered on the second ring.

"Giada? Hi, how are you?"

Her casual tone made my stomach church. How could that traitorous bitch spew lies about my husband to the FBI and then speak to me like nothing was wrong?

"Good. You?" I said, holding my breath to avoid revealing my agitation.

"I'm great. Just finished a long shift at work and was about to head home."

"Oh. You've been at work all day? No breaks or anything?"

"Uh, no. Why?"

God, she sounded so relaxed. I gritted my teeth. "No reason. Listen, I was just thinking that we are basically like sisters now, and I've never had a sister. Maybe we should get to know each other."

"You want to get to know me?"

"Yeah. Of course. Maybe we could meet…" I paused to think

of a crowded public place we could meet. "For lunch somewhere?"

Julia was quiet for a moment.

"We could work around your schedule, of course," I added.

"Um, sure. That would be great," she finally said. "But why now? I've been with your brother for over a year now. You've never shown any interest in getting to know me before."

I dug my nail into the side of my finger. "Uhhh, well, yeah. Sorry about that. It takes me a while to warm up to new people is all."

"Oh, okay," she replied. "I thought maybe it was because you saw me with Agent Michaels today."

My blood ran cold. *She knew?* "You…saw me?" I stammered.

She breathed a laugh. "Yeah. But don't worry, I didn't tell anyone. Look, I figured he was talking to you, but I wasn't positive until I saw your reaction when you spotted us together. Talk about a bad poker face."

All of my thoughts jumbled together. "Wait, what did you say his name is?"

"Agent Arnold Michaels," she replied. "No need to be coy Giada, I know you know who he is."

I tried to swallow the lump in my throat, but my mouth was too dry. I was positive I'd seen her with the same man that I knew as Agent Grady. So apparently, he'd given us both different names.

"Look, don't tell Luca you saw me. Let's grab lunch together and we can discuss, okay? I work tomorrow, but the next day is wide open. Okay? Can you keep all this to yourself until then?"

"I…" I paused and inhaled sharply. I didn't need to be so sheepish. This woman tried to throw my husband under the bus. "I don't know, Julia. You completely betrayed Luca. And me. You're a rat. I should tell him right away."

I rubbed for temples as the full implications of her behavior hit me. "God, was that you that went to the police about the murder, blaming him?"

"No! I had nothing to do with that. Giada, you've got to believe me. I'm on your side. We're basically family, remember?"

I'd never felt like family with her, and especially not now. But I had no proof of anything.

"Please, after we talk and you hear me out, you can tell Luca everything. Maybe he can even help us. Just give me forty-eight hours, okay?"

Reluctantly, I agreed, right as my stupid grocery order arrived. We hung up, but I no longer had the energy to cook dinner. I told Luca I wasn't feeling well and went to bed early.

I hated keeping secrets from him.

CHAPTER 19

Giada

Despite having gone to bed early, I barely slept. I kept questioning myself, wondering why I was willing to keep a secret—even for a matter of mere days—from my husband, all for someone I didn't even like.

Yet somehow, I resisted telling Luca the truth. I told myself it was for the best, avoiding stressing him out until I knew more. He was headed back to Atlantic City that day with Alessio, so I wouldn't even see him again until after I met with Julia. In the meantime, I needed a distraction. Anything to keep my mind off reality until I decided if I could trust Julia. Luckily, Gabby was free to spend the day together.

We met up for iced lattes, but as soon as we'd ordered, I got a call from Thomas. He said Luca asked him to tell me that my shipment had arrived—but was docked near Bridgeport, and they didn't have anyone available to go fetch my stuff for two more days.

I groaned and hung up the phone.

"What's wrong?" Gabriella asked before tilting her head down to capture the straw of her iced coffee with her lips.

"The boat that has the stuff on it that I bought in Italy was supposed to arrive days ago, but it was delayed. And now it's apparently docked and being unloaded but in Bridgeport."

My friend wrinkled her nose. "That sucks. When did you tell the client you'd get everything to them?"

"They expected it by yesterday." I shook my head, knowing once the items were off the ship, it might be days before someone figured out where they were supposed to go. I'd taken so much time off for the extended honeymoon that it was a miracle I hadn't already been fired.

Gabby sucked on her straw until it made a loud slurping sound. Then she shook the cup and grimaced. "That went down way too fast for how many calories it had."

I nodded in agreement, although I'd barely touched my drink. All of the stupid shipment stuff was stressing me out, and with Luca gone, I didn't have any strings to pull to get my items sooner.

"The worst part is that it is all smaller pieces. Lamps, a mirror, an accent rug, and some vases and decorative figurines. I mean, I could've just mailed this stuff, and it would've arrived by now, but Luca was so insistent that it go on the damn boat."

I glanced down at my phone, debating what to say to my boss. I didn't really know of any way to spin it so I didn't come off as a total fuckup.

"We really aren't too far from Bridgeport," Gabriella said.

I gazed up at her, confused by her newfound eagerness.

"Do you know what boat it's on?"

"Sort of. I mean, I have the numbers and everything so I should be able to find it."

"Then let's go get it ourselves. We don't need to wait for the men to sort it out."

I had a feeling it was a terrible idea, but her enthusiasm was contagious. And Gabby had a point. The guys had fucked this up, so it really didn't make sense to wait for them to fix it. I tried to envision how big the mirror was.

"I'm not sure it will all fit in my trunk."

"You could put some stuff in the back seat," she pointed out.

My smile widened. "You are brilliant. Let's go."

Gabriella filled me in on her latest boyfriend while we drove, but thanks to traffic, it was dusk by the time we arrived. The shipyard wasn't one of the main ones, so it had been tough to find, and the area was so poorly lit that I couldn't even tell if we were in an actual parking lot.

I pulled my car close to the metal gate at the end of the gravel lot and killed the ignition. We both climbed out slowly, disoriented.

"It sure gets dark early out here," Gabby commented, glancing at the thick row of trees on the other side of the lot which fully blocked the last rays of sunshine.

"Property owners only," I read off the sign plastered to the locked gate just before my car lights shut off, bathing us in darkness. "Well, shit."

"You are a property owner," she said.

"I think they mean you have to own the boats, not the glass bunnies on the boat."

"Bunnies?"

"They're really cute," I insisted. Actually, anything made from authentic Murano glass was amazing, but bunnies were particularly trendy this year.

Gabriella hoisted her purse higher on her shoulder and walked around the gate. "If they really didn't want us on the dock, they'd do a better job of blocking it off," she pointed out.

I had to agree with her there. I trudged through the grass around the gate then followed her down the metal dock. There was a streetlight offering a little light by the first boat we passed, but the next two lamps had burned out.

"I can't read anything," I said, squinting to read the label on the last boat. It was a larger one, and a shipping crate sitting on a platform beside the boat looked like the type I'd seen Luca's company use before.

Gabby used her phone's flashlight to illuminate the sign.

"Yes! That's it," I said, confirming the details matched with the text Luca had sent me earlier confirming the shipment arrival.

"Shit!"

I followed my friend's gaze to the giant padlock covering the loading door for the crate. Why hadn't it occurred to us that the damn thing would be locked? Of course, we hadn't banked on arriving so late. In my mind, the dock would still be bustling with people paid by Luca, and I would've just had to say my name and they'd flock to help. I hadn't imagined the area would be pitch black, deserted, and totally creepy.

"This was a dumb idea. I'm sorry," she said.

I stepped closer, reaching for the lock, figuring I might as well try a few different combinations since we'd driven all this way. As soon as my fingers touched the cool metal though, I realized it wasn't fastened.

We both exhaled with relief.

I tugged the lock out just as we heard an engine in the distance. I paused, painfully aware the car was getting closer. I knew it was stupid to be scared, but we were completely isolated and on the end of the dock, we didn't exactly have anywhere to go. I clutched the lock in my hand as I swung the door to the crate open.

"Am I the only one thinking that this seems an awful lot like the start of a bad horror movie?" Gabriella joked.

I agreed completely. Even the knowledge that I had a loaded gun in my purse didn't make me feel any better.

The sound of tires crunching on the gravel was followed by complete silence as the driver parked the car and switched off the ignition.

"At least if we get trapped in here now, there is someone nearby to let us out," I joked. I peered into the crate, but it was pitch black. "Shine the light in here. If we at least have a couple things unloaded, we're a lot less likely to look suspicious to whoever that is,' I said, gesturing to the car. Now that its lights were off, I really couldn't see the vehicle either, but I knew it was still there, and I'd rather look like I belonged here when its driver reached the docks.

Gabby turned away from the car too and raised her flashlight. What we saw wasn't what we expected.

"Holy fuck!" she said, much louder than necessary.

There were no words to capture my thoughts as I stared ahead at what had to be close to a hundred semi-automatic weapons. There were locked cases throughout the container, but everything had been unlocked and most were partially open, as though someone had begun to take stock of the contents.

"Shit," I mumbled. "This is definitely not the right container. Let's just go," I said, tugging on the door with all my might.

"Uhh Giada," Gabriella said, shining her flashlight in the corner. There, wrapped up in a healthy amount of bubble wrap, was a mirror. My mirror. Beside it was a tightly rolled rug.

I no longer cared about my stuff, though. Something was wrong, and I didn't need the dozens of bells and whistles sounding in my head to tell me that. "We should go," I repeated.

I slammed the door shut right as Gabriella screamed.

CHAPTER 20

Giada

My mind flashed to my gun, but as I turned to my friend, I knew it was too late for that. A lanky guy with a baseball cap held a knife to her neck, and the guy behind him already had a gun pointed at me. Neither of them looked even remotely familiar.

I raised my hands slowly, keeping my eyes locked on the man with the gun.

"This is private property," he said.

"We're leaving," I said. "We don't want any trouble."

The guy with a knife laughed. "Seems like you came here looking for trouble."

"We're just lost. After you let go of my friend, you can watch us walk to our car."

There was a lengthy silence.

"Yeah. I don't think we can do that. You see, sometimes when people trespass, they see things they aren't supposed to see."

"We didn't see anything. We couldn't even get the doors open. They're too heavy."

"Liar, liar pants on fire," knife guy said. Then he turned to his friend. "What do we do with them?"

"I guess call the boss," the second guy said. He stepped closer to his friend, and the moment he glanced away, I reached into my purse for the gun.

I wished I could get Gabriella's attention so she could create a distraction long enough for me to actually get the safety off, but she was focused squarely on the knife at her throat. I couldn't fault her there.

"We can't let them go since they saw." The guy turned back to me and swung the gun around. "Freeze, or I'll shoot!"

I froze.

"Raise your hands back up."

Reluctantly, I complied.

The gun guy came forward and snatched my purse. "Jesus, this one's got a gun," he said to his friend. They snatched Gabby's purse too, but found no such goodies there.

"You really don't want to mess with us," I said. I still couldn't tell if these guys actually worked for Luca or were in the process of robbing someone, but either way, my name tended to carry weight amongst local criminals. "Do you seriously not know who I am?"

The gun guy was silent, but the knife guy spoke up. "You aren't that chick from the Mexican soap opera are you?"

Shit. "I'm Giada Conti Marino. My husband is Luca Marino. My father is Marco Conti. My father-in-law is Salvatore Marino. Do any of those names ring a bell to you?"

It was apparent from the lack of reaction from either of them that no, the names meant nothing to them. We were fucked.

"Luca owns this shipping crate. He owns the whole boat, for Christ's sake. If you're trying to rob him, he'll have you killed. If you even think about hurting us, he'll kill you too."

"We aren't stealing anything," knife guy said.

"Shut up," the other man said to him. "Put them in the crate, and then we'll call the boss." Then he turned to us. "If you fucking scream, I'll shoot you."

Screaming and fighting seemed like a much better option than willingly letting ourselves be locked in an airtight crate with two thugs and a billion weapons, but the threat of being shot made it impossible for me to muster even a peep. I told myself it would be fine, that they would call their boss and realize their mistake.

I focused on my breathing and tried to stay calm. Gabriella on the other hand, looked awful. She was pale and sweaty, and her tears had left black mascara streaks on her cheeks.

"It'll be fine," I said as they nudged us into the crate. "Luca will fix this." I turned back to the man. "Seriously, who do you report to? Alessio Rizzo? Giovanni Costa? Thomas Verratti?" I cringed at the realization that I didn't know the full name of any of Luca's other guys.

"Stop talking lady. I don't know any of those guys." Gun guy shook his head and turned to his buddy. "You watch them, and I'm going to look for some duct tape to shut them up until the boss gets here."

Then he left us alone with the crazy knife guy.

"You ladies are awfully pretty to be walking around here alone at night," he said.

I saw Gabriella's eyes widen but didn't realize until she shrieked that he was fondling her with his free hand.

"Don't you fucking touch her!" I said.

"Why, you jealous?" he teased, licking his lips and then tracing his disgusting tongue along my friend's cheek.

My stomach churned.

Luckily, his friend returned then, and he backed away from Gabby. The guys moved us to what appeared to be a small storage facility or warehouse. There was one door and at least two windows, which was a relief, but I didn't see a way to escape with the two guys watching us, especially since we were still tied up.

After what felt like an eternity, a third man arrived.

Knife dude looked relieved. "Hey, Michael, they—"

The guy who apparently was named Michael glared at the first guy so harshly that he shut up. "What did I say about announcing our names to everyone?"

The first guy scowled. "She said her husband owns that boat or something."

I winced as they peeled the tape off. "I'm married to Luca Marino," I said. "If you don't believe me, call him." Then I listed the roster of groomsmen from my wedding and all the names of my male relatives. "Or call anyone who's anyone in this fucking world, and they'll tell you to let us go now."

I barely finished my rant when I saw Michael's expression changed.

"Shit!" He turned to the other two guys, anger in his eyes. "You had better hope she's not who she says she is," he mumbled, reaching for his phone. He dialed, then waited a moment before speaking. "We got a problem," he said. "Two of my guys were at the B docks unloading, and two girls were snooping around." He paused. "My guys think they saw everything."

I glanced at Gabriella during another pause. She was still fighting her duct tape gag and crying.

"They got the girls restrained here, and they're both fine, but um, one of them says she knows you." He paused again, then turned to me. "What's your name again?"

"Giada Francesca Conti Marino," I said, deliberately enunciating.

He repeated my name, and I held my breath for his response. He paused then handed me the phone. I didn't know who it was, but I wasn't about to pass up an opportunity.

"Hello?" I said, leaning towards the phone since I was unable to hold it independently with my hands taped together. "This is

Giada. My husband is Luca. Help us, please. My husband has money, and—"

"Giada," the familiar voice said before swearing. "Are you alright?"

"I don't know. Who is this?"

"Thomas."

I blew out a sigh. We were going to be okay. "Gabriella is with me. These guys don't seem to know who Luca is and we're both…"

"I'll be there in a half hour," he said. "Stay put until I arrive. Put Michael back on."

I didn't exactly have an option about staying put, but as Michael took the phone back, it was obvious Thomas was chewing him out. My chest heaved with relief.

"It's okay," I mouthed to Gabby. She didn't seem convinced.

After several minutes, Michael came back, looking stressed.

He walked around and peeled the tape off my wrists. I could tell he was trying to be delicate, but it still hurt as the tiny hairs were yanked free.

"They didn't know who you were," he said apologetically. "I'm really sorry."

"Untie my friend," I said.

He hesitated, then went to Gabriella. She pulled away from him in terror, so I came over and nudged him out of the way to untie her myself. I pulled her to me and held her close for a hug. She was shaking, but it wasn't that cold.

I wasn't able to completely relax until Thomas arrived. I didn't know him as well as Alessio, but I believed Luca when he said that his men would be as loyal to me as to him.

Thomas brushed past Michael and immediately came to me. His eyes traveled up and down my body before casting a quick glance to Gabriella.

"Are you okay?" he asked me.

"Yeah, I mean, this was awful, but…just take us home." I paused. "Did you get a hold of Luca?"

He shook his head. "He's in a meeting. I'm sorry. Alessio will be here in a few minutes."

"I want to go now," I said, glaring at my creepy captors. I needed away from them immediately. Gabriella did too.

"Yeah, I just… we have to wait for Alessio. I don't know how he wants to handle…" Thomas' eyes darted over to the captors as well.

"I can't look at them another minute." I said.

Thomas turned to Michael. "Wait outside. All three of you."

They left, and Thomas went over to a side room. He flipped on the lights and opened the door. Glancing in, I saw it was set up like an office, but with a couch. "You guys can sit," he said.

I dragged Gabriella into the other room. Thomas followed, opening a small fridge and offering each of us a drink. I took a bottle of water and held it out to Gabriella.

"Alessio will deal with…them, and then I can take you both home," he said.

I nodded, and then a sick feeling came over me. "When you say he'll deal with them…"

Thomas shook his head. "Don't worry about it."

"You can't let him kill them!"

Thomas shot me the sort of look that I'd been getting from the men in my life for decades. But this time, I wasn't going to butt out.

"Kill who?" Gabriella piped up.

"No one," I said. "No one is being killed."

She turned to me. "That guy held a knife to my throat. I want him dead."

Thomas cast me an "I told you so" look. I shook my head.

"My car is here," I said. "We don't need to be here for this. We're leaving now. You and Alessio can both 'deal' with those guys."

I motioned for Gabriella to follow me.

Thomas stepped into the doorway. "Luca would rather someone drive you home."

"Luca isn't here."

He glanced at Gabriella and made a face.

"What?" I demanded.

"Can we talk?" he asked, motioning to the other room.

"I'll be right back, Gabby," I promised. "I'm just going right here," I said, motioning to the main warehouse room.

Thomas shuffled his feet uneasily for a minute. "Look, I can take you home whenever you want, but we can't let your friend go anywhere until we're sure she's not going to talk."

"Talk to who?"

"Anyone! Friends, neighbor, therapist, but especially not the cops."

Now I understood what he meant. "She won't go to the cops."

He looked skeptical.

"She's my best friend in the whole world. You can trust her."

Thomas' expression didn't change a bit.

Exasperated, I made my way over to my friend. As she sat on the couch, her arms were wrapped around her, and she was hunched over her legs like she was about to be sick.

"You doing alright sweetie?"

She sniffled loudly then shook her head. "No, I'm really not."

I placed one hand on her thigh and rubbed her back with the other. "Look, Thomas is going to drive us home in a few minutes. You remember him from the wedding, right? This was all just a misunderstanding."

Gabby wiped her nose on the back of her hand but didn't say anything.

"They just want to make sure that we are all on the same page about that,' I continued.

"About what?" she asked.

"Well, that this was just a misunderstanding." I paused. "They want to confirm you didn't see anything in that shipping crate and that you didn't notice anyone else."

She didn't move initially, but then just when I thought she was about to agree, she shook her head furiously. "I saw a billion friggin guns, Giada. And you did too. I don't know what kind of messed up Twilight Zone we are in now, but—"

"Shh," I whispered, hearing noise at the door.

It was Alessio.

"Thank God," I mumbled. "Come on," I said to Gabby before turning to Thomas. "We are ready to go now."

He glanced at Alessio and shook his head.

Alessio gave me the same overly thorough up and down that Thomas had, so I answered the question before he asked. "I'm fine," I said. "Let's go."

"Either Thomas or I can take you home whenever you want Giada, but um, we can't leave Gabriella alone just yet," he said.

"I have no intention of leaving her alone anytime soon. She's terrified! We need to get out of here and then you guys can sort out your mess later."

"Do you want Luca going to prison?" he asked, lowering his voice. "Because that's what will happen if she talks to the cops about any of this."

"She won't go to the cops," I said.

"Like hell I won't," Gabriella shouted.

Thomas and Alessio both exchanged a look.

I rolled my eyes. "Christ. Where the fuck is Luca?"

"Atlantic City," Alessio replied.

"Still?" I groaned. Even now that it was late and there was virtually no one else on the road, it was probably a five-hour drive.

"He should be on the road soon."

"I want to talk to him," I said.

Alessio shook his head. "As soon as he's out of his meeting. It's important."

"I'm important," I replied.

Alessio rubbed his temples like he was getting a migraine. "Can you please just get her calmed down?" he asked. He turned to Thomas. "Why are the two nimrods still alive?"

Thomas shrugged right as I spoke up.

"You're not killing anyone."

Alessio slumped forward. "Seriously, Giada? What do you think Luca is going to do the second he gets here if they're still here? Leave him out of this. He doesn't need the extra stress."

I agreed with that part, except that nobody needed to be killed today.

"We can all go back to the house once they're no longer an issue," Alessio said, shaking his head and stalking to the corner of the small office.

~

Luca

I'd planned to spend the night in Atlantic City, maybe even look into some other business prospects in the morning, but the second Alessio cut out early, I knew something was up. He'd said everything was fine and that he'd take care of it, but I assumed I'd be leaving for home the second my meeting ended.

Still, when I'd finally called him to say I was on the road, I hadn't expected him to start his explanation of what happened with "Giada's fine, but…"

I repeated his words in my head, told myself she was fine the entire drive, but I didn't fully believe it until I arrived.

I saw Giada's car the second I pulled into the lot, and a beat-up Hundai was parked behind it. I hurried up to the warehouse, startled to see Thomas outside with two scruffy looking guys.

"Who the fuck are they?" I asked Thomas.

"Who the fuck are we? Who the fuck are you?" one of the guys said.

My gun was in my hand in a second and I fired a shot two inches from the guy's head without a moment's hesitation. Part of me hoped I'd miss and actually hit the man. Sadly, I didn't.

The guy jumped around shrieking, so I still didn't get the answer to my initial question. The front door opened and it was Alessio, with an overly eager Giada behind him. I shoved the gun into my waistband without even bothering to secure it into the holster, and rushed to my girl.

"Giada," I murmured, pulling her to me. I squeezed her so tightly that her shoulder made a popping sensation, and as I relaxed my hold on her, I inhaled sharply. She smelled delicious, as usual, but I hadn't realized how much I appreciated that scent until I really considered the possibility of losing her.

I leaned back and ran my hand over her, checking for injuries.

"I'm fine, Luca," she said, her eyes meeting mine.

"Not a scratch?" I asked.

She hesitated. I gritted my teeth together so firmly that it hurt.

"Which one?" I asked, reaching for the gun again and turning to the guys.

"Luca!" she scolded. "Neither. Nobody hurt me. They just… there was a misunderstanding, and they put duct tape on my wrists and mouth.

I flashed Alessio a look. It had to be done, and it might as well be done quickly. I reached for Giada to shield her from it all, but she swatted at me.

"Don't you dare kill anybody. Either of you! Jesus." She shook her head. "Gabriella is right inside there. Are you going to kill her too?"

"Why don't you guys go inside for a minute, get caught up?" Alessio suggested.

God, he was a lifesaver. I tugged Giada's hand, but she didn't budge.

"Luca, look at me," she said. "They had no way of knowing who I was because they didn't even know who you are. This is not their fault."

"Yeah, listen to your girl!" one of the jackasses said.

I couldn't help myself. My gun was in my hand by the time I whipped around to face him. Just as I pulled the trigger, though, Giada knocked my arm down. The bullet ricocheted into the dirt then sprung up into the idiot's shin.

"What the fuck, Giada?" I said, swiveling.

I nodded to Thomas, and he tried to cajole her into the house.

"Jesus," Alessio mumbled, his frustrations mirroring my own. "Pick her up."

Thomas did so, but it looked like Giada may have actually bit him. I was about to turn back to the more pressing problem when I remembered something.

"Shit. She might have a gun in her purse!" I started towards the door. For all her talk on the merits of not shooting, I didn't have a doubt in my mind that she'd fire on Thomas if he got in her way at the moment.

"I have it," Alessio said, lifting his shirt to show me not one, but two guns tucked into his waistband.

I breathed a sigh of relief, but just then the other jackass, the one I hadn't just grazed with a bullet, took off towards his car.

"You don't have your keys!" I shouted after him. "And if you make us chase you, we will shoot to kill."

The moron took another two steps and then turned.

I shook my head. "I fucking hate loose ends, but she won't forgive me," I said to Alessio.

"I'm sorry," he replied. "I wanted to take care of this before you even got here, but she's…"

"Scary?" I supplied.

"I was leaning towards persistent," he answered.

I nodded. I understood exactly what he meant. I hated the feeling that this was going to bite me in the ass someday in the near future. I motioned for the guys to come closer and sit at the picnic table. They reluctantly did, the one still bitching about his poor shin. A third guy came out, and Alessio explained that he was Michael, one of Thomas's new hires. I silently cursed my papà and his dumb plan to add more guys without "accountability" as he'd phrased it.

"That woman saved your life," I said to the idiot sitting before me. "Both of you, actually. And I'd just love you to give me a reason to change my mind about sparing you."

They wisely remained quiet.

"Sit. Stay." I commanded. "If either of you moves, we shoot."

I pointed to Michael. "You, come here."

He followed.

"This is all your fault," I said. He opened his mouth to speak, but I shushed him. "If you were dealing with my papà and not me, you'd be dead right now. I hope you realize that."

Michael nodded.

"As it is, I'll let Thomas deal with you. But you three should all be ashamed. Grown men don't threaten women. We respect women. It really isn't that fucking hard." I turned to Alessio. "Do you have all their guns?"

He nodded. That was good. We could save them and plant them at a future crime scene if we needed to cast shade on any of them. "If any of you speak a word of any of this to anyone ever, we will kill you. If you ever speak my name or say anything about my family, we will kill you. And if you ever so much as glance at my wife ever again, I will personally pull off your fingernails one by one, cut off your toes, and then kill you. Any questions?"

They all shook their heads and mumbled responses.

"Good. You can go. But you're all going to report to Thomas at eleven a.m. tomorrow morning. If you don't show up, we'll kill you. If we have any trouble finding you, we'll kill your closest male relative and then still kill you once we find you."

I blew out a sigh, then turned to go join my wife.

❧

Giada

I didn't hear any more gunshots, so I decided that was a good thing. Whatever drug Alessio had me give Gabriella seemed to be working. She was still semi coherent, but no longer frantic. I was actually a little tired too. I stretched out on the couch beside my friend and let my eyes drift shut. What a fucking mess today had become.

I was nearly asleep when a sudden noise at the door jolted me wide awake. I gazed to the door to see Luca standing there, alone. I rose to my feet and walked to him, careful not to wake Gabby.

He looked even more exhausted than I felt, and the mixture of concern and anger on his face was all too reminiscent of the past.

I stopped directly in front of him and peered into his eyes, waiting for the lecture. After a moment, his piercing stare grew uncomfortable. It was like I could feel the glaring disappointment radiating off him. I dropped my eyes to the ground and inhaled slowly, counting as I exhaled.

"We should get home," he finally said. "It's late, and we both need sleep. We can talk in the morning."

"You mean you can lecture me," I corrected.

"Yes," he said, reaching for my hand.

"I need to go wake Gabriella."

"Alessio will drive her home."

I looked back up at him. He had to be kidding, didn't he? "She won't go with him."

"She's unconscious."

"I'm not leaving her alone with him."

"He won't hurt her."

"She'll be terrified when she wakes." I shook my head. "Seriously, what is the plan here?"

"My plan is to get you home so we can both sleep. In the morning, Alessio will bring her over, and you can talk some sense into her."

"She can ride with us to our place."

"I can't watch her while driving."

"So bring Alessio too!" I insisted, not bothering to remind him that she was currently unconscious.

"We have too many cars here."

"Then I'll drive myself and Gabby, and you boys can do whatever the fuck you please," I said, spotting my keys on the desk. I snatched them up and walked out the door, slamming straight into Alessio.

Looking around, I realized he was the only person outside. I hadn't heard a gunshot, but that didn't mean…

"Where are the other guys? There were three other people here," I said, my voice sounding more panicky than I'd hoped.

"Your husband sent them on their way, unharmed," Alessio said.

I wanted to believe him, but… I turned back to Luca.

He nodded. "If they blab to anyone or give us shit, we still might have to kill them. Or we might end up in prison. But for now, they're alive and well. You'll see their cars are gone."

Watching Luca as he spoke, I decided he seemed to be telling the truth. I'd ask him again later, when we were alone, to confirm though.

Luca turned to Alessio. "Can you drive my car to my place and sleep on the couch?"

Alessio made a face.

"Giada is concerned her friend will respond better if she's not alone with you, so Gabriella can sleep in our guest room tonight."

"That bed sleeps two," Alessio said.

I felt my eyes widen but Luca actually cracked a smile.

"Pervert," I snapped.

"Tell Thomas to take Giada's car home and park it at my place, then come back here with Giovanni to get his car, then carry Gabriella to the Escalade," Luca said, ignoring me.

"I need our purses," I mumbled, turning back into the warehouse. I grabbed my bag and Gabriella's, then followed Luca to the car.

He opened the passenger door for me to get in, then once I was seated, I watched as he helped Alessio position Gabriella into the back seat. Her eyelids fluttered, but she didn't seem aware of anything.

"What did you give her?" I asked.

"She's fine," Alessio said. Then he leaned forward and whispered something to my husband.

The drive home felt long, which it was. I shifted uncomfortably in the seat, then finally wedged my purse under my head to rest.

By some miracle, I actually did fall asleep, waking when Luca switched off the ignition. Groggily, I turned to Luca, a peaceful feeling passing over me as we locked eyes. I smiled, out of habit I suppose, and then all at once I remembered everything that had happened the last eight hours.

I turned abruptly to the door and tried to open it. The door didn't budge.

"Did you seriously lock me in?" I asked.

Luca's expression changed then too, but he leaned over me, gripped the same handle I'd been trying, and swung the door open with ease. *Whatever.*

I climbed out and stalked up to our apartment. I was still bone tired, but I needed to wash the day away before I could sleep. I started towards the shower, then remembered we'd have guests. I switched on the bedside lamp in the guestroom and folded down the covers, then went to the kitchen and grabbed a bottled water, a banana, and some granola bars to set on the nightstand. I snatched the extra pillow off the bed and located a blanket from the closet, and dumped both of those items on the couch for Alessio. He could scrounge for his own snacks.

As if on cue, Alessio came through the front door then, cradling my best friend like a child. He headed towards the couch, and I shook my head, pointing to the guest room. He groaned but complied, placing her gently on the bed.

I tugged off her shoes and pulled the sheet up over her. Since she'd worn leggings and a stretchy top, she might actually stay comfortable enough to sleep in that all night, but I wasn't too confident. Her eyes fluttered open, and she had the same dazed look on her face I'd seen in college after our nights of too much drinking.

"I'm so tired," she murmured.

"I know," I said, gently smoothing her hair away from her eyes. "You're going to sleep in my guest room tonight, and we'll do brunch or something in the morning. Okay?"

She yawned and peered around the room before her eyes drifted shut again. I waited a minute, then switched off the lamp and left, closing the door behind me.

The men were standing in the kitchen, talking softly. They stopped abruptly when they noticed me.

"If she wakes up, you come and get me, okay?" I said.

Alessio glanced at Luca then agreed.

"I'm taking a shower and going to bed."

As I walked to the shower, I regretted not getting myself a glass of water and a snack, but no hunger was enough to make me want to walk past those two again. I turned on the faucet and undressed while the water heated up.

Just as I stepped into the steam-filled glass enclosure, Luca entered the bathroom. A bottle of water was in his hand, but that gesture still didn't justify the intrusion. I hated that our bathroom had no lock on the door. The bedroom did, but it was one of those tiny locks on the handle that Luca could pick with a hairpin in under two seconds, so there was no point in even bothering with that.

He began undressing quickly.

"You are not joining me," I said, my tone conveying the appropriate sense of finality. "If you touch me, I will kick you in the balls."

"I'm not seducing you, Princess. But we need to talk, and since we aren't alone in our place tonight, thanks to you, this is our best bet for privacy."

"Thanks to me? Um, no Luca. My preference would be for both of our friends to be sleeping at their own homes tonight. You were the one who insisted on kidnapping Gabriella." I paused, letting the water hit my face. "You don't want to talk to me. You just want to yell."

He breathed a laugh. "And you don't want to yell at me?"

Luca had me there. I wanted to yell and kick and scratch and bite. I wanted to shake him until he realized what a fool he was.

He stepped into the shower, and overtaking most of the space in the stall. I backed up, suddenly needing air, but quickly hitting the tile wall. Luca stared at me for a moment, and I wasn't sure if it was disappointment, sadness or concern in his expression.

"What were you doing there tonight?" Luca asked, handing me the shampoo.

"I was trying to get the pieces I needed for my job. They expected them last week."

"Delays happen, Giada."

I assumed the delays were more frequent when illegal weapons smuggling was involved, but I kept quiet.

"I told you I would get the items as soon as I could. You need to trust me."

"You aren't exactly a trustworthy guy," I said. I rinsed the shampoo out of my hair and stepped away from the water. I squeezed my hair, wringing out as much water as I could, then massaged conditioner into the long strands.

"How did you even know where it was?"

"You sent me the confirmation stuff. It had the shipping container on it."

Luca rolled his eyes. "Jesus, Giada. I only sent that to you so you could give your boss an estimate, not so you could hunt down the ship, trespass on private property and nearly get yourself killed."

He paused, but not long enough for me to protest his logic. "Did it really not occur to you that I would have people guarding my shipments? Giada, they could've shot you the second they saw you. That's how we are trained, shoot first, ask questions later."

I winced at the way Luca lumped himself in with those cretins, but at the moment, I didn't disagree. He was a lot like them.

"I can't keep you safe if you go around doing stupid shit all the time," he said.

"You wouldn't need to keep me safe if you weren't finagling illegal arms deals on the side!" I shouted back, my voice echoing in the enclosed space.

Luca's jaw twitched. "I'm not getting into that with you now. My business is my concern, not yours."

"Your business nearly got me killed! And that asshole held a knife to Gabby's throat. She's probably scarred for life."

Luca turned, submerging himself under the water.

Neither of us spoke for a moment. I hoped he was taking this time to think about what a colossal dick he was being, but apparently, no such luck.

"You can't keep interfering, Giada," he said as he swiveled back to me. "When I showed up tonight, to sort out the mess you caused, you should've stayed out of it." He shook his head in disgust. "You can't hit someone's arm when they're holding a gun.

Do you have any idea how dangerous that is? You could've made me shoot Alessio."

"It would serve him right for the shit you two do."

"We wouldn't have had to do anything tonight if you weren't so damn impatient!" he yelled.

"You can't just go around shooting people who annoy you!" I shouted back.

"Annoy me? You thought that guy was an annoyance?" Luca flung his hands up, knocking my facial scrub off the tiny corner shelf. "Giada, I was terrified. Those guys were alone with you for hours. They could've hurt you, raped you, killed you. They had no idea how important you are to me. They were criminals, and they kidnapped you."

"They are no more criminals than you are, Luca," I said, surprised by the coldness of my tone. "I couldn't just let you kill them."

"I don't need you to monitor my conscience. My soul is already tarnished enough, and I'm less worried about that than having two brainless morons running around pissed off at us."

"Maybe it isn't your soul I was worried about, Luca. Did you ever even consider that? If I let you kill that man, those deaths would be on me. If I hadn't gone there last night, you would've never come, and..." I paused, determined not to let my faltering voice betray my emotions. "If they died, it would be because of my actions. And I'm not okay with that. But I'm sorry if my unwillingness to kill anyone who gets in my way inconvenienced you."

I turned away quickly. I thought I'd feel relief after speaking my mind, but I didn't. I felt much, much worse.

Luca didn't say anything, which was fine by me.

I squirted bodywash onto my loofah and hurriedly washed, eager to get away from Luca. When I reached my arms though, I noticed the sticky residue coating my wrists hadn't washed off at all. Instead, there were bits of black fuzz stuck to it now. Even just looking at it reminded me of the horror and helplessness I'd felt, tied up with two men who didn't know me.

I scrubbed harder, feeling the tears well up in my eyes. My skin—already sensitive from the adhesive—turned red, but it was still sticky. "Damn it," I mumbled, my eyes blurring over to the point that I could barely see.

Luca reached around me, gripping my hand tightly until I stopped scrubbing. He tugged the loofah out of my hand and tossed it to the side. Then he inched closer, wrapping his arms around me tighter.

"I can't…" he began. "The thought of anyone hurting you makes me crazy."

His chin pressed against the top of my head as his fingers slowly stroked my wrists. After a moment, he moved so he was facing me, and he lifted one wrist, inspected it closely, then kissed it. He shut his eyes as he repeated the gesture with my other wrist.

"I'm sorry," he said softly, his eyes still closed. "I'm so sorry."

It was hard to stay mad at Luca when he was like this— calm, gentle, vulnerable. It didn't hurt that he was dangerously handsome sopping wet. His lips lingered at my wrist, so I slowly pulled my arm out of his grasp. Luca opened his eyes, his deep brown stare locking on me for a moment, and then he kissed me.

His kiss was so tentative at first that I couldn't help but wonder if he thought I'd follow through with my threat. Honestly, it was still a possibility, but it wasn't foremost in my mind anymore. I was still furious with Luca, and we still had so much to work out, but right now, nothing sounded more comforting than being fully enveloped by my husband's strong arms.

As I kissed him back, he deepened the connection between our mouths, holding me close with his hands on my cheeks. Losing my balance on the slippery tile floor, I reached for his hips. Luca, clearly interpreting that as an invitation, stepped forward, pinning me against the wall.

His hands left my cheeks, stroking my hair, my arms, and the sides of my breasts. From where he stood, I could feel how much he wanted me, and in a way, that comforted me, too. A few hours ago, I hadn't known if I'd ever see Luca again, and the thought had terrified me. Now, I couldn't get close enough.

Breaking away for a breath, Luca pressed his forehead against mine. "I love you," he whispered.

I didn't have the energy to repeat it back to him. Instead, I reached down and grazed his prominent erection. Raising to my toes, I captured his mouth with my own, moaning into him at the eroticism of it all. He broke off the kiss again after another moment, his lips moving to my breast, licking and tugging at one nipple then the other.

I reached for his hips, and didn't have to say a word. Luca lifted me up, using both hands to steady us as my back rest against the wall. I wrapped my legs around him, using one hand to guide him into my entrance before looping both arms around his neck.

Our movements were limited in the shower, but it didn't seem to affect either of us. All the tension I'd felt throughout the last several hours rapidly rebuilt deep in my groin as the slippery body of the man I loved—faults and all—moved against me.

I thought about how scared I'd been, compared to how safe I felt now, connected in every way possible with Luca. He was my perpetual savior, my eternal downfall.

My orgasm swept over me with such a sudden intensity that I thought I might black out. I was loosely aware of my moans growing louder just before Luca joined in with his own, softer moan, but the sounds were all lost in the steamy cocoon of the shower.

I was dizzy as Luca lowered me to my feet, steadying me with his arm as he gently wiped my thighs with the loofah. He shut off the faucet and wrapped me in a towel before I could even remember if I ever washed out my conditioner.

"Drink," he said, handing me the water.

I did, despite his bossiness. Then I accepted the toothbrush Luca handed me, already adorned with toothpaste. I finger combed my hair before twisting it into a loose knot on my head so as not to drench my pillow. When I joined him in the bedroom a minute later, he held out my nightgown. As I slipped it on, I remembered our guests.

"I should check on Gabby," I said.

"Alessio will keep an eye on her ,and he'll get us if she wakes."

I reluctantly crawled into bed as Luca turned off the light. A minute later, I was still wide awake.

"Go to sleep, Giada." Luca ordered.

As if it were that simple. "I can't. What's going to happen to Gabriella?"

"She'll be fine. I promise." Luca pressed a firm kiss into my forehead before flipping onto his side, facing away from me.

He never faced away from me unless he was angry, I realized. But if he was angry, well, so was I. I had even more reason to be upset than he did. And telling me Gabby would be fine didn't make it true.

I was certain I'd be up for hours, stressing over the events of the past day and the new traumas the future promised, but I was wrong. Somehow, I fell asleep within minutes.

Luca

I awoke to the pounding in my head. Casting a glance at Giada, curled up in a ball in the farthest possible corner of the bed, I confirmed she was both still asleep and still upset with me. I winced, and the thumping repeated.

I groaned, realizing the hammering wasn't in my head so much as at the door. I crept out of bed, rubbing my eyes, and went to the door. Alessio stood on the other side of the door. I imagined I looked every bit as exhausted as he did.

"She's up," he whispered.

I closed the bedroom door behind me and peered over to the guest room. The door was shut, and Gabriella was nowhere in sight. I turned to Alessio for an explanation.

"She tried to leave, and I told her to wait until Giada woke up. She said Giada could call her later but that she was going. I let her know that wasn't an option, so she went back to her room. I'm surprised the slamming of the door didn't wake you."

"We had a late night," I said, aware that he, too, had a late night. Except rather than go to bed right when we got home,

Giada and I had spent a fair amount of time arguing and then making up.

"Yeah, I heard," he mumbled, heading into my kitchen. He eyed the coffee maker like it was a spaceship.

I motioned for him to move so I could brew a full pot. I suspected Giada would need all the coffee in the world to get through today.

"What exactly did you hear?" I asked.

Alessio chuckled. "Well, first there was you two yelling at each other, and I was half scared that I was going to have to come in there and stop your wife from murdering you."

I smiled, relieved that was what he meant. But then he continued.

"And then all the yelling was replaced by even louder noises of a different nature."

I cringed, feeling heat rush to my cheeks. "You heard that?"

"The entire building probably heard that," he replied. "Well, her anyway. She is loud. Kinda hot, actually. Listening to her, I almost get why you're willing to put up with how high maintenance she is."

I turned to my friend and glared until he took the hint and shut up. I supposed I should've been comforted it was only her that he heard, although I felt oddly territorial of Giada's more intimate noises.

Before I could say anything, our bedroom door clicked open. Giada had changed into a pair of thin cotton shorts and a long-sleeved tee shirt and somehow managed to look both adorable and semi-alert.

"Good morning," I said. "Coffee?"

She padded into the kitchen, glared at Alessio, flipped her middle finger at me, then poured two cups of coffee. As she went into the guest room, Alessio turned back to me.

"Yeah, I really don't get how marriage works."

I sighed and retrieved two more coffee mugs from the cabinet.

~

Giada

"Hey, how are you feeling?" I asked, handing Gabby the coffee and perching on the end of the bed.

She took a sip then froze. "How do I know this isn't drugged?"

I rolled my eyes, snatched her cup, and downed a large swig. It scalded the back of my throat as I handed the mug back to her.

"Your husband's creepy friend said I couldn't leave until you were awake. I really don't like being told where I can and can't go. I don't even remember how I got here."

"Sorry. Alessio is…an acquired taste. And I gave you something last night to calm you down. You were really freaked out after—"

"After we were kidnapped at gunpoint by weapons dealers and a creepy man groped me while holding a knife to my throat?" she supplied. "Yeah, I was freaked out. Still am. And you have a lot of explaining to do."

I nodded. She was right, except, I wasn't even sure how to explain that.

"It was a big mix-up," I began. "Luca's dad owed a favor to someone and let them ship some stuff along with Luca's normal shipment, and no one knew that was what they were going to ship."

"No one knew it was a crate filled with really big guns?"

"Shh!" I glanced at the door. "Look, obviously there are some really bad guys involved, and I didn't realize that or I would never have brought you there; but it's probably best if you just forget what we saw. In fact, just forget we ever went there at all. Let's pretend we just went for coffee and then did some window shopping and dished about guys the whole night."

Gabriella looked completely unconvinced. "I don't know what is going on here Giada, and honestly, I think you're right that I don't want to know. But we need to go to the police. They need to know that a huge shipment of guns is sitting at the docks. They need to go catch those guys that kidnapped us."

I shook my head. "You can't go to the police. Those guys—they weren't acting alone. This is bigger than you realize, and the police can't keep us safe. Besides..." I began, then I stopped myself.

"What?" she asked.

I shook my head, appalled that I'd almost actually told her the truth. I sipped my coffee, wishing I were lounging in bed drinking it like any other Saturday, wishing I were anywhere but here, doing anything but trying to convince my best friend she hadn't just seen a massive shipment of guns.

"Luca is involved, isn't he? That's why you don't want me to go to the police."

I hesitated, then nodded. She was my best friend, after all, and she'd seen enough to know that much was true.

"God, tell me you didn't know about this before."

"I had no idea we'd have any trouble at all last night, I swear. I didn't know anything about the...contents of the shipping crate or the guys at the dock. You have to believe me."

"That's not what I mean," she said. "Did you know Luca was mixed up in this shit?"

I couldn't answer that, but of course, my silence told her everything she needed to know. "It's not what you think, Gabby. Really. He's a good guy. He doesn't have any choice in all of this. You don't know what his father is like."

"A good guy? Giada, be real. He knew exactly what was going on last night. He carries a gun." She shook her head so vigorously it was as though she was trying to shake up all the bad thoughts flying through her mind. "He's been involved in this crap for years, Giada. And you've known it all along, haven't you?"

Gabriella paused her rant, but not too long. Clearly, she knew I wouldn't respond. "All those times he was overprotective, all those times he seemed suspicious and creepy or violent…it's because he is. He's a criminal, Giada. Why would you marry him?"

"He's not a bad man, Gabby. He just…he's not perfect, but—"

"No buts. He's a sociopath. And so are you if you stay with him."

She finished her coffee then looked around for her shoes.

"I'd like to go home now," she said.

I rubbed my forehead and sighed. "You can't go to the cops, Gabby," I repeated.

"That's not really your call."

Fuck. "Gabby, you don't understand. This is bigger than you and me and Luca. I'm not asking you to keep this quiet. I'm telling you that you have to forget it all."

"Or what?" She turned to me, hands on her hips.

"If you weren't my best friend, you'd be dead already," I said, hating that it was the truth. "Those guys with the guns—they don't care about anything except money. If they know there were witnesses, they'll kill you."

Her eyes brimmed with tears.

"I'm so sorry, Gabby. I never meant to drag you into all of this. If I could go back in time and stay away from the dock last night, I would. You're the best friend I've ever had, and I can't stand the thought of losing you."

Her hands trembled against her hips, but she didn't shift her position. "I'd like to go home now," she repeated.

I nodded softly and slipped off the bed. I closed the door behind me as I left the guestroom. Luca and Alessio were in the living room, but they both stood as they saw me.

"Is she okay?" Luca asked.

I shook my head. What a dumb question. "No, she's really not, but I explained it to her, sort of, and she's not going to tell anyone."

"She won't go to the cops?" Alessio asked.

"No," I said, rolling my eyes since that was clearly covered by my previous statement.

He turned to Luca.

"I'll talk with her," Luca said.

"I just told you both that I took care of it."

Luca squeezed my shoulder. "We need to be certain she got the message."

I shook free of his hand, feeling the opposite of comfort from the condescending gesture.

"Your things are in your car," Alessio said, interrupting my frantic thoughts.

"What?" I turned to him.

"A mirror, lamps, rug, some other stuff… I don't know what all. Thomas and Giovanni loaded it into your car before they brought it back. If you want me to help bring it up here—"

"It's fine," I snapped. "Thank you."

I resented that he could be so cavalier when my best friend was struggling. She was terrified, angry, and confused, and I couldn't blame her at all. I wasn't sure our friendship could survive this.

Luca

*T*urned to my wife's friend, inhaled slowly, then launched into my speech.

"I understand you're scared, Gabriella, but there are forces outside our control at play here. Bad guys that you don't want to piss off. If you go to the police or tell anyone at all anything you saw last night, they will kill you, and probably your entire family. Trust me when I say the police can't protect you. Alessio and I made sure that no one who saw you last night will ever say anything, but if you tell anyone you were there or that you saw anything at all, we can't protect you."

Gabriella stared blankly at me.

"I need to know if you understand what I'm saying."

"You're saying I have to pretend that last night never happened."

"Yes. No matter what. If the police question you, if anyone at all ever questions you—about the men that took you, about what was in that crate, about me or Alessio—you know nothing. You saw nothing. Do you understand?"

She didn't speak.

"They will kill you if you talk. So, I need to know that you're hearing what I'm saying."

"If I pretend nothing ever happened last night, that Giada and I just went shopping after our coffee, then nothing happens?"

I nodded.

"I'll never see those guys again and nobody will hurt me?"

"Yes. That's right."

She cast a disgusted glance at Giada. "Fine. It's forgotten. Can I go home now?"

I turned to Alessio to confirm I hadn't left anything out. He nodded. "Yeah. Do you want one of us to drive you?"

"I'll drive her," Giada piped up, rising quickly to her feet.

Gabriella grimaced. "No thanks. I'll take a cab."

Giada was visibly hurt by this response, but there was nothing we could do now. I knew this was inevitable at some point, and all we could do now was hope someday Gabby got over it and forgave Giada.

I reached into my wallet and pulled out a small stack of hundred dollar bills. "For the cab," I said, handing it to her.

Gabriella eyed the money then scowled at me. Shoving my

hand to the side, she reached for her purse. "I don't want your blood money or bribes or whatever it is. I don't know what shit you're mixed up in, and I don't want to know. You should be ashamed of yourselves, all of you." She turned to Giada. "Especially you. You know better. God, you are such a hypocrite."

"Gabby, I—" Giada began.

Her friend cut her off with a wave of her hand. "I don't even want to hear it. Nothing you say could ever possibly make up for what you put me through or make me ever want to associate with the likes of you. You disgust me. I don't ever want to see you again. Any of you," she said.

She glared at Giada a moment longer, then stalked out of the apartment.

I turned to Giada, who looked like she was about to crumple to the floor, and quickly went to her. But as I started to wrap my arm around her to comfort her, she swatted me away.

"Don't touch me! Don't you ever fucking touch me again." She stormed into our bedroom, slammed the door, then turned the lock.

I let my head drop to my chest as all the drama of the past day washed over me, bringing a wave of exhaustion that seemed utterly insurmountable.

"So…" Alessio said after a moment. "I'll just let myself out." He cleared his throat, clearly aware that I'd forgotten he was still there. "I'll see you at the club later?"

I nodded weekly. He hesitated, then left.

Defeated, I stared at the locked bedroom door for several minutes. Giada and I had more than our fair share of fights over the years, but this was the first one where I truly didn't know if she would ever fully forgive me.

CHAPTER 22

Adrian

When Marco summoned me to the house under the guise of wanting to find out how everything at the firm was going, I'd prepared myself for anything. Another assignment, a test, a demand that I return the "favor" they'd done for my sister, or even an interrogation about the gun I had, finally, procured the legal way.

I had not prepared myself for a cozy family dinner. Maybe not so cozy, I supposed, since there were nine other people at the oversized table. Luckily, Angelo was one of those, so I could at least attempt to return to him the gun I'd borrowed. His girlfriend Julia was there too, so I waited until he was alone with the guys to bring it up. Not surprisingly, he'd ruthlessly mocked me.

"I got my own now, so I can return yours," I explained.

"I've got plenty," he said, as though we were discussing an ink pen and not a handgun. "You can just keep it."

I hesitated, then opted for honesty. "I really don't want it. Since I have a permit for mine, I figure I might as well keep things legal…"

He actually snorted. "Are you expecting the feds to raid your place sometime soon?"

"No, but—"

"Fine," he interrupted, holding out his hand.

"It's in my car. I'll go get it."

Angelo rolled his eyes before I turned.

I had just retrieved it from my car when lights from another vehicle temporarily blinded me. I considered stashing the gun back in the car, but instead slipped it into the back of my pants.

The car pulled to a stop beside me and out climbed Giada. I was surprised to see that it was Enzo, and not Luca, in the driver's seat.

"Hey there," she said, leaning in for a hug. I pulled back, giving her the awkward sort of middle-school hug, not wanting her to feel the gun at my hip.

If she noticed my discomfort, she didn't say so.

"Fancy seeing you here. Were you here for dinner?"

"Yeah," I said. I smiled politely at Enzo as he passed, carrying magenta pink Louis Vuitton luggage past me. "What are you doing?"

She chewed her lip, casting a stare at the luggage.

"You and Luca didn't…"

"No, no. We're fine," she said.

I actually felt relief. Not because I actually wanted them to be happy together, but only because I couldn't stomach the thought of being thrown back onto that carousel of loving her, then hating her, then loving her again. As long as she was married to Luca, the boundaries were clear. Giada wasn't an option, and I was free to be happy with someone else. Or single.

"He's in Atlantic City for the weekend for business. The last night he was away didn't go so well, so now I'm staying here where I can be babysat like a child."

"Oh," was all I said.

"Were you on your way out?" she asked.

I hesitated, barely remembering where I was going. "No, I just needed to get something from my car."

"I would love a drink, and I am desperate to avoid Julia. Want to meet me back by the pool? I'll bring the alcohol."

"Uh, yeah. Sure," I agreed. I followed her inside, waiting until she'd greeted her mother and then started up the stairs, before approaching Angelo. I thought it was odd that Giada didn't question more why I was there, in her home, for dinner. I couldn't help but wonder if Luca told her I was working with her dad. Something told me she'd view me differently if she knew. Of course, she'd known for ages what Luca was up to, and that obviously didn't bother her.

I discretely handed the gun to Angelo, who simply dropped it on the accent table beside him and then reached into his pocket for a business card. He held it out to me, and I accepted, confused as to why Angelo had just given me a card for the manager of a condominium building.

"Dad thought you should have a bigger place, in case your sister wants to stay with you sometime," he explained. "Plus you're kind of old to still rent."

I opened my mouth to point out that Angelo himself still slept at his parents' house most nights, but instead opted to remind him that the vast majority of New Yorkers rented.

He shrugged. "Yeah, well, call this guy, and he's got a unit to show you. It's a two-bedroom, and your work will cover the down payment."

I quirked an eyebrow. That sounded promising. "Where is this location?" I didn't recognize the address.

"Close to the firm and to your real boss," he said with a wink before sauntering down the hall.

I blew out a sigh then made my way to the back to talk with Giada.

"How's Annie doing?" she asked.

"Good. She's, uh, resilient," I said.

Giada nodded, settling back against her chaise lounge. I sat beside her, feeling awkward to be sitting fully clothed in a poolside lounger next to my ex-girlfriend.

"So, what is Luca doing in Atlantic City?" I asked, eager to make conversation to break the painful silence.

"Business," she said.

I wondered if she didn't know more specifics or just wasn't telling me. "And what happened the last time he went that was so bad?"

Giada made a face. "Gabriella and I went someplace we shouldn't, saw some things we shouldn't, and, um…now Luca is terrified to let me out of his sight, and Gabriella will never speak to me again."

I hadn't expected all of that. It took me a moment to decide where to start. "I'm sure Gabby will forgive you."

"I am quite positive she won't."

"It couldn't be that bad."

"Whatever you're picturing, it's ten times worse," she replied. "I almost got her killed. And then when I explained that she couldn't ever tell anyone, well, it didn't go over too well. She already hated Luca, but now she hates me, too."

"How exactly did you almost get her killed?"

"There were some guys that weren't thrilled that we saw what we saw."

"What did you see?" I interrupted.

"Stuff," she said with a pointed stare.

"Oh." I tried to imagine what could possibly be so bad that Luca wouldn't want her telling me. Then I found myself wondering if Angelo knew.

"Anyway, the guys worked for Luca but didn't know who I was and weren't the nicest guys around. Hence the trauma."

I set my drink down, suddenly queasy. "Did they hurt you?"

Giada shook her head. "No, they didn't. We were both fine." She paused, and her expression changed. "But they could have hurt us."

"How the fuck does Luca have guys working for him that don't know who you are?"

"That's a whole different story. The point is, I lost my only friend in the whole world, and there's no point in me even trying to make a new friend because it's inevitably going to end the same."

There was a depressing truth to her statement. We both focused on our drinks for a moment.

"I'm your friend. So is Lorenzo."

Giada snickered. "Enzo is literally being paid to spend time with me this weekend. And you…well, you are an enigma. I'd like to be your friend, but I seem to recall you saying that would never happen."

I considered her words. I thought about telling the truth, that there were a lot of things I now did that the old me swore would never happen. But that version of me was long gone. No point in dredging up the past. So instead, I shrugged. "Well, here we are, chatting amicably."

Giada smiled, then seemed to notice something out of the corner of her eye. "Shit," she whispered.

I gazed up and saw Julia pacing near the pool house. Suddenly, I remembered Giada saying she was avoiding her brother's girlfriend. Not that I was surprised by that. The two had never gotten along.

"Want me to distract her so you can run?" I offered.

Giada giggled. "Thank you, but I'll just get it over with."

I nodded, finished my drink, then made my way back into the house.

~

Giada

*J*ulia barely acknowledged Adrian as she barged over to speak to me.

"I'm surprised to see you here after you blew me off and didn't return my calls," she said, perching on the edge of the chair beside me.

"I sent you a text that something came up. I've had a rough couple of days, okay? I didn't blow you off," I explained.

The witch rolled her eyes. "This is important."

"So was the shit I've been dealing with the past two days," I said between gritted teeth.

"God, your brother is right. You really do think the whole world revolves around you, don't you?" Julia didn't pause long enough for me to reply. "I'm busy too, you know? But I can still show up when I say I will. It's called respecting other people's time."

I downed the last sip of my drink, shaking my head. "Yeah, well, I think we've chatted enough. I'm going to bed." I swung my legs off the side of the chair, but before I could rise to my feet, Julia gripped my wrist.

"Giada, we need to talk. Remember?"

My eyes focused on the spot where her frighteningly long nails touched my skin. "Get. Your. Hand. Off. Me," I said.

Julia dropped her hand. "Look, Giada, I'm sorry. This has all just been really stressful, and I thought you understood how important this all was. Us girls need to stick together. We could be friends if you would just get to know me."

At the mention of friendship, my stomach churned, and my thoughts turned to Gabby. God, how I missed her already. If she were still talking to me, I could head up to my old room and call her to vent about Julia. Gabby would call Julia a cow and tell me how perfect she is for my awful oldest brother.

"Giada, come on. We are in the same boat, you and me," Julia continued.

I snapped out of my daze. "But we're not, though. You've apparently been talking with an undercover federal agent."

"So have you."

I shook my head. "I haven't said a damn thing. But, apparently, you've been spouting lies about my husband, and God knows what you've told him about the rest of my family."

Julia's lips parted as if she was surprised by this. "I haven't lied about anything. And I haven't even told him everything. He promised he'd keep you safe. I'm looking out for you."

"Julia, I'm tired. I don't know what you want from me, but I'm going to bed."

"Giada, you aren't listening. We need to get our stories straight."

"Does Angelo know what you've been doing?" I asked, locking my gaze on hers in hopes of being able to ascertain if her response was truthful.

She hesitated, then shook her head. "No, but I'm doing it for him. And, I mean, I'm only telling the truth."

Julia paused and swallowed loudly. I actually believed her, and for a moment, I actually felt sorry for her.

"I see you in church. You claim to be a good person. Don't you think it's time you act like it?" she asked.

"By betraying my husband?"

She rolled her eyes. "Like he hasn't betrayed you. He's probably off fucking hookers in Atlantic City as we speak."

All of my sympathy dissipated. "Julia, if you want my advice, stop talking to the FBI. I am not going to help with whatever smear campaign you've got going on, but I will see if Luca has any ideas for how to get you out of the jam you created."

Her face blanched. "You can't tell Luca."

"He needs to know, Julia. And I'm not keeping this secret from him." I paused, grimacing at the awareness that I'd already kept it from him too long. "He'll know what to do," I said, certain that was the truth.

"He'll have me killed!" she cried.

I sighed, slowly rising to my feet and stretching. "No, he won't. That's not like him. What he will do is figure out how to fix this mess."

I grabbed my empty glass and turned to walk back to the house.

"Giada, please! You're not going to tell him tonight, are you?"

I thought about that. I probably should, but Luca already had enough on his plate. He'd be back after another night, and we'd have a whole day to relax together and catch up. I'd have plenty of time to tell him then. Although, we were heading to Giovanni's birthday party together the night he returned, and I knew Luca was looking forward to the chance to just unwind with me and his friends. He deserved a stress-free night.

I turned back to Julia, surprised to see the desperation etched in her features. Her eyes were damp and red, her breath ragged and uneven. "Calm down, Julia. I promise Luca isn't killing anyone, not even you. You clearly need to get to know him better if that's what you think."

My words didn't seem to calm her in the slightest, so I continued. "No, I won't tell him tonight. I am going to call him as soon as you stop pestering me with your rants, but I don't want to stress him out. He's got enough on his plate, and he doesn't need another thing to deal with now."

"When then?"

"His friend's birthday party is Sunday night. I'll talk with him after the party. Why don't you text me sometime you're free Monday, and we can get coffee like we planned before and I'll tell you what Luca says."

Julia wrinkled her face, but said nothing.

"In the meantime, don't talk to any cops. Okay? Just trust me on this. You may think you're helping, but you're not. You're putting yourself and everyone else in danger. Luca will know what to do, okay?"

"Sunday night?" she repeated, still looking panicked.

I nodded, declining to add that depending on how much Luca drank at the party, I might table the discussion for Monday morning. Julia didn't need to know the details.

"Good night," I said, hoping my tone conveyed the sense of finality I felt about the conversation.

I shivered as I walked back to the house. The temperature had dropped considerably, and after talking to Julia, I needed a palate cleanser conversation. I changed into my pajamas then curled up in bed to call Luca.

~

Luca

*J*had just brushed my teeth when my phone rang. Alessio instantly shifted into high alert, glancing my way, but I nodded dismissively as soon as I saw the caller ID.

"Giada?" I said as I answered, half expecting it to be someone else calling on her behalf.

"I didn't wake you, did I?" she asked. Her voice was soft and warm, and reminded me exactly of the way she looked when she first woke and was still half asleep.

"No, we just came back to the room a little bit ago," I said, loosening my tie and dropping it over the chair where I'd draped my suit jacket.

"We?"

"Oh, uh, Alessio is here." I held the phone out.

"Hi Giada," he called from the bed near the window.

"You guys share a hotel room?"

Her surprise made me smile. I supposed it was odd, but it seemed a waste of money to book separate rooms when neither of us slept much. "We rarely book separate rooms when it's just the two of us, but sometimes, Alessio meets some mentally unstable dancer with low self-esteem and ends up in a different room for the night. Tonight it looks like we might actually be roommates." I paused. "Why aren't you sleeping? You're at your father's, right?"

"Yes. I can't sleep. I miss you."

I sat on my bed and inched my way up to the headboard, stacking pillows behind me. "I miss you too," I said, surprised she sounded like she meant it. Giada clearly hadn't forgiven me for everything with Gabby yet, so I was eagerly taking any scrap of truth she offered.

Alessio groaned, dumped the magazine he'd been reading on the floor, then took off to the bathroom with a stack of clothes. After a moment, I heard the shower running. I supposed that was his way of giving me privacy.

Giada asked about my day, so I told her the basics, then asked about hers. She told me about meeting with a new client and how awkward it was to have Lorenzo driving her to a work lunch, but she seemed to accept it.

I assumed the only reason she hadn't protested even more than she did when I'd insisted on her having a bodyguard again was because I'd arranged for Lorenzo to fill this position, largely thanks to her father.

"I ran into Adrian," she said, the uncertainty in her voice telling me she wasn't sure how I'd react to this news. "My father apparently invited him over for some family dinner."

I wasn't shocked, honestly. Angelo told me he'd been working with them some. No actual jobs yet, but slowly Marco was apparently pulling him into the periphery of his family. Angelo mocked him endlessly and didn't seem to understand why his father wanted anything to do with Adrian. I'd wondered that as well, initially, but after some thought, the rationale had become clear to me. Adrian's motivation for keeping close to the family was harder to discern, though.

"I wasn't there for dinner, but we had a drink on the patio later. Just the two of us," she added.

I felt the corners of my mouth curve upward. "Are you trying to make me jealous?"

"Just seeing if you were listening, really." She paused, and I pictured her yawning. "Now that I have no friends, it was nice to be able to talk to someone."

There wasn't even a hint of blame or bitterness in her tone, which was depressing. I didn't like the fact that I'd ruined her best friendship, but I'd known for ages that it was inevitable. Living the lifestyle I led, friends outside of the family weren't an option. For me, it wasn't a big deal because my friends were all part of the inner circle. But for Giada, it was different. She knew too much to talk freely with women outside the family, and the other wives and girlfriends on the inside were largely oblivious to the true nature of our business.

"I think it's weird that Adrian is spending so much time with my father and Angelo lately. Don't you?" she continued.

I didn't have a clear answer for that. "Did you ask him about it?"

"I asked my dad, and he said Adrian was a family friend. When I mentioned it to Adrian, he got all weird and changed the subject. You don't think my dad roped him into doing some crazy favor for him, do you?"

I hesitated. "I think Adrian is a big boy who can take care of himself. You don't need to worry about him. If he doesn't want to get mixed up with your family, he'll say so." From the start, when Adrian was an oblivious outsider, he'd had no problem standing up to Marco, Angelo, or me. I didn't doubt that he was impervious to Marco's charms now, either. If he wanted out, he'd get out.

Giada's silence suggested she wasn't so sure. "You didn't really answer my question. Is Adrian working for my father?"

Leave it to Giada to be blunt. I took my time answering, careful to phrase it all perfectly. "I don't think Adrian has done any recent jobs for your father. None that I know of, anyway."

As always, she read between the lines and pressed onward. "Why is my father keeping him around?"

"I don't know."

She sighed loudly. "You obviously have a guess, though."

I hesitated. "I think your father sees some potential in Adrian. He's smart, loyal, and he likes you."

"Not anymore he doesn't," she interrupted.

I ignored the interruption. "From what I've gathered, I doubt your father actually envisions Adrian doing any real work for him, but he does seem like he's maybe training Adrian."

"Training him for what?"

"You," I replied.

"Huh?"

I regretted letting her drag me down this path, but now felt compelled to fully explain. Knowing Giada, she wouldn't let it drop until I told her all of my thoughts anyway. "I think your dad wants to keep Adrian in the fold as a potential suitor for you."

She actually laughed at this. "My dad basically forced me onto you, but now that we're married you think he wants me to switch to Adrian? He knows how I feel about divorce."

"He doesn't want you to leave me for Adrian. Nor do I," I added. "But I think it comforts him to know Adrian could take care of you if something happened to me."

Giada was uncharacteristically quiet. For a moment, I actually thought she'd fallen asleep.

"You're saying my dad is training Adrian because he thinks you're going to die?" she finally said, her voice louder.

"No, of course he doesn't think that. It's just a precaution."

"And what do you think?"

"I don't think I'm going to die anytime soon," I said. "At least not for another seventy-five years."

"Then why are you okay with Adrian being back in the picture?"

I squeezed my eyes shut, trying to remember why I'd gone down this path with her at two in the morning.

"Amore, come on. I don't mind if you and Adrian are friends because I trust you. And I have no intention of dying, but it does make me feel better knowing you'd have someone to take care of you if something did happen to me."

Alessio walked out of the bathroom, wearing sweatpants and a He-Man tee shirt. He flopped back onto his bed before flashing me a look of pity then flipping through his magazine.

Giada sniffled softly into the phone.

"Baby… It's late. Alessio is all tucked into bed here, and you need your sleep too."

Alessio flipped me off without glancing away from whatever article he was reading.

"I don't like that you talk about dying like it's normal."

"I mean, it is normal. Everyone does it eventually."

"But everyone doesn't think about dying in their mid-twenties. I hate that your lifestyle makes it more likely you'll die young than some random person."

"Car accidents are the main cause of death for young people," I said, hoping that was still the truth. I ignored the quizzical look Alessio shot me and continued. "It could happen to anyone. But I'm not going anywhere. I promise. And you know I'm a man of my word."

She sighed, and I relaxed, knowing I'd satisfied her, at least for the night. "Is what you're doing now dangerous?"

"No. We're just learning some stuff about running the casinos. Just checking out the possibilities. No one here knows who we are, and even if there were some danger, my personal bodyguard is snuggled up only a few feet away."

She laughed. "Will you stay on the line with me until I fall asleep?"

"That might disturb Alessio," I said.

"If you have phone sex while I'm right here, I'll shoot you myself," Alessio said, his voice loud enough for Giada to hear.

I pressed my hand over the phone. "Thanks, asshole," I mumbled.

"Tell me more about your client meeting," I said to Giada. So she did.

As she talked, Alessio eventually set down his magazine and occupied himself with his phone, instead. I didn't notice feeling particularly tired, but I must have fallen asleep.

The next thing I knew, the entire room was dark. I was still holding my phone, but my hand had dropped down to my side. Across the room, Alessio was snoring softly, his back to me. I glanced at my phone, satisfied that Giada must have fallen asleep also, since I had no missed calls or texts from her. I stretched my neck, then stood to change out of my button-down shirt.

As I made my way to the bathroom, I heard a rustling noise in the hall. I paused, thinking it was odd for someone to be wandering the halls when the large, obnoxiously bright digital clock by the bed read 4:15. I reasoned that it was probably hotel staff, distributing the bills under the doors of guests scheduled to check out in the morning, but just to be sure, I crept up to the peephole and looked out.

A kid—who couldn't have been more than fourteen or fifteen —stood in front of our door. He wore black jeans and a black sweatshirt and had a grotesque-looking lip piercing. I wasn't sure what to make of the kid until he pulled some sort of tool out of his pocket and reached for the electronic lock above our doorknob.

I glanced back to Alessio, who was still asleep. I considered trying to wake him, but if the kid was breaking in, I'd prefer he not know that we were awake. If he heard noise within the room, he'd realize he wasn't catching us asleep and off guard. I snatched my gun from the dresser then spotted Alessio's switchblade beside it. I gripped the switchblade in my right hand and moved the gun to my waistband.

I snuck one final glance out the peephole, then quietly flipped open the chain. It was the flimsy kind that one solid kick could break through, but I hoped to resolve this situation as quietly as possible, regardless of what exactly was happening.

The lock clicked open, and I made a mental note never again to stay at a hotel with such shitty locks. I scooted back to the wall and waited, hoping the kid would try to open the door. He did.

He turned the knob delicately, then slowly pushed the door open two inches. His eyes focused in the direction of the beds, probably checking we were both still asleep. After a minute, he crept fully inside the room. I waited until he turned to softly shut the door before I made my move.

I lunged forward, wrapping my left arm around him at an angle that forced both of his arms to his sides. I swept my right hand up to his neck. He struggled against me, forcing me to press the knife into his flesh. In the dark, I couldn't tell how deeply I'd slashed, but the kid yelped.

"Move and you die," I said.

"What the fuck?" Alessio mumbled, flying to his feet across the room. I heard him click the safety off his gun.

The kid jerked his arm upward, forcing me to angle the knife so the tip pierced the side of his neck. He froze instantly, not even daring to breathe now.

"Lights would be good," I said.

"Where's the fucking switch?" Alessio said.

A moment later, light flooded the room, and I winced, my eyes struggling to adjust.

"Fuck," Alessio muttered again, joining me near the kid.

"I...I don't want any trouble," the kid stammered. "Please don't kill me."

I glanced at Alessio, who reached forward and performed a quick and very thorough pat-down of the kid. He retrieved his wallet, cell phone, some e-cigs, and a knife.

"On the floor," I said, waiting until Alessio also snatched the gun the kid had dropped on the floor.

Alessio stared calmly at both of us, then nodded. I backed up, walking the kid with me, until we were close to the beds.

"Sit down, hands in the air," I commanded, releasing the kid with a shove.

He complied, his face filled with terror.

Alessio turned to me and rolled his eyes. "I was having the most incredible dream," he said. "There were these two blondes, and..."

I glared.

"Nevermind," he said, taking the hint. "I'll tell you later. The point is this is just my fucking luck that now, not only am I not with two blonde chicks, but there is some tween bleeding to death on my bed."

The kid's eyes widened even further at this.

"Jesus, please don't piss yourself," Alessio said. He turned to me, then pulled out the desk chair. "Can he sit here instead?"

I rolled my eyes, pretty sure Alessio's focus on his sleeping conditions for the rest of the night was misguided. By the time we resolved this...problem...it would be morning. "Fine," I said. "Go to that chair."

"Please don't kill me," the kid repeated, moving to the chair.

"Shut up," I said.

Alessio handed me a school ID from the kid's wallet.

"Aaron McNeilis," I read aloud. "That's you?"

He hesitated, then nodded.

Alessio held his phone out in front of him. The kid looked bewildered.

"Unlock it," Alessio said.

The kid tried several times to use his thumbprint, but his hands were shaking too violently.

"Christ," Alessio mumbled. "What's the code?"

Aaron told him, and Alessio successfully unlocked it. Alessio grimaced at the corner of his bed where the kid had sat, then positioned himself on the other side of the bed as he began to look at the phone. I aimed my gun at the kid.

"Do you know who we are Aaron?" I asked.

He shook his head, but the lack of eye contact told me he was lying.

"Why did you break into this room?"

"I…needed money," he said. He raised his hand to his neck, winced, then pulled it away. As soon as he saw the blood on his fingers, his eyes widened and his skin paled.

"Can you get him a wet towel or something?" I said to Alessio. "You're fine," I told the kid. "I barely nicked you."

"Why did you try to break into our room if you needed money?" Alessio asked.

Aaron hesitated, cringing as Alessio approached him with the towel, then relaxing as Alessio leaned back against the far wall.

"I saw you guys in the casino. You were throwing around cash like it grows on trees. I didn't think you'd notice if some were missing."

"What was your plan once you got in here? Shoot us and take our money?"

"I wouldn't have shot anyone. I figured you were drunk and might not even wake up. The gun was just to scare you. I didn't…"

Alessio finished thumbing through the kid's phone and tossed it to me. "Looks like he's just some random fuckup," Alessio said.

The kid opened his mouth to protest, then stopped.

I snapped a picture of his school ID, then stuck it back into his wallet. "Here's the deal, Aaron. If you want money, get a job. You lack the stealth you'd need to be a pickpocket, and you're too stupid to get involved with the guys that run this place. You need to watch your ass in this world. There are men in this casino that would slice off your toes and eat them for lunch if you woke them up like this."

Aaron nodded eagerly, still looking like he was moments from pissing himself.

"We'll dispose of the gun for you. You'll get the fuck out of our hotel room and never tell anyone any of this. Understood?"

He continued nodding.

"I need a verbal response, Aaron."

"Y—y—yes," he stammered.

"Okay. If we hear about or see you ever again, there will be consequences that you won't like. I've got a copy of your ID here, so we know where to find you if we need to. Got it?"

"Yes," he said, tears dripping down his cheek.

Alessio and I exchanged tired glances, but the kid didn't budge.

Alessio rolled his eyes. "Go," he said, motioning to the door.

The kid stood on shaky legs and started to the door.

"Hey!" Alessio shouted.

Aaron turned, wincing as if he were about to be executed. Alessio held up his phone and wallet, then dumped them in the kid's hand. He locked the door behind Aaron, then watched through the peephole for a minute.

"Fucking moron," Alessio mumbled, stumbling into the bathroom.

I glanced at my phone, yawned, and decided I could use a few more hours of sleep. I tried not to think about the fact that, hours after promising my wife I wouldn't die anytime soon, I almost got shot by an errant teen trying his hand at B&E.

Alessio returned to the bedroom, scowled at the foot of his bed where the kid had briefly sat, then knocked the top cover to the ground. He grabbed a new blanket from the shelf facing the beds then climbed under his covers. "Fucking kids today," he mumbled. "Interrupting my goddamn dream."

I bit back a laugh, settled into my own bed, then soon drifted off to sleep.

CHAPTER 23

Giada

I'd worried that the rest of my time at my parents' home would be tense, thanks to my stressful talk with Julia, but she and Angelo didn't come by the rest of the weekend. Also, my awareness that Luca would know exactly how to handle the situation when he returned home enabled me to relax and put it out of my mind.

Luca picked me up late Sunday morning. I considered telling him about Julia and the FBI agent during the drive back to our apartment. Luca informed me that some wacko teen tried to rob him in the middle of the night, and it was the perfect opportunity to share my crazy news, but I didn't. I'd been without my husband for nearly three days and wanted to simply relax in his arms once we got home. The moment I told him about Julia, he'd switch into work mode. He probably wouldn't even have time for me before the party, and I'd end up having to wait another night.

Julia texted me shortly after I left my parents, confirming I wasn't going to speak to Luca until that night. I wasn't sure why the timing mattered to her, but I replied that I'd chat with him after Giovanni's party. She'd then asked about the location of the party, which was even weirder. I told her the name of Luca's club where we'd be, but politely emphasized that it was a private event in hopes that she'd take the hint and not try to sneak in.

"Who's that?" Luca asked, retrieving my bags from the trunk.

"Julia," I replied, forgetting my plan to not bring it up until later.

Luca frowned. "Your brother's girlfriend Julia?"

"Yep. That's the one," I said, switching my phone to silent and wedging it back into my purse.

"I didn't know you two were so close."

"We're not. I still hate her. We talked some on Friday night though, and she wanted my help with something." I paused. "Remind me after the party, and I'll tell you then. Right now I have some more important things to do."

He unlocked the door to our apartment, then followed me inside. "Like what?"

I flashed him my most wicked grin. "You."

Luca dragged me to him, holding me close enough that his erection pressed against my stomach. "I'm on board with that plan," he said, winking before kissing me. His tongue tickled the seam of my lips before darting into my mouth. He tasted of coffee and I deepened the kiss, eager for more.

"I missed you," Luca said in a gruff voice that made the muscles in my belly clench.

He hiked me onto the counter, raising my sweater over my head. His smooth olive-toned hands caressed my breasts until a soft whimper escaped my lips. Luca reached around, unfastening the bra and letting it fall off my arms before lunging forward, nipping at the sensitive peaks of my breasts.

"Oh God," I panted as his tongue swirled around one nipple, then the other. I reached for him, burying my fingers in his soft hair as I held him to me, encouraging him to continue his work.

His hands worked their way up the long skirt I'd worn and I

grinned, realizing he was about to notice I hadn't worn panties. He growled against my flesh when his fingers reached the bare, damp apex between my thighs.

"You did miss me," Luca teased. His hands roughly parted my thighs as his lips moved lower. His tongue traced the length of my slit before circling the swollen bundle of nerves at the top.

I could've come like that, and that was probably his plan, but I wanted more. I always wanted more when it came to Luca. I relished the next few strokes of his tongue, then spoke up.

"I want you inside of me, now."

"So bossy," he murmured, continuing to kiss and lick me for another moment. Just when I thought he wouldn't comply, Luca rose to his feet. He dropped his pants in record time then gripped my hips, scooting me closer to him on the counter. He pressed a finger inside me, then used my moisture to coat his length.

Just as I was about to protest the delay, he thrust into me, filling me completely. I moaned, and he swallowed the sound with his kiss, pressing his lips to mine. After a moment, he released my mouth, lowered me back to my elbows, then pounded into me like he was on a mission. The tension built in my belly at a dizzying pace, and as I bit my lip to try to hold off longer, Luca rewarded me with a throaty moan.

I hooked my legs around his hips as if I worried he'd stop, but as my breath quickened, I knew I could only resist my orgasm for another minute at most.

"Come for me, Giada," Luca demanded, maintaining his relentless stride. "I want to feel you come on my cock."

His dirty words pushed me over the edge. My vision blurred, and I cried out as the waves of pleasure propelled through me. Luca's hips stuttered and a string of words I didn't understand flew out of his mouth. His warmth filled me, then he dropped his head to my chest, gently nipping the top of my breast before settling against me.

My legs were trembling too much to hold them around him

any longer. They dropped to his sides, dangling off the counter. Luca eased out of me with a groan.

"You're way better at that than Alessio," he teased, a boyish grin on his cleanly-shaven face.

I swatted at him right as he laughed. He scooped me into his arms and carried me to the bathroom.

"I need a shower before the party," he said. "I assume you want to join me?"

My legs felt like Jell-O, and I wasn't sure they'd support me after that orgasm. "I'm thinking a bath instead."

Luca considered that. "Okay, I'll get your bath started, then order food for lunch."

"Will you join me in the bath after?"

He bit back a grin. "Of course, but then we'll probably need another shower later."

I didn't mind that prospect in the slightest.

~

Luca

We'd closed down Rize for Giovanni's party, plastering a "Private Party" sign on the door. We'd ensured his favorite foods were prepared, and his wife had sent us an extensive list of people to invite. Since most of those guests were unfamiliar to me, I couldn't quite relax the way I would if the room were filled solely with men loyal to me and their dates. Alessio and I both pledged to stay sober…not avoiding alcohol entirely, but pacing ourselves so that we remained capable of driving and quick thinking.

There were a handful of people I needed to talk with, some to confirm loyalties and some to figure out their connection to Giovanni and Lauren. I realized now that Giovanni was married, he'd have new people in his life, thanks to his wife, but the process of vetting everyone could be tedious.

Still, after the afternoon I'd enjoyed with Giada, nothing could truly stress me out. Giada and I enjoyed the food, then separated to make the rounds of the room. She returned to my side in time to sing to the birthday boy and enjoy the multi-layer round cake coated in edible confetti and adorned with giant glittery numbers declaring Giovanni to be thirty years of age.

"You have to at least taste it," Giada said, her eyes fluttering shut as her lips closed around her second bite. The soft moan that escaped her lips had me hard in an instant. I growled and pressed my hand to the nape of her neck, bringing her mouth to mine. I appreciated the sweet lemony tang of the cake on her lips, but when we parted, it wasn't more cake I was craving.

"You taste better," I told her.

"Maybe we should get a slice to take home and see what other parts of my body taste good covered in frosting," she suggested.

"I would happily eat those parts all day without the icing," I reminded her.

Giada's cheeks flushed. "You're trouble. And I told Lauren I'd help her brainstorm some ideas for their guest room. So if you'll excuse me..."

She quirked a brow and waited until I kissed her again before walking off to Lauren. Thomas appeared by my side, and together, we chatted with a couple of the neighbors Lauren had invited to the party. As soon as we could politely excuse ourselves, we moved closer to the bar, where no other guests were within earshot.

I'd asked Thomas for an update on his work. He'd handled the trouble with Michael and those other two morons, but moving forward, I pledged to have more involvement with all of our men. Even if they weren't aware of my identity, I needed to know theirs. Never again would I allow Giada's safety to be compromised.

Thomas agreed with the plan, and shared his thoughts on how to make it all work.

As Thomas spoke, I gazed across the room, my eyes flitting aimlessly until I found her. She was still leaning against the edge of the bar, where I'd left her, but Alessio had taken my place. His body angled in front of hers in a way that would lead a casual onlooker to assume he was flirting. I interpreted his position differently. Alessio was protecting her.

I watched as my beautiful wife ran her fingers through her hair and then tossed back her head, laughing like she didn't have a care in the world. When she regained her composure, she glanced my way. Her cheeks broadened into a sweet smile the moment our eyes met. She pursed her lips together as though kissing the air, and my chest tightened at the gesture.

How had I gotten so lucky? I'd done nothing to deserve Giada's love. She was so good to me, so perfect for me, that I physically ached to think about a life without her. Our whole lives stretched before us to spend together, but already I knew no measure of time with her would be enough. I would always want more.

Giada's gaze intensified as though she were reading my thoughts. Alessio, following her eyes, turned to me as well. He raised an eyebrow and lifted his glass in a distant toast. I felt my lips part in a smile. If someone had told me a few years earlier that Giada and Alessio would ever be friends, I would've laughed.

But somehow, it had happened. My two favorite people in the universe had somehow found common ground—other than their connection to me. It was a miracle, and one for which I was grateful every single day.

Alessio said something else to make Giada laugh, then she pressed her palm against his bicep and turned to me. Then, at the exact same moment, she and Alessio each tapped a finger against their wrist to alert me to the time.

Beside me, Thomas snickered. "They're friends now," he said, his expression filled with confusion.

"They are friends now," I confirmed.

"And that's a good thing?"

I felt my head bobbing before I realized I should probably answer out loud. "It's a great thing. I'm…relieved."

Giada's eyes twinkled as she smiled, and I couldn't even remember what important matter Thomas and I were supposed to be discussing.

"Excuse me," I mumbled, patting him on the arm and crossing the room to rejoin my wife.

As I neared her, Giada drifted towards me as though pulled by a magnet. Alessio laughed.

"She made me do it. I told her, you never rush the boss, but she seems to think she's exempt from the rules," he joked.

"She is exempt from everything," I said, my voice softer than I intended. I weaved my fingers between hers and drew her closer. I inhaled slowly once her face was mere inches from mine.

"Why do you smell so good?" I asked her.

"Because I like to make you squirm," came her whispered reply.

I suppressed a groan, but appreciated that her closeness provided a full shield for any reaction my body had to her delicious fragrance.

"So are we getting out of here soon?" she asked.

"Depends. What's in it for me?"

"I think you know the answer to that."

I dropped my gaze to our feet, letting my forehead dip against hers while I tried to recall if there was anyone else I needed to talk with before we left.

I had all but forgotten we were surrounded by others in a very public place when Alessio cleared his throat loudly and with purpose.

"No, he's mine!" Giada replied before I could even glance up.

I breathed a laugh at her response, gripping her hand tightly as I turned to my friend. He recapped in Italian the two remaining tasks we needed to complete before leaving.

"Low blow, Alessio. Low blow," Giada said, always resentful when we switched languages to prevent her from understanding.

"You could learn the language," he reminded her.

I bit back a smile and turned to my wife. "Fifteen minutes, and then I am all yours. Okay?"

She angled towards me and I met her in the middle, relishing the taste of amaretto on her soft lips before finally releasing her hand and going to talk with the next person on my list.

~

Giada

"I love that you are comfortable with Alessio now," Luca said as he started the engine.

I raised an eyebrow. I had thought Luca liked us becoming friends, but stupid Angelo had told me Luca would never 'allow' me to have friends who were male. "Well, it turns out he's sort of a cool guy."

He was silent for a moment, then gazed at me for a moment and spoke again. "You looked beautiful tonight. It was distracting."

"Hmm. My apologies. I'll make sure to look ugly next time we go out."

"Not possible."

"You looked quite handsome tonight, too," I told him. "I really like you in a suit. You'd think I'd get over it, since you're always dressed up these days, but...nope. You plus formal wear...I don't know, it just does something to me."

"I thought you liked my joggers."

I felt my eyes widen and my nostrils flare at the suggestion. I did like Luca in his joggers, especially the thin grey ones. They were so soft and the material hid none of what he had underneath. I turned to watch my husband as he drove. He was devilishly handsome in whatever he wore. My extreme attraction was distracting, and a tad confusing. I supposed we were still newlyweds, but I had expected the insane, over-the-top desire to wear off by this point.

Somehow, it hadn't. I still wanted Luca every bit as much as I had on our wedding night. My heart still raced when I saw him without his shirt. My skin still flushed when he stood so close to me like he did tonight, where I could feel the cool material of his suit against my silky gown but couldn't openly grope him like I wanted. And I still blushed when he looked at me in that way that told me his thoughts were every bit as inappropriate as mine.

Maybe it was a hormonal imbalance. Or maybe I just had the sexiest husband out there.

"What'cha thinking about?"

"You."

"Me?" He glanced at me for elaboration.

"I love you. That's all."

"Ti amo anch'io," he replied. I didn't need a translator to tell me when he said he loved me, too. If I ever did take an Italian course, I'd sail through all the romantic stuff and all the dirty things Luca said in bed. And probably the bad words, too.

I traced my fingers along the top of Luca's hand as it rested on my thigh and gazed out the window. It was a gorgeous night. Maybe a tad cold, but the sky was so clear that I could actually see stars. Something about the wonder of the night sky made me feel so small and insignificant and so completely undeserving of all the blessings I'd received. And that made me think about the future.

"How set are you on using Italian names for our babies?" I blurted out.

Luca grinned and raised an eyebrow.

"Down the road, I mean. Whenever we end up having babies," I clarified.

His smile remained. "It might be negotiable. Maybe we use American names for the middle name?"

I shrugged. I was okay with that. "I like Adelina or Aurelia, for a girl, and either Rocco or Dario for a boy. Or Elio."

"Hmm." He moved his hand back to the wheel as he signaled to turn. "I was thinking Galilea or Fernanda. Ooh, or maybe Antonella for a girl. And Elmo for a boy."

I chewed my lip, trying to choose my words carefully. Luca peered over at me then back to the road several times. "I mean, maybe Antonella could work for a middle name," I finally said.

He turned to me and laughed now, eyes wide, and I realized he had been teasing me all along.

"Jerk," I mumbled. I dropped my hand onto his lap, and he quickly wrapped his own fingers around mine. I lifted his hands to my lip and kissed.

"You're lucky you're guaranteed to make such cute babies," I said.

He gazed at me again, his smile broader. He opened his mouth to say something, and then his expression changed instantly.

"Down!" he shouted, dropping my hand and forcefully shoving my head towards my lap. My head knocked into the glove compartment box just as an explosive noise rang out. Glass shattered all around me. Luca shouted something, but my ears were ringing.

The car swerved wildly, and I heard a cracking noise as my head slammed into something. A dull pain started in my neck, intensifying as it spread. Just when I feared I couldn't tolerate the pain for another second, everything went black.

Luca

struggled to gather my bearings as the car crashed to a stop, then I focused on the immediate risk. I reached for my gun, wincing as searing pain radiated down the side of my arm. I fought through the pain, clicking off the safety and aiming out each window. I kept my hand over Giada's back, ensuring she stayed down in case they returned.

"Stay down for another minute," I said, realizing I didn't even see the car that had shot at us. I dialed Alessio, knowing he and Thomas weren't too far behind. Alessio stayed on the line until they arrived, wanting him to confirm when it was okay for us to get out of the car. We'd hit a fucking tree head on, so my car wasn't going anywhere else tonight.

"How are you doing, baby? Keep your head down. Just a little longer," I said to Giada.

"Pulling up now. Don't see anyone," Alessio said.

I watched as his car pulled past us.

"Giada?" I asked. It wasn't like her to be so quiet. She usually panicked.

"They're gone," Alessio confirmed. "You guys okay?"

"Giada?" I repeated, dropping my gun. I gingerly reached for her shoulders as the horrific realization washed over me that she might have been shot.

When I looked at her face, all bloodied and already starting to bruise, a scream ripped through my throat.

Alessio tugged open my car door, then hurried around to Giada's side.

"She must have been shot," I said. "No, baby, no…"

"She has a pulse. And she's breathing, Luca," Alessio said.

I tried to cradle my wife in my arms while Alessio seemed to be checking her for other injuries.

"She wasn't shot. I think she hit her head," he said. "Call 911."

"But…"

Thomas pulled out his phone and dialed. Then he stood and yanked my gun out of my hand, jogging back to his car.

I walked around the car, barely able to breathe let alone think straight. Giada still wasn't speaking, wasn't moving.

"What have I done?" I mumbled.

"Ambulance is on its way, Luca. She'll be okay," Alessio said.

"No, no, no," I mumbled. Dozens upon dozens of adorable baby names flowed through my brain now, like a freight train I couldn't stop. "Baby, come here. Open your eyes!"

"Luca!" Alessio's shout was too sharp to ignore. I gazed up at him. He reached out and touched my arm. I roared at the sudden stabbing sensation.

My friend swore. "Luca, you've been shot."

"But Giada…"

He shook his head, clearly frustrated. But I couldn't tell why.

"Are you okay?" he asked.

"I'm fine. But why isn't she moving?"

Suddenly, sirens were blaring and lights shone on us.

"Follow my lead," Alessio said. Then he stood and turned to the paramedic who'd already caught up to us. "I lost control on the turn and hit a tree. I think she hit her head."

The next few minutes were a blur. Alessio pulled me off of Giada while paramedics fussed over her and shouted meaningless acronyms to each other before finally loading her onto a gurney. Police arrived and though normally that would rachet my blood pressure up, I didn't even care.

"He's her husband," Alessio said, pointing to me.

The paramedic motioned for me to join them in the ambulance, then told Alessio and Thomas what hospital we were headed to. They buckled me into a seat in the corner where I couldn't even reach her hand.

I couldn't take my eyes off of Giada. They said she had a concussion, that her vitals were stable. But until she woke up… I couldn't even think of the alternatives.

"Sir!" The female paramedic's tone suggested that she'd said something to me before. I gazed up slowly. "Are you injured?"

I shook my head.

"You're bleeding," she said, gesturing at my arm.

I glanced at my arm, trying to recall what Alessio had told the paramedics. I was certain he wouldn't have said anything about a gunshot. "It's not my blood," I said, ignoring the look of skepticism on her face.

"What is your wife's name?" she asked.

I replied, then fielded questions about her age, allergies, and other pertinent health information.

"Any chance she's pregnant?"

I started to shake my head, then paused. As far as I knew, she wasn't, but I supposed the baby name game could've been a prelude to her telling me. "I'm not certain. Can't you test?"

The paramedic nodded. "The police are at the scene with your friend now," she said. "They'll probably check if he was drinking."

Alessio hadn't been drinking, at least not more than one or two drinks over the course of the last five hours. Neither had I, not that it mattered now. He could handle the police though. He'd explain the accident, make sure no one searched either car… Everything would be fine on that end.

But Giada…

"Wake up, baby," I said, reaching for her.

I couldn't lose Giada.

The End

SNEAK PEAK OF MAFIOSA PRINCESS- REDEMPTION (BOOK 7)

Luca

Chapter 1

"Luca!"

My eyes flew open at the sound of Alessio's voice. I jerked back to the present. The Emergency Room lights were blindingly bright, and every few minutes, sharp, ear-piercing beeps pierced the otherwise tolerable ambient noise.

I pushed away from the window that had been supporting my weight, wincing with the pain of the movement. Giada was on the other side of that glass, but they'd kicked me out of the room.

"She's in there," I said, pointing with my good arm. "I wanted to be close, in case I could hear something, or..." I shook my head, confused as to what had just happened. "Did I fall asleep?"

"No. I think you passed out. Luca, you've been shot. You're bleeding everywhere."

I glanced down, realizing the droplets of blood surrounding where I'd been standing. Just then, Thomas appeared out of nowhere, clenching a wad of paper towels. He crouched down and wiped up the mess.

"Luca, you need to get a bandage and change your shirt. This place is filled with doctors, plus the police want to question you, and they're going to notice you bleeding everywhere," Alessio said.

"I can't leave her."

"I know. Look, we've got some supplies to clean you up. We're just going to walk over to the bathroom right there," Alessio paused to point down the hall. "You'll be back here in one minute. Thomas is staying here. He'll be with Giada."

I shook my head no, but Alessio was already forcing me down the hall. My legs tingled with an unsettling numbness, and my brain felt too foggy to protest the movement. The bathroom he nudged me into was an individual room, the kind intended for a woman and her small children or possibly someone in a wheelchair. Not for two grown men. It was the type of bathroom Giada and I might have snuck into for a quickie.

I groaned as Alessio nudged me backwards.

"Sit," he barked.

I didn't have the energy to fight him. I sat. Alessio pulled out a knife and sliced through the sleeve of my shirt, baring my injured arm.

"Gesù Cristo," he mumbled. He dampened several paper towels and then dabbed around the wound.

I winced and turned away.

He returned to the sink, getting fresh paper towels and soap. "This will sting," he cautioned.

It did, but I didn't mind. The ache had started to dull and that didn't help with anything. As long as the pain was sharp, I couldn't focus on anything else. Right now, I needed that distraction.

He tore open a small packet and unfolded an antiseptic wipe, then rubbed it over my arm. He leaned in closer, shining his phone flashlight on my arm, then set down all of his supplies and helped lift the remnants of my shirt over my head.

"You're a lucky bastard," he said. "It just grazed you. Took a chunk off the side of your arm, but doesn't look like it hit anything else."

I didn't feel particularly lucky. I felt cursed, sitting alone in a bathroom with Alessio while my wife suffered.

"Hurry up," I spit.

He squirted some ointment onto my arm, then pressed one large square bandage over it and coated that one with a second identical bandage. "You need stitches," he said, "But this should hold for now."

Alessio pulled a new shirt out of his bag. It was a button down, thankfully, since I didn't think I could lift my right arm. He slid my injured arm into the sleeve, let me handle the second arm, then crouched in front of me to do the buttons.

"I can button my own shirt," I said, swatting his hand away.

"It's my shirt and I'll be faster anyway. You want to get back to Giada quicker? Sit still."

I complied.

"The cops asked if I had been drinking and they did a breathalyzer. I passed. They wanted to know why I was driving your car, and I said because you were on a phone call. I said I looked away for a minute and lost control at the curve and then overcorrected. Thomas was behind us and saw it all." He paused. "They want to talk to you so that's the story, okay?"

"My car?"

"I called a guy. It's getting towed. I moved all your stuff to my car. Oh, and Thomas has Giada's purse."

I winced at the sound of her name. "Giada," I repeated.

Alessio nodded and helped me up. He shoved the shirt and bloodied supplies into the trash under everything else, then washed his hands. As he dried, I washed mine as well. He reached into his pocket and handed me a packet of pills.

"Oxy," he said. "For your arm. Wait till after you talk to the cops to take them."

Then he also handed me a bottle of artificial tears. My eyes were bright red and puffy, but I doubted any eye drop could help.

"I did this," I said, turning to Alessio. "I pushed her down. If I hadn't—"

"If you hadn't, she would've been shot and killed," he interrupted. "You saved her life, Luca. She just has a concussion. She'll be fine. Come on."

He unlocked the bathroom door and led me out. I ignored the questioning stares of the nearby nurses, who probably wondered what two grown men were doing together in the bathroom.

Thomas was standing where we'd left him.

"No update," he said, "but cops are here." He gestured down the hall.

"They can wait," I said, stepping closer to the glass again.

Unfortunately, the police saw me standing there, and came down the hall. Alessio tried to head them off, but they insisted it would only take a minute and that they could question me where I stood outside her room.

I didn't take my eyes off the glass as I retold the entire story. Luckily, the cops didn't seem too interested in digging and quickly left.

Right as they did, a door swung open and a young female doctor came out.

Stay Tuned for the Release of Mafiosa Princess- Redemption!

ACKNOWLEDGMENTS

I always assume it'll get easier to write books, the more I've written. Yet somehow, that's never the case. So with each new book I release, I'm filled with even more gratitude for the behind-the-scene people supporting me. Sarah P- I truly appreciate your quick and on-point edits. JD Designs- I'm eternally grateful for your gorgeous covers and willingness to make a trillion tiny changes at a moment's notice. Thank you to all of my beta readers and reviewers…and to every blogger who promotes my books. Finally, to my family—you're my favorite distraction.

ABOUT THE AUTHOR

Liza Malloy writes contemporary romance and women's fiction. She's a sucker for alpha males, bad boys, dimples, and muscles, and she can't resist a man in uniform. Liza loves creating worlds where her heroine discovers her own strength and finds her Happily Ever After. When Liza isn't reading or writing torrid love stories, she's a practicing attorney. Her other passions include gummy bears, jelly beans, and the occasional marathon. She lives in the Midwest with her four daughters and her own Prince Charming.

Visit her website at https://authorlizamalloy.wixsite.com/lizamalloy

Join her email list at http://eepurl.com/gnuROD